STORMBORN SAGA

GUARDIAN OF THE SEAS

J. T. WILLIAMS

DWEMHAR REALMS

Copyright © 2017 by J.T. Williams

All rights reserved.

No part of this book may be reproduced in any form or by any electronic or mechanical means, including information storage and retrieval systems, without written permission from the author, except for the use of brief quotations in a book review.

DWEMHAR REALMS BOOKS

STORMBORN SAGA
Stormborn
Mage Soul
Elf Bane
Stormborn Saga Trilogy
Ranger's Fury (Ranger Trilogy #1)
Black Moon (Ranger's Revenge #2)
Aieclo (Ranger's Revenge #3)
Epochs (Clockmaster's Shroud #1)
Shards of Etha (Clockmaster's Shroud #2)
Shadow Cry (Clockmaster's Shroud #3)
The Dark Compass (The Lost Captain #1)
Eyes of Storms (The Lost Captain #2)
Heir of the Sea Captain (The Lost Captain #3)
Cataclysm
Ascension

THE ROGUE ELF

Half-Bloods Rising
Seer of Lost Sands
Shadow of the Orc Star
Necromancer's Curse
Wrath of the Half-Elves
The Last Dwemhar
Of Shadows and Blood
Trials of Eschal

ROGUES OF MAGIC
Rogues of Magic Trilogy

LOST TALES OF THE REALMS
Ranger's Folly (Ranger's Revenge Trilogy Prequel)
The Dwarven Guardian
A Stranger's Quest
Wizard Trials
The Thief's Sin

All books listed here are within the same world. For further information, please head to my website! www.authorjtwilliams.com

CONTENTS

STORMBORN

1. Of Eels and Dwarves   3
2. An Ancient Secret   23
3. Sunrise   46
4. Valrin of the Sea   68

MAGE SOUL

1. Shadows of Old   91
2. Mysterious Friend   123
3. Underrealms   148
4. The Black   166
5. Sacred Bonding   190

ELF BANE

1. Wind Temple of Swia   209
2. Songs of Harrodarr   226
3. Ghosts   244
4. For a Friend   266
5. Slavers   286
6. Realms   325

STORMBORN

BOOK ONE

1

OF EELS AND DWARVES

It was an early morning in the southern Glacial Seas before the sun had risen over the white-capped waves, when to his own desires, a young boy pushed off his blanket and sat up.

He was a determined young man, and though the house was warm and a breakfast was an arm's reach away, he had always felt alone. This was his home, as much as he could call it one. He had no mother and he had no father. He was Valrin, the orphan of eels, or so he had playfully been named now that he spent his mornings gathering them. His Aunt Tua looked after him. She wasn't his true aunt, but he was thankful for her. There were few warm arms to be had in the fishing village of Travaa, and there was even less warmth outside.

Valrin chewed on a fish cake with red berries and strapped up his boots. Donning a slightly bigger-than-needed coat, he slipped on his gloves and pushed open the door.

It was just now entering the months of fall in the southern lands, but the polar lights greeted him. One of his few friends in this desolate port town.

The town itself was built into the rocky shores that went up from a cove that was frequented by fishers in sour weather. The few houses that had sprouted up were generally guest homes used only during the fishing season.

As he went toward the water's edge, he checked two traps for eels. The fishers loved eels and he wasn't too sure why. He never had much luck fishing with them himself but perhaps it was different out at sea. He had never gone fishing on one of the massive ships and actually seen what they used them for. He always hoped to, but he never had a chance.

"Two," he said to himself. "That ought to get me a bit of coffee."

Coffee was a much sought-after substance that Aunt Tua loved. She had looked out for him for as long as he could remember, and she was actually part elven. It got her in trouble by some of the other fishers. The people of the Glacial Seas sought to keep to themselves and their own races. There were no other elves on the island but she was okay with that. It was strange, in a way, but her careful watch always made Valrin feel like something was different about him. For a while, the fishers said he was good luck. There was even a rumor he had washed ashore during a horrible storm and was chosen by the storm itself to live. Aunt Tua was never very specific on how he came to be.

For years, he heard the names "Storm Child" and "Ocean Soul," but he never felt offended by them. He loved the ocean and storms. As powerful as they could be they made him feel truly alive. As he grew older and now edged toward the years of being a man, by the standard, there were even more peculiar looks at him.

As the sun began to rise, he passed one of the fishers who was much older than the rest.

"Valrin, have you gotten any of your slimy bastards?"

He nodded. "Yes, sir, I do. Were you needing one?"

"Nope, but I have a feeling you will have some traders coming in. I'm going to go fish myself. There are dwarven vessels on the horizon. You know they always bring good wares."

Dwarves were the best for the oddities, and Valrin pranced up the hill to where he could see the other side of the island and the approaching ships. There were several in the outline of the orange sky. He quickly ran to his other traps and began to sack his catches. Running from one part of the island to the other, he went to every nook he'd hid his traps. The people of the village cared little to search for eels themselves. Besides, why do it when they could have a young boy like Valrin do it?

As he returned to his house, Aunt Tua looked him up and down.

"Now you're looking a mess this 'morn."

"I am. Thank you for the fish cakes. You know how much I love them."

"That I do. I was feeling a bit restless last night. I couldn't concentrate. I will be happy when the dark winter comes. Did the other fisher leave out like she said?"

"She did. Her boat is gone."

For the past few weeks, Valrin had spent his days with an elven minstrel fisher named Evia. It was a strange combination, a minstrel fisher, and she was a rare sight. A woman of younger years, and one who took a liking to Valrin.

"Vals," she would say, "you mustn't worry about what others do unless it is their actions that cause harm. Then you must deal with them."

Valrin remembered this and kept it in his mind. He had heard many sayings of the wise, but this one made sense to him more than any. He had seen many misgivings in the port. He had even seen men killed over money.

There was much evil in the world, and he could only do so much to not be saddened by it.

Though Aunt Tua would have rather he waited until they had settled in, it was clear the dwarven vessel he had seen at sunrise was approaching the wooden docks. He quickly carried his simple creatures to see what the dwarves would trade. He knew Aunt Tua wouldn't mind. She stayed indoors during the day and always told him she loved the night, and though it was strange to many, he understood it. As he came near the docks, he noticed this was no fishing ship as he had seen before.

It was a large ship, with green rails and massive pointed crossbows along its deck.

Many stocky dwarves stomped down a gangplank, and a few of them had blood on them.

There was one man who stood in front of them. Valrin didn't like the look of him. He seemed to like bones and was not afraid to shake some poor sea creature's skull at the fishers who had come to greet him.

"I say to you all," he began, "I am a simple dwarf. I only seek a dangerous man who has thus far evaded my capture. There is a ship. Its center mast is destroyed. It has a rough crew of the most dangerous types. Elves. Men. A woman who casts magic from her hands. We need your help. If you see this ship, if it makes port, with great care, simply cast the contents of this bag in a fire."

He handed the bag to one of the fishers.

"I will personally pay the entire island a sum of one thousand pieces of gold and supplies to last the winter tenfold for the capture of this crew."

"Tenfold?" the man taking the sack asked. "What could a crew do so much as to be worth this kind of reward?"

"Do not worry of it," the dwarf said. "Just know that their captain is dangerous and none of them can be trusted. I had some of my own betray me to him, and I would like to deal with the deserters."

The dwarf smiled, and the others with him laughed as they went back to their ships.

Valrin dropped his bag. The dwarves were already leaving.

The men talked among themselves of the vast reward they had been offered. Whoever these wanted people were, they would not be wanted for long.

Valrin was down for the rest of the day. The dwarves, though of a fleet of many ships, were not interested in trade, and it seemed no other ships would come in. Valrin sat on a bluff overlooking the harbor as the sunset began to fall.

"I know where the wind does blow,
Over icy waters blue,
Forever wandering the depths,
Of a sailor's life, I wish I knew

Sunrise high and across the sky,
Sun sinks low and starlight shines.
A long night, winter cold and dark,
The polar lights of godly signs.

'Ever a night, I think and wish,
For my parents to come from the sea,
Take me back and teach me why,
I only remember a stormy sky."

Valrin closed his eyes and lay back. He looked up at the sky and thought of the island he had called home for so long. The winds blew over him, and he took a deep breath. He then heard something. Something that seemed frantic in nature.

He looked up to see that a ship was coming into the harbor but not very quickly at all. It had red sails, and the center mast was broken down the middle. Men used rows to move the ship onto the shore.

As night began to fall and the sun was just leaving the sky, Valrin jumped up and ran down the bluff to the shoreline.

He wondered if this was the ship. The vessel the dwarves searched for. He was one of many who were now on the shore. There were several crewmembers looking out, and several more looking behind them.

A tall man jumped to shore and immediately put his hands up at the rather rowdy group of islanders.

"I am Edanos of the free vessel *Truest Bliss*. We come with no arms drawn, seeking peace."

One of the fishers stepped forward. Valrin knew him as Guna. In his hand was the sack given to them by the dwarf from before.

"We had heard of a ship. Dwarves are lookin' for you."

The crew of the *Truest Bliss* seemed to become disgruntled. There was a shorter man next to Edanos who whispered up to him. A woman stood to his right and pointed to the tree line, and Edanos looked and seemed to nod in agreeance.

"People of this isle, I do not have the fortune of the

dwarf captain, nor do I seek to buy your loyalty. I have a small supply of grain for payment to take one of your tall trees on the bluffs. We will need no assistance in harvesting it, and by morning, or sooner, we will be gone."

Guna drew a small blade, as did other fishers, while a vast majority lifted up an arrangement of spiked hoes and even a gigging stick.

"You will not be going anywhere. You will be staying, and we will have a happy winter courtesy of a dwarf's reward."

The many crew aboard the ship drew back longbows. Valrin noticed they were elves. The shorter man grasped a hammer.

Is he a dwarf? Valrin wondered. He didn't seem to have an issue with this captain.

The woman beside Edanos lifted her hands, and a blast of fire landed just before Guna.

"We may be kind," Edanos said, "but do not threaten my crew, fisher."

"Braei, send the man to the afterlife," the shorter man said. "Archers, prepare to release!"

About that moment, Aunt Tua pushed her way through the crowd.

"What kind of nonsense is happening here?" she asked.

Guna pointed. "These are wanted men, and a good reward is wanted for their heads."

"And how is a wee man like you going to get that reward with several elven arrows in your chest? Not to mention that war hammer." She turned to the captain.

"Your crew is welcome to my house, and ignore these rascals. They are only here for a season. It is just me and the boy Valrin here all the time."

Valrin joined her, and Edanos signaled his crew to stand down. Those fishers gathered seemed to do the same, except for Guna.

Edanos went to Aunt Tua and bowed. "Thank you. I assure you we will be here only as long as necessary."

The fishers all went their own way as the bulk of the ship's crew disembarked. Guna shook his head, obviously disgruntled, but having lost his support, he, too, sank away.

Valrin watched as many elves stood on different parts of the ship. They were tirelessly watching the opening of the cove.

As a large group of the crew, including the one called Braei and the dwarf, went to harvest the tree, the captain was beckoned to Aunt Tua's house.

Valrin was amazed of the man. He had no hair on his face, a strange fact for those of the Glacial Seas. He wore a dark tunic with metal brooches and a curved sword.

"Mr. Edanos, will you sit and have some tea? I have a large stew I've been cooking and a store of dried meat. If it is not enough for your crew, my apologies. I didn't expect such an arrival this time of year."

"Your kindness is almost overbearing. I will gladly accept, and thank you for your words against the men outside."

She smiled. "They are too simple-minded to even be called men. They are pigs, in truth, and I'm happy when they leave. You have an attractive woman with you. I'd say watch her."

Edanos laughed. "Braei can well take care of herself in an unscrupulous crowd. I promise."

As Valrin stared at the captain, he looked away as he was noticed by Edanos' careful eyes.

"Do you live here, son?"

"I do."

"Your father a fisher?"

"I do not know him. My father and mother were lost to me. I came here in a storm."

Aunt Tua seemed to look at Edanos as he nodded and centered his gaze. "A boy of the storm? There are legends of such boys and girls, at least among the seafaring folk. A lost race of long ago, before the seas covered these lands, was said to bless the realm with certain souls who would be born of storms who had access to the old knowledge. They actually created souls. Can you believe it?"

Valrin nodded but he wasn't actually sure he believed it.

"I have spent much time on the many seas of our lands, but these seas call to me. There is something to be upon these waters with the story I just told you. I, too, have no parents to call my own, but the sea has been good to me. I have great friends, and we do what we can to help those in need. These pirates are the worst kind. They may promise riches, but they will take over your island. You will be taken care of, but only as slaves."

"A bit rough for a young boy to hear?" Aunt Tua said.

"True, but this world is rough. A world full of the coddled is a world in chaos. I find it is better to accept truth as it is."

There was a knock at the door, and Edanos jumped, his hand to the hilt of his blade. Aunt Tua opened the door, and in stepped the short man.

"Looking for our captain," a man said.

"Come on in," she told him. "He is here."

As he stepped into the house, followed by the woman, Aunt Tua beckoned them to sit as well.

"The wood is in place," Braei said. "It will hold until we can get to a proper shipwright. But we should avoid any run-ins until we have a proper job done."

"Aye," the short man said, "and storms, or we'll be fishing our sails out of the seas!"

"Braei, Rortho, this young man is Valrin of the seas."

"Another?" asked Rortho.

Aunt Tua seemed to be more disgruntled. But Valrin wasn't sure if that was exactly the emotion. She was suddenly more distant than before.

"Yes," Edanos confirmed, "one like me. One destined for the water."

As it was now clear to the others that Aunt Tua was upset, Braei stood to help her serve the food.

"Thank you, ma'am, for the hospitality. The fishers are tending to our other crewman. It seems your words have caused a change of heart from the others here."

"Yes," she said plainly.

She served the food to them and sighed before going towards her room. Valrin was curious of it but then turned to the others as they ate. Edanos took out a ring he kept in one of his pouches. He handed it to Valrin.

"Have you seen one of these?"

Valrin shook his head. The ring had a brilliant speckled white glow in the center of a blue field.

"It allows you to go under the surface of the water but not drown. It is only usable by some. Put it on. Let us see if you possess what I believe you do."

Valrin put on the ring slowly, a bit concerned over what he was actually doing. As the metal rested on his finger, it began to glow slightly.

Edanos smiled. "We are brothers of the same world, Valrin. I'm happy we have met."

It was at that moment that Aunt Tua emerged from her room. She had a single silver chained piece of jewelry in hand. She handed it to Valrin with tears in her eyes. He was confused. He had never seen her so upset, and he was worried of why. As the fire glowed behind her, she sat down at the table.

"I knew at some point the truth would be known, but I did not know it was now."

Edanos sat up in his chair.

"You have only been with me for just over twelve years, but when you came here, I was already older than you may believe. I came to the north for the darkness. I was infected some time ago with a kind of curse that while I received a potential cure, it did not remove my sensitivity to the harsh sun.

"I had prayed to Wura to give me purpose in this desolate place, and that night, you washed ashore with that amulet. I took up my guard of you. I accepted my curse and remained here, watchful. I had a purpose and I rid myself of my cure to assure I could protect you." She gave him the amulet. "I know not what it is, but I do not believe in coincidence. Not anymore, at least. Perhaps this man can tell you more of it. I have a feeling about him."

Edanos leaned in, looking at the amulet in Valrin's hand. He touched it with his hand and then nodded, looking at the boy.

"This is special, something that's a sign of—"

A hurried knock on the door cut off the captain's words. He stood up as Braei made it to the door before anyone else. It was one of the elves.

"Captain! The men are all sick; they put something in our food."

Those within the house stumbled out. Valrin immediately noticed that many of the crew were lying on the ground, grabbing their stomachs. It also seemed that other members of the crew had not eaten, and angrily held their weapons out at the fishers. It was then Valrin looked up to the bluffs. The other fishers had lit a large fire, and a white glowing plume filled the sky over the island.

"It is a signal," Rortho said." They are signaling the fleet."

"Then we must go now," Edanos ordered. Valrin and Aunt Tua stood back as the three sailors moved toward their crew on the ground. Gura stood between them and the sickened crewmembers. A large group of dwarves came from the ship.

"We see our old master coming this way quickly. We must go now."

Edanos drew his curved blade, holding it toward Gura. "I only kill when I must, and this is looking to be a situation that doesn't fair well for you, fisher."

Valrin noticed several ships on the edge of the cove making a slow but deliberate approach. From what he could see in the moonlight, none of these looked exactly like the ship that had been here before.

"Stay, Valrin," Aunt Tua told him.

She began to walk at a hastened pace toward the confrontation between the crew of the *Truest Bliss* and the fishers.

He followed behind, although kept back far enough to hopefully not alert his aunt.

"You can strike me, Captain," Gura said, "but I assure you, you will die by the hands of one of the many on this island."

Aunt Tua walked up to Gura and pushed him in the chest. "You have had good catches this year. The gods have blessed you, and this is how you repay them. By selling out a crew who has not shown any violence to you."

Gura pushed her back and pointed at her face. "You inbred elf, why don't you act normal for once in your life. I should have waited until morning. I wouldn't have to see your scarred face, you filthy bitch. I know who else spends their nights up, but you're not even an ounce as attractive as a harbor wench from a few islands over. You're old, washed out, and weak."

Gura kicked her in the stomach, and she fell to the ground. He spat on her, and then Valrin noticed she was to her feet in a flash, to the utter surprise of the fisher.

"You know not who you speak to, human," she yelled.

It was that moment when from the darkness of the bluff came several figures. Edanos looked up.

"Rugag," he said to the others.

As the figures approached, the captain from before, Rugag, was clapping.

"Very good, very good. I knew they would come here. I had hoped to get at least some sleep, but we were never too far away."

Rugag went to Gura and handed him a bag of silver.

"A payment on a promise to be had in time. You've done good for your island. It will now be a port for the dwarven lord of Barbs. All upon the island and the waters surrounding it, are now under the protection of His Majesty and all property here is now his."

A sudden grumbling roar came from the other fishers.

"Keep calm, keep calm," he said. He then walked toward Edanos, lifting his ax up as he did.

"Come quietly, you sea wretch. I have enough men to take three dwarves and ten Rusis. I can take you, alone."

Rugag then looked down at Valrin. His eyes

widened, and he stepped past Aunt Tua. He pointed a chubby finger at him.

"A Stormborn here? This amulet, it is what we need. Come here, boy!"

Valrin stumbled backward and began to run just to have Rugag grab him.

He began to scream, kicking and punching before taking aim with his fingers and digging into the dwarf's eye. Rugag threw him onto the ground and cursed.

"Damn boy." He lifted his ax up to strike when Aunt Tua suddenly jumped over Valrin, grabbing the ax, and her face turned white. She let out a blood-curdling scream. Her mouth elongated, and sharp fangs glistened in the moonlight.

"Vampiric bitch!" He punched her in the face, dropping his ax and driving a jagged dagger into her throat.

"Aunt Tua!" Valrin cried.

A blast of magic struck the ground near them, and Valrin felt a hand grab him. He looked up at the deck of the *Truest Bliss*. Elven archers fired into pursuing dwarves as he was carried up the gang plank. Valrin was tossed on to the deck of the ship by Edanos, who then shouted to the crew.

"Cast off! We must go now!"

Braei stood on the plank, helping the few of the crew who could still walk, and pulling another who just happened to be on the ground right near her.

"They're killing the others," Rortho said, tossing two more of the crewmen on the deck.

"We have to raise the sails. The other vessels are upon us," Edanos said.

Braei began to pull up the plank to the ground when several dwarves came upon her. Valrin watched from the railings as she reached out, a blast of fire throwing one back. Another slammed his ax just over her head, and she turned, attempting to pull herself on deck.

One of them grabbed her leg, and in a shrieking flash, Aunt Tua was on them. Her face was covered in blood, and her body had multiple stab wounds.

"Aunt!" he cried out, but she turned her attention to other dwarves.

Rortho pulled Braei up and then the gangplank as the ship began to lurch forward.

"Valrin! Stay down!" Edanos ordered. A series of bolts flew across the deck, and he fell to his stomach, crawling away from the fire that took many elves and men off the deck of the *Truest Bliss*. He had thought of sailing many times, but he never imagined it as this.

From his spot behind a stack of crates, he saw the massive ships on either side of them. Braei ran along one edge of the ship, casting bolts of lightning from her fingertips as ropes with claws came along the railings of the ship. Men cut them and slashed at dwarves who attempted to board them. A loud and harsh horn called from the two ships, and several more dwarves came in waves upon the deck.

Edanos, who had been at the helm of the ship, dropped down to the deck level and began fighting the intruders. In several swathes and parries of his sword, he forced his way along one side, cutting the hold the ship on their right had, before turning to the one on the left.

"Kill them!" Valrin heard shouted from the shore. "Kill them all, except Edanos!"

The wind seemed to increase. The sails of the ship lifted up, and they broke away from the one ship; however, the other ship was still boarding them.

"Their sails!" Rortho shouted. "Take out their sails, Braei!"

The Rusis shot a blast of fire toward the other ship, catching one sail aflame before another crossbow bolt flew into the side of the ship.

Valrin stood up, seeing the tensed rope in the ship. It was just out of range of sword, and it seemed the Rusis was now engaged with two other dwarves. Valrin saw a large spear. He grabbed it and ran to the edge, stabbing the rope, attempting to fray it and break the hold the ship had on them. Smaller bolts began to fly toward him, striking the wood around his head. Dwarves on the ship saw him, and they had no issues with killing someone as young as Vals, especially aboard this ship.

As a massive crank on the ship began to pull the *Truest Bliss* into a fatal position, a screech split the air, and Aunt Tua appeared on the deck of the opposing ship. She tore apart the mechanisms and slashed her clawed hands into the dwarves who faced her. She then jumped onto the rope holding them in place and bit the line. The rope dropped, and she jumped back to the edge of the dwarven vessel. Several ax heads cut into her head, and she fell into the water.

Valrin began to cry.

"Now, lift sails. Let's get out of this place!" Edanos said.

Valrin followed the captain up to the upper deck as they moved with haste out of the cove. There were many ships on the other side of the island, but in their folly, the dwarves had not expected them to escape. They reached open sea and began heading north, Valrin's home well behind them.

Valrin collapsed on the wooden deck. Edanos gave the wheel over to Rortho. Braei came up to the same area, and he tapped her on the back.

She looked to him. "That was close, Captain. We lost at least thirty men, but—"

He cut her off and dropped down to Valrin. "She was your only family you had known?"

With tears falling down his face, he nodded.

"Do not worry, son. You are with us. Your aunt was a kind woman, and her curse, as she called it, ended up saving your life and the lives of my crew. I, too, was like you with no family. You will call this ship home."

Valrin looked up and forced a small smile.

Edanos pulled him to his feet. "You need rest, and this ship is far from danger, and for now, we can assure you sleep. We can talk more of our futures tomorrow."

Edanos took him to a lower level and a single door with a golden outline around it. This was the captain's quarters.

Valrin looked around at the large collection of books, trinkets, and sea charts. He had seen something like this when he was only a few years old. A large vessel came to port and he got to go aboard. He had never forgotten that. Now, he was on a ship himself. As he explored more, he noticed that there were several simple beds with small circular windows looking out to the sea.

He sat down on one, and Edanos smiled. "Sleep well, young Valrin. There is much we will speak of tomorrow."

2
AN ANCIENT SECRET

VALRIN HAD NEVER ATTEMPTED to sleep on a ship at sea. In fact, of the many small boats he had been on in his life, this was the first actual ship he had really spent much time on at all. He awoke to sunlight coming through the window above his head. The rank smell of the wood by his head caused him to curl his nose, and he threw his feet over the edge of the bed. He stood up, surprised he had not awoken earlier, and then immediately thought of his Aunt Tua.

Now he understood why she did not like the light. Why she only was in the dark. She had the blood of a vampire. She had been bitten, and that was what she had run to the north for. He touched the pendant around his neck and exhaled. He was deeply saddened by the events, but there was a curiosity in the air, a feeling under his feet, like there was much more within reach than before. The ship lurched, and he struggled to stand. His stomach turned and felt queasy.

He needed fresh air. He made his way to a dark wooden door and pushed it open. The blow of a salty but icy breeze hit him, and he looked around to see glaciers. It was very bright outside, too. He recoiled back just as Edanos came around the corner.

"You're going to need a bit more warmth out here than you're used to. The winds of Dimn blow upon us with a howl."

It must have been obvious to the captain that Valrin wasn't feeling well, because as soon as they were back in the captain's quarters, Edanos handed him a jar of crushed herb.

"For the ocean shakes your stomach is having. You will get used to it in time."

Valrin took a few of the leaves and chewed them. They were harshly bitter and sent a tingle to his nose, but in just a few seconds, he was feeling better.

Edanos went to a wooden chest with black brackets and pulled out a large coat.

"It is a bit big for you, but I believe it will work until we can find something better. I can get you something more appropriate soon. Rortho's repairs are holding, but we need to resupply and perhaps find some more men."

"Thank you," Valrin said, "for taking me in."

"Do not thank me. I only did what was right. I know that in time, all of our paths will make more sense. I had thought it was the end of our quest when our center mast was destroyed, but now I have more faith in it overall."

Edanos went to an alcove in the room where a

kettle was hung. He touched it with his fingertips. "Good, it's still warm. Do you like coffee?"

He nodded.

After serving two cups of the black brew, Edanos sat down with him.

"What questions do you have for me?" he asked.

Valrin couldn't think of any questions on the fly. He stared at the captain, who drank his coffee and simply waited. He didn't feel rushed; he didn't even feel nervous. This was the first stranger he had felt completely calm with in his entire life.

He took a sip of his coffee. It was a bit bitter but still good. He looked down at the pendant around his neck.

"Storm Children or . . . Stormborn, you say you are one too?"

"Aye, I am. That necklace shows your tie to the sea and passage to a place that, well, you are lucky to be able to go to."

"So you have one too?"

"I did, but it was taken from me when I was very young. You were lucky to be left on an island like you were. I was not so lucky. I ended up on an island of unscrupulous characters and many just simply hoping I was worth something on the market. I spent time as a servant boy, if you can imagine it, and the only valuables I was left with were my hands. I had a few friends, if you could call them that. My necklace went to the king of the Barbs, the dwarf king Rugag spoke of, but he never knew what it was, not yet, at least."

"So they know what it is. They could go to this place, too."

He nodded. "They can. But they cannot find it. There is an old secret, a weapon in both sight and words. It is a powerful object and unlike any other attainment to children such as you and me. It is something that binds to your very life force. It becomes a part of you. I have never seen it, but I know of it."

Valrin laughed. "It sounds like some spiritual thing."

"Yes." He laughed as well. "Something like it, I guess. In the end, my goal has been to get my jewel back. I have traveled over many waters and, for many nights, stared at the stars, looking for my purpose. I have found it, and we will go to a town where there is someone who can help us."

Edanos stood up. "Was there anything else you wondered? You are on a ship for the first time. Do you want to see the rest of the ship, perhaps climb to the crow's nest and see the view?"

Valrin finished his coffee and thought of Edanos' question. He knew what he wanted to do, but he wondered if it was too soon or too forward. It wasn't something the captain had suggested. He stood up and decided to see if it was possible.

"Can I steer the ship?"

The captain smiled. "I would like nothing better."

They exited the Captain's Quarters, and Valrin looked out across the ocean as they ascended the stairwells to the upper deck. The sea was vast and empty, a light blue in all directions, with a bright sun that was floating lower in the sky. Rortho had the helm of the ship and gave it up to Edanos as he approached.

"Valrin, come here."

He went up to the wheel and placed his hands on the wood.

"A ship should be a part of you," Edanos began. "When you feel the rock of the waves and your weight shift from one boot to the next, you enjoy it and imagine the ship as your body and your body upon the sea itself. When you change course, it should feel as if you are simply moving over the surface with ease."

Valrin could feel the tug of the rudder, and then shifted the wheel to his left, sending the ship to his right in a lunge.

"Easy," Edanos told him. "Keep it straight for now."

He shifted the ship back the other way and, this time, did it with grace.

"Good," Edanos said.

He looked down at the crew moving on the deck below. Some worked on ropes, others sharpened spears and swords, while watchers looked out from the deck for other ships.

He then looked up into the sails. They were a mix of patchwork and different colors. The masts had marks from flames, and even a few arrows stuck in parts of the ropes. A flag was at the very top of the masts. It was dark blue with no adornments.

"We fly the flag that is the color of our life-giving force. By our, I mean we, as Stormborn. The ocean is our life. We come from it, and we will, in time, return to it."

Braei, the Rusis woman, joined them now. She came from below decks and held a bag of tobacco.

"We are running out," she said.

She began to scrape out a black pipe before packing the bowl and lighting it with a small firestick from a brazier at the aft of the ship.

"We will get more," said Edanos.

"You take us north. Where might we go to get something like that?"

"Merea," he told her.

She looked at him in surprise that even Valrin noticed as he glanced back.

"Then you have told him? You mean to go through with it?"

"We did not survive the night before to pass on this chance. He knows of the secret. He is excited about it."

Rortho now took out his own pipe. He packed it and began to smoke almost as quickly as he had grabbed the pipe.

"My kin will figure out that we are up to something. Before, we guarded the migrating humpback whales, and now we abruptly go north. He knows you have the amulet."

"I do not have the amulet; the boy does. I will not take from him what is not mine."

"Do you know what power you could give up?" Braei asked.

"No, I do not. Neither do you nor do you know

exactly what will happen before we can get there. We will go to Merea and speak with one who can guide us. I know this isn't exactly what we planned, but I need to face that I may never get my own back. The boy came to our lives by the will of the gods. We will not spit upon their workings."

Valrin continued to hold the wheel. It was obvious that the two main crewmembers of the captain were a bit perturbed by his decision involving himself. He didn't understand why, but for now, he knew it wasn't his place.

Though she was a bit abrasive, Braei offered to take him below deck. Rortho took the wheel again, and Edanos was to retire to his cabin for some time. He followed her across the deck and into the belly of the ship.

The crew area was tight quarters compared to that where Valrin had slept.

"Our crew changes frequently. Normally law breakers or some just trying to get away from their problems. We even have dwarves of Rugag. They were left on an island to freeze to death, and while I was okay with it, Edanos seems to not be able to do what is needed."

"Isn't it good he helped them?" Valrin asked.

She laughed uncomfortably. "You are young, innocent in the world. I do not doubt my captain, but I would have left them to die. Dwarves, at least in these parts, are not the type you help. Rortho has been friends with Edanos since Edanos was your age. He is the only dwarf this Rusis trusts."

"What about you? How did you join the crew?"

"I was rescued by him from a southern vessel that came to attempt to find 'exotic' slaves. If you can believe it, even Rugag's fleet helped Edanos in the effort to protect the northern waters. I was very young, and the only memory I have is of men wearing red garbs shouting and dying around me. Edanos pulled me from a cell and said I did not need to fear. That was twelve years ago."

"So how old are you?"

She laughed. "Old enough to tell you that you're asking too many questions now!"

She led him to another area of the ship, walking past many stores of food to an area with an assortment of bladed weapons.

"They may not like it, but you need one. Pick something out; make sure it feels good in your hand."

He looked over the many curved and straight blades of varying lengths. He picked up a sword but found himself unable to lift it. He pushed it back on its side. He then took an ax in hand, but it felt too sloppy.

"I don't know. What would you pick?"

The woman opened her hand, and a small ball of fire illuminated the room. "I need no bladed weapon, but pick one you can at least use and not be tired after your second swing."

He pulled a curved blade, similar to Edanos'.

"A scimitar? That will be tiring. Go with a shorter blade for now, like this one." She pulled a short but polished blade from the rack. "Now, come on, above deck. We will be nearing port soon."

Back topside, he walked along the deck, touching engraved wood and jumping from the snaps of the sails as the winds shifted. The air upon him was like the icy blows of a winter storm, but he felt invigorated. In the distance, he began to see an island.

In time, he went to the front of the ship, staring at the outlines of buildings on a snowy and rocky cliffside town. The port area of the town was actually under a monstrous overhang of the city itself. Atop the massive cliffs was a snow-covered dome of sorts. As they came underneath the city itself, he noticed that the dome actually had a fire burning within it and suspended gardens just visible from the docks, spiraled vines that had frostbitten ends hanging down the cliffs.

"A wonder of our world," Edanos told him. "Merea grows food for the many regions of the Glacial Seas. It is a place of both wonder and corruption, but it's a free city and not under the influences of Rugag's types."

"How has it remained unaffected by the Barb king?"

Edanos pointed above them.

"Do you see the red crystals growing out of the rock?"

"I do."

"Those are marvelous dwarven constructs, back when the dwarves of this region were not as they are now. If danger threatens this small town, the weapons activate, and any ship caught in the water meets an untimely fate."

"Have you seen it?"

"No, but the fear of such an action keeps the dwarves far away. We are safe to do our business here, and while the ship is worked on, you and I will go into an older part of the town. Cover your amulet up. We do not want questions before the opportune time."

The ship moved along the dock and was quickly tied off. They stepped off the ship, and Valrin was careful to bind his cloak around him. The docks themselves were made of stone and had runic etchings on the path they walked.

"These docks are actually older than you can imagine. The dwarves simply built their buildings above it. The sea people from before were an ancient race, powerful beyond most magic. Their true culture was lost long ago."

They left the regions of the docks and took a road through tall stone buildings with many people of varying races walking around. Though he had lived his life at sea, Valrin had never seen a person with gills like a fish on their necks.

He tried not to stare, but it was such an odd sight, he couldn't help it.

"They are elves crossed with merpeople. Do not stare—they've been known to ink someone. I understand it is not the least pleasant at all!"

The smell of the salty air was stronger here than the actual sea. Cured fish hung in alleyways that were open to the cold sea breeze. They were walking up a hill, and with each step, Valrin's legs burned. They came to a flat area with many stalls on either side. Edanos went to the stalls and grabbed several different garments, stopping to look at Valrin.

"I think, um, I guess it's right."

He paid the stall keeper and gave the clothes to Valrin.

"You can dress properly once we get inside the chapel. The woman we meet will keep us waiting. It is what she does. It will give you time to become more comfortable."

Valrin didn't know where they were going, but he felt that at the very least he would happily put on new clothes.

They began up a narrow stairwell that wrapped up and around a series of buildings that rose up in an almost badly constructed tower. At last, they came to a single double gate and a long pathway that went over the sea. Edanos opened the gate, and they entered. The pathway actually was open to the sea at just past Valrin's hips. He felt nervous, and he even thought he felt a sway to the stone bridge way with the cruel glacial winds.

He bound his coat over his head and watched Edanos' feet to lead his path. They came to a large building with a single crystal atop. It had a window, a lone circular lookout that wrapped around one-half of a crowning tower just off center from the crystal.

Edanos knocked on the door and waited. At least

the area they stood in now was shielded from the outside winds.

"Go ahead, change. It will be a moment."

He quickly took off his coat and put on the new clothes bought by Edanos. It felt weird wearing something not made from sheep's wool by his aunt. It fit well, though partially tight along his chest.

"You will get used to it. Floppy clothing makes a poor man. You should look your best, particularly if you are captain of a ship."

Valrin wasn't a captain, but he valued the guidance from his new friend.

"It has been some time since I came here. She will wonder of why I have been away. Let me converse with her before you speak."

The door cracked open.

"Edanos, you leave me alone too long," a voice said.

"I come to see you now."

The door shut. Edanos knocked.

"I am not here. Go away."

He knocked again.

"She is not here. Go away," the same voice said.

"I really must speak with you," he said into the door.

"Did you bring me something?"

"Yes." He shook his head, looking at Valrin. "A new friend."

"Can I eat it?"

Valrin closed his eyes and dropped his head.

"I forgot. She likes a snack. Just, just wait here and don't fall for her crazy stories. She likes to entertain."

Edanos immediately began into a quick jog, and Valrin had no clue where he was going.

"So are you human, I guess? Or elf? I normally can smell elves and holy dwarf dung. I know you're not one of those sea cucumbers. What is your name, Stormborn?"

How does she know that? he wondered. "Valrin."

"A name of importance, like Edanos, but better, stronger. Have you ever been to Merea?"

"Um, no. Never. I came from a small island to the far south."

"I see. The storms of old blew further than that, but many never awake to their paths. It seems you have. There is much to speak of, but I fear that there is not the time for all to be spoken. We will talk again, after our meeting, at a different time. A time when you will wonder why I said this, but fear not. I do not just babble as some might say."

It was a few moments later, and Edanos returned.

"She wasn't babbling on, was she?"

"I told you," she said from the other side of the door. "Do you have it?"

Edanos held a fish in his hand.

"Yes, I have your gift."

The door creaked open, and Edanos straightened the collar of his jacket. "Come on, and don't touch anything," he warned him.

The brightness of the outside was a stark contrast to

the shadowy interior Valrin found himself in. It was an entryway with multiple candles in tiny recesses in the wall. There was a circular room sunken into the floor ahead down eight steps. The entire room had water flowing in a circle around the floor even though Valrin looked out the window and could see the expanse of the sea. He had no idea where the water was coming from. There were stone pews in a half moon facing a large statue of a mermaid. A fountain was below the statue's feet, and he heard the voice of the woman again.

"Feel the power of the Storm Children, together, interwoven in fate and action to seek out the one place they both desire for their destined fates so long ago foretold."

"Do you intend to game, or will you show the boy your face?"

"Testy human, we of the merfolk do as we want. Fish. Now."

"You're not a mermaid," he said plainly, tossing the fish into the water.

There was a soft laugh through the halls and the sounds of water rushing to and fro around the room. Valrin noticed the water flowed without sense, moving up and around the room and then back down to the pool before the statue. At last, the water all moved toward the statue, moving up its form and then sticking to the stone itself. The stone seemed to come alive for a moment, its eyes glowing brightly, and then a watery figure stepped into the pool. The fish turned to blood and was absorbed by the entity.

Valrin reached out, and Edanos slapped his hand. "Do not touch the messenger of the god!"

"Let the messenger decide of whom can touch her," the watery form said.

The hand reaching out was just as Valrin's, except there was no bone or flesh, just water. He had retracted his hand, but now he took her beckoning and touched her.

"Of the sea, of the streams, of all that is and was and will be, water, giver, and taker of life in equality of life and death. I am the shroud between this world and the next, and the giver of words from Meredaas to his followers."

"Meredaas, the god of the seas?"

He had heard the name before. Aunt Tua had a book about the gods of the North, and he remembered that image.

"Yes, young Valrin, the great Meredaas, he who, as water, has taken many forms."

"Are you really he?" Valrin asked.

The vibration of the water seemed to change and move quickly. The figure laughed. "I am not, but I do like your questioning. I am a sprite of the temple grounds. None come here. None come from the city named after the Great One. So many are lost."

The figure turned and pointed to Edanos. "I sense it upon him. You bring him to claim the birthrights of all Storm Children?"

"The dwarves threaten the seas. They attack the free peoples; they bring war and bloodshed to the waters. It was by the will of the gods that I found this boy, and he is headstrong and capable. He has a heart about him, and that is needed to bring peace to these waters."

"There will be no peace in these waters, but there will be a change. It was foretold and in time will come to pass. The Storm Children must prepare and be ever watchful of that."

The sprite moved back to the pool before the statue.

"There is a power in the Glacial Seas. These were once high holy lands of the sea peoples of old before they were known as sea people. Their power is still in the lands, but it is hidden. There is magic here untouched by the dread of the old gods of the South. There is purity, but there is also great evil contained throughout these vast frigid waters. The line between the realms of the living and the realms of the gods blur within the depths both above and below the sea.

"Valrin of Travaa, you are young and know not of this world, but beneath your shirt, I sense your offering to the god of the sea, a binding contract to protect the waters of the vast seas, to guard the creatures of the ocean, and to contain an old magic within yourself. You are a Stormborn, one of the very few chosen at the formation of your soul and body to take this charge. Do you wish to embrace the path of the god's servant?"

Valrin wasn't sure, and he looked to Edanos.

"Have you?" he asked him.

"Alas, I could not. It is your choice alone, but know there is much to be done by the one who takes this charge. I cannot force you, but I believe you can, as a fellow Stormborn."

"I will do it," Valrin said.

He finally felt a purpose, finally something beyond eel traps and desolation. He would embrace what he was born to do, though he still did not fully know what that was.

The sprite receded into the pool, and there was a grinding sound behind them. The stairwell they had walked down split in two, revealing a doorway.

Valrin walked forward. Edanos followed behind him. "I have never seen this place in all of the times I have come here."

They went forward, and Valrin pushed open the doorway. There was a glowing room ahead. It was dark but had a blue hue. As they walked into the dome-like structure, a voice spoke from the walls around them.

"Stormborn, you seek the path to your birthright. I tell you this alone. Follow the path north of Merea, through the many teeth of the Jagged Glaciers, and enter the fog realms, following the direction of moonrise. There, look for the whales and fish and the shell horn that sounds at dawn. It is upon that place you will find a doorway with a single star. Present your token and pass through. It is there you find what is yours. Complete your binding, and I take you into my house of protection until it is decreed you are to be no more."

A pedestal rose from the floor, a single crystal.

"This shall be your light in the fog realms. Only place it upon your ship, and the fogs will not hinder your progression."

The room then went dark, and the doors behind them opened.

Valrin took the crystal and turned to see Edanos on one knee.

"That was the voice of the one, the god Meredaas. He gives you this charge."

"I'm not sure where he wants us to go."

"Do not worry, Vals, I will get you there."

"Vals?"

"I can say Valrin if you'd prefer."

"Vals works."

"Come now, boy, let us get to our ship."

They exited the room, and the stairwell closed. They pushed open the doors leading out, and the voice spoke one last time.

"Carry upon the seas with haste and forever embrace that which is the fate of all that live upon the sea."

Edanos shut the doors behind them. "Her riddles and stories, she does love them."

They began back toward the ship when Edanos suddenly diverted from the road and went to an overhanging lookout. He reached into his pocket and pulled out a golden tube that he put to his eye. "Indeed, it seems our friends have followed us this far."

"Are they attacking?" Valrin asked.

"We couldn't be that lucky. They are waiting. We have passage through the cave of the city, but they will be watching. If we keep a good pace, we should be able to shake them. They do have quite a few ships. It seems the secret around your neck has attracted much attention."

Making it back to the docks, Rortho greeted them. "We have hermit crabs on us, Captain. I guess we did not have enough time to fully shake them."

"They do what they do."

Braei approached with a mug of ale.

"I do hope you found more crew where you found the fine drink."

"Aye, Captain, I have at least twenty deckhands, elven lot for the most part and one eager human. He can do tricks with a bow or so the tavern wenches said."

"I don't need tricks nor anyone that would have wenches to vouch for his skills," Edanos stated. "I need a good crew."

A man with a long white bow approached them. He had a beard and wore a dark blue coat.

"Captain?" he asked.

"Yes, Edanos of the *Truest Bliss*, and your name is?"

"Fadis, archer, servant to a simple man."

"You're the trickster, then?"

The man smiled and took Braei's ale to his lips, taking a large sip.

"I am, and I've been called worse."

Braei dumped her ale and pushed the man in the chest. "You said you wanted to join our crew, but that does not make you better than a mere deckhand. You can scrub the decks. Work those trickster arms of yours."

Fadis looked at Edanos.

"Well?" Braei asked.

The eager trickster, as he was dubbed by Braei, shrugged and boarded.

"So we make it through the passage and you hope we will get a good lead? Where to afterward?" Rortho asked.

"North, through more treacherous waters."

The dwarf shook his head. "We just got the ship back together. We don't need to tear it apart! But I will rally the crew." The dwarf went up the gangplank. "Prepare to sail!"

Valrin boarded and watched as the crew worked in a rocky harmony as the new crew melded with the old. He went up to the wheel and stood by Edanos.

"The new crew seems to not get along with the old."

"It does happen, but know you must have a good crew who you trust. If you are good to them, they will respect you. We are not pirates like those dwarves. We respect those we work with."

"Yes," Braei mocked, "even if they drink your ale!"

They pulled the holding lines from the moorings and began to move around the actual rocks of the foundation of the city. In the inner portion of the mountain was a large passage that led to the other side. As the ship moved through the passage, Edanos pointed to the ceiling and the carvings in the rocks.

"Vals, it is said that giants carved this passage and

set the foundations of the city, but I say giants do not make runes so intricate."

"Who did it, then?"

"I do not know for sure."

"Dwemhar?"

"Ha!" Braei laughed. "Dwemhar? You have the boy talking about myths."

"No more mythic than the Rusis. I do not know who made these, but within the Glacial Seas, all such things as this are considered work of the sea peoples."

"True you are, about the Rusis," Braei said, "but we actually survived and outlived them. Wouldn't it be a strange thing to come upon one now, after so many years? I do not know of a Rusis that wouldn't obliterate a Dwemhar at first chance."

"Rusis, you talk like dwarves do of elves and as elves do of dwarves in the South. If we are not careful, we shall all be the last of our races. Have you even seen a Rusis other than yourself?"

Braei was silent.

"Take note, then, Vals. Peace. That is what must be aimed for in this world. That is the only way any of us can survive."

"It is a nice gesture for hope," Braei muttered, "but peace only comes for those who win a war."

They came to the end of the passage, and the open sea was before them.

"All sails, tighten ends and keep your cloaks bound!" Rortho shouted. "We move to colder and more violent waters!"

. . .

As they pushed forward the sun set before them. They began to make subtle movements around large standing stones that jutted out of the water, not as icy peaks of glaciers or massive mountains, but as literal towers of stone as if a submerged structure with steeples was just below the surface.

There was a storm in the far distance, but it moved away from them. They didn't need the crosswinds to knock them off course, especially now in such turbulent water.

Valrin kept an eye out behind them, as did Edanos. The dwarven ships would likely follow, but they both prayed they would not catch up.

Twice Valrin went to lie down but found himself tossing and turning. He sat up and looked at the amulet. He noticed that the jewel within was pulsing with the beat of his heart. He put his hand against his chest and held the amulet with the other hand. It was not his imagination. It was the same. He couldn't guess what it meant, but he wondered if the place he was going to would explain it.

He wondered if there would be another sprite, or perhaps Meredaas himself? The book he had read before said the gods could take many forms. He questioned if he would even recognize the god if he was standing before him.

He went back outside and noticed that many of the crew had retired. Edanos was leaning on the back of the ship as Valrin approached him.

"Look, Vals," he said, pointing to the sky. "Do you know of the constellations?"

"I know of some, but this time of the year the first one Aunt Tua told me of is harder to see. I believe she called it Etha's hand? She said it was an elven star pattern praised for its assistance in enchanting."

"Yes, you speak of a power constellation, and when combined with a full moon or a black moon, it increases magical properties by quite a bit. But that is not what is important upon the Glacial Seas. Look upon the horizon, Vals. Just above the crest of the world, you will see a large bright star. That is the sea snail. After that will come the sea horse. Once it is above us, you will have four to six hours until sunrise. Once the polar night begins, there are other ones such as the penguin that would correspond with mid-morning. This becomes more important during that time. The first time I had to deal with the unending night, I about went crazy trying to align myself."

"I understand the path of the stars and the passage of time, but what is a penguin, Edanos?"

"Dear Vals, there is much I must still teach you."

3
SUNRISE

The night was well over them. The sign that Edanos had told him to watch for was now above the ship. He had seen sea horses only once, and now he could make them out in the grouping of stars floating over them.

He had gone to sleep for a while, but Edanos had begun evading more of the towering stone structures, and massive glaciers drew up on either side of them. He couldn't sleep anymore.

Valrin stood by the wheel of the ship.

"Vals, I insist," he said, offering him the wheel. "The best way to learn is sometimes by literally doing it when you have no choice."

"But you're piloting the ship."

Edanos stepped away from the wheel. "No, I'm not."

As the wheel spun and the ship began to move off course, Valrin gripped the wheel and looked forward, keeping the bow of the ship angled between the icy mountains. Though Edanos could grab the wheel at a moment's notice, Valrin wasn't sure he would. He carefully maneuvered the vessel, a harrowing feat considering this was only the second time he was at the helm.

"You're a natural man of the sea. You will be a greater sailor than even I, in time!"

As they maneuvered through the icy chasms, he began to hear a tune. At first, he thought it just the wind, but the longer he listened, he heard more of a song.

Shivering souls upon our sea,
Slicing slashing cut them free
Siren's songs so sweet so soft,
Help their souls to flee aloft.

Bodies aching from lack of touch
Let our hands take care of such!
Come to us and let us play
All of your troubles we shall slay!

"Sirens," Edanos told him nervously.

The glowing hands of the creatures grabbed the railings and smiled, looking up at them.

"The worst part of sirens is that most of your crew will be at severe risk. You are too young for them to affect you, but you are nearing the cusp of manhood. You will deal with them in time. I once fell for the seduction of these sea creatures. They may be of Meredaas, but I still do not care for their sort."

The sirens began to sink away, finding none they were capable of seducing on deck. The glacial path opened up. A great plume of fog hung before them.

"Sea of fogs. I will take the helm. Go place your crystal near the front of the ship. Put it somewhere it will stay put."

Valrin nodded and ran down to the lower deck. A few of the crew had emerged from the lower level, obviously seeking the sirens that were well behind them. He went to the pole for the foremasts and noticed a notch behind one of the ropes that was large enough for the crystal to fit. He placed it and then went back to Edanos.

"Let us see what your gift can do for us. Do you remember the words of Meredaas?"

"'Keep the path of moonrise.' So, we must turn east?"

"Yes, into the fogs we go, and my only prayer is that our path will show!"

As the fogs began to run over the deck, the crystal glowed and a bright fiery light pierced the fog in a large open swathe, clearing the sea and opening a path for the ship. Almost immediately, Edanos wheeled left to avoid a large rock jutting up from the sea. Valrin looked behind them and noticed the veil of the fogs covering their path.

"No ship in their right mind would enter this region without some form of a device such as this."

"So I assume we will have no more pursuers?"

"Never assume, especially when dealing with the one known as Rugag. Always keep the sails ready. That pirate has chased after us for some time, and I can say he is anything but dumb. Here, Vals, take the helm again. I will get us some coffee."

Valrin stood at the helm, looking through the vast bleakness before him, and was amazed at the magic of the crystal and its ability to burn away the fog.

He had gone from a boy gathering eels to sailing with one of the greatest captains he could ever imagine in the span of just a few days. He did think back to his aunt, Tua, though. He was saddened by her death, but he tried to believe as Edanos did. There were reasons for the workings, but he felt they were beyond his understanding.

Edanos brought both of them mugs. The hot coffee was a welcome drink in the frigid cold he felt to his very core.

"A bit of cinnamon in this cup. A rarer herb from the very far south. It will help stave off a sore throat, or so they say."

The taste was strange but good. As he piloted the ship through an almost constant path of fog, they began to pass through a series of large archways. The remnants of other vessels dotted the rocks. Weathered and long-rotting wood with the frayed ice-covered ropes were an ominous sign.

"This region of fog has only existed for the past

forty or fifty years. I remember a time when ships just called this a cursed region. It didn't keep ships from sailing here. Treasure hunters, mainly. The fogs came upon the surface, and afterward I can say far fewer dared to come here."

"Where did the fogs come from?"

"If I knew where these fogs came from, I would tell you. It is one of many mysteries of these seas. Perhaps one day you will discover it!"

"I could never do what you do. I can barely guide the ship! I'm not even too sure I could get us back out from where we've come so far."

Edanos smiled at him. "Time is both your enemy and friend. It takes time to learn how to navigate the many oceans, but it also wears on your men. It takes time to develop cunning to deal with the many dangers of sailing, particularly where dwarves are concerned, but I'd say I have done it well. But that has taken time from what some may call a more normal life. Marriage. Children."

"Do you find yourself wanting that?"

"Sometimes."

There was a silence between them. Valrin watched as wisps of fog rolled between them. There was a flash of lightning behind them, and Edanos looked down at him.

"I then remember that I am not of this world. I am Stormborn. I am a man of the sea. In my travels of late, I have sunk a ship of the Barb king and rescued another like me." He nodded toward him. "I am happy with the events so far. I have dreamed for many nights of going where we go. In the end, I hope it is worth it."

They had been progressing through the fogs at a rapid rate. They were to sail until dawn and then look and listen for signs of a horn sounding and whales within the waters. The dawn sun was still some time off, but there was a glow in the sky.

"I do not know what this is, but the lord of the sea did not tell us of any such sight as this," Edanos told him.

The *Truest Bliss* began to grind the sea bottom, and Edanos turned the wheel to the right, attempting to navigate the obstruction. The bow seemed to grind and churn, the current of the ocean pushing them back and forth and forcing the aft of the ship to slap up against a rock.

The crew rushed to the deck and grabbed large spears. They went to the side of the ship and drove the spear points into the rocky ice. The currents shifted around them, and for the moment, they could not move away from the rocks.

Valrin looked through a split in the rocks and noticed a glowing crystal.

Braei wiped the sleep from her eyes and then looked at Edanos as she pointed. "A strange path, Captain. Did you mean for us to come here?"

"No," he said, walking to where he could get a better view.

Rortho climbed up on the pathway, nervously looking down to see what he could spot from afar.

Fadis strung his bow and jumped onto the path.

"Only the captain can order crew to leave the ship when we are at sea," Braei told him.

"The captain needs eyes that can see beyond the fog, and weapons that can reach enemies that are just out of reach. I can do both for our captain."

Valrin looked down the path, and Edanos looked to Rortho.

"You have the helm. Keep the ship steady. Once the current shifts, keep yourselves against the rocks and light torches along the bow. We did not end up here by accident. I will take them and check whatever this place is."

"Aye, Captain. Just don't go joining the fish. It'd be a shame in this desolate cold place."

Fadis walked ahead of them, moving up the path until he came to a large stone. He ran up to the top of it and knelt down. As Edanos and Valrin nearly got to the spot where he was, he turned and jumped down. "It looks good; there is no one here."

Braei shook her head. "I wouldn't expect someone here. It is a bit desolate."

"I'm just trying to keep myself as a worthy member of the group. Besides, my eyes can see that no snow or ice has been disturbed along this path in some time. If you do not want further help from me—"

"We're just a few yards from the ship, so it is likely that no one would be immediately attack us until we were further in, but thank you," Edanos said.

Braei shook her head.

There were many more glowing stones the further they went along the path. The road itself had dropped in to actually run slightly below the edges of a wall that came up to Valrin's chest. The road climbed up and through several swathes of ocean, breaking stone pillars.

In the distance, there were several dark statues just visible in the moonlight. The road passed between two of them, and further on, a large domed structure was encrusted with a deep layer of ice.

A frigid wind gusted over them. Valrin brought his coat around him and kept his head down, but he tried to follow Edanos the best he could.

Fadis made a loud sound with an audible shiver. "So cold! Hey, Braei, do you think we could share some heat together? I could use some warmth."

"Bastard human," she responded. "Keep your thoughts to yourself or I will give you some heat."

"Hmm, sounds like an invite for a bit more fun."

Edanos stopped and turned. He drew his blade and pointed it at Fadis.

"One more remark, and I will dispose of you into these waters. You test my patience beyond what any of the rest of the crew has."

Fadis had his hands up. "No worries, good sir. I'm just testing what I can do with your lady."

"She isn't mine."

Edanos began to walk again, and Braei pointed for Valrin to follow him.

"Boy," Fadis said to him.

"Yes?"

"Learn well from the captain. He has a moral resolve that is admirable. Not claiming himself a woman and all. I'm just a bastard. I struggle the line of what is right and what is. . . what is not so great. I have tried for a few years to right my wrongs but it seems I have failed in that so far. I do care though. I hope you've learned that from the recent interchanges between us all."

Valrin ignored him. He thought about responding, but that would've just opened up another avenue of conversation, and his mind wasn't on actual talking.

He looked up at the massive statues and noticed they each wore crowns with large spikes that came off their heads. Snow drifts twisted around their bodies, and the road was covered with ice here. He could hear the pounding of the waves beneath them. The salty spray reached up to the path.

Braei used her powers to melt the ice and give them a wet but walkable path. They came to the large door. There were two torch basins, but neither of them were lit. Not surprising considering where they were. Edanos took out a torch stick, and Braei lit it for him. The bright fire felt good against Valrin's face. They were about to enter. Valrin felt a tug in his stomach, wondering what was beyond the closed doors. He questioned if it would be a treasure of some kind, but in truth, he just hoped for something of interest and not deadly. To find an abandoned structure this far out in the middle of the Glacial Seas was strange to all of them.

"It is not elven," Edanos said. "I cannot even read this text."

"It is of the sea people," Fadis said. "There is

writing like this back in the floating city. Some say it is Dwemhar, but I've always known it as sea speech."

Edanos pushed open the door. It was a simple enough feat, but it was just the first of a set of doors. As they went to the second door, the first one simply flapped in the wind. The second door was a bit more difficult, but it too, was forced open by Edanos and Fadis.

As the archer stepped into the next room, he immediately notched an arrow and snaked his way to the right of the door. Edanos pointed his sword in front of him. He scanned the surroundings, and then Braei and Valrin followed.

There were old bodies everywhere. Most of the bones were no more than dust, but a few still had shape. They did wear a silverish armor, but there were no markings on them.

"What do you think killed them, Captain?" Braei asked.

Edanos knelt at one of them, feeling along the bones. "I do not know. These skeletons are so old, I cannot even guess.

Valrin walked away from them and thumbed through a book on the table. *Enchanting*, the book was titled. He glanced up at a large basin in the center of the room. He then saw a crystal underneath its edge and went to it. As he rubbed his finger on the edge of it, the crystal started glowing before a roaring fire came to life in the basin.

"Wow," Edanos said, "a strange find, indeed!"

The warmth from the fire was nice, and Valrin was

so close that the last thing he wanted was to move away from it. But Fadis had noticed something, and so had Braei. A doorway, that, unlike the other wooden doors, was not very dark, had appeared surrounded by torches. As Edanos approached it, the doorway opened, resulting in a lighted hallway with large glowing stones above their heads.

"The strangest thing," Fadis said.

Several tall figures appeared before them, and at first, there was a general shuffling of weapons, but the specters did not seem to see them or care to interact with them. They began to walk down the passage.

"Should we follow?" Braei asked.

Edanos led them. It was a long passage overall, with no windows or drawings or anything to distract them from simply following their guides. There was another room here. This one had large, ice-sheeted windows on the far half edge of the room. The ocean was visible here, with a ribbon of green polar lights observable just above it.

"What is this place?" asked Braei.

Edanos shook his head. Valrin looked to those around him, but it seemed they were as perplexed as he was.

"I will have order in this assembly!" a voice rang out.

It was sudden, and the speaker materialized before them, but he was speaking away from them. The specters they had seen before began to appear clearer than they had seen them.

It was a large group of people. They were not elves

or dwarves. They appeared as men but wore strange tall headdresses that were weird geometrical shapes. Everything about them was alien to him.

"We must flee this place. The wars have come to close! The waters will flood the cities on lower ground," one of them said.

"You think as the elves. We are above them, and we must act it," another said.

The original speaker who had called them to order stretched out his hands.

"It is written that we shall uphold ourselves with mindfulness when faced with tragedy. One cannot descend to panic, to simple pleasures of the flesh. We cannot lose faith in what energy we put toward our minds."

"But, master, the storms are getting closer. We cannot pray to the gods; they have abandoned us. We are here alone."

"We are not alone, for we will always be a part of this place. Our spirits will live on, and our presence will become as the sea. Forever. Our ancestors are within every rock of the mountains high. The world is but a step from us. The realm of the gods is within reach to us if only we claim it."

The original man who had called for them to flee now spoke again. "We are without the ability to claim such a thing. We are without connection to our brethren. We will die here and become part of the sea. With storms we shall be remembered, thunder rolling across vast oceans. I have seen it. I have seen the future. Our world will fade away, and few of any who call themselves of our blood will ever know we existed."

Lightning flashed outside the windows, and Valrin wasn't sure if it was real or if it was part of whatever vision they were witnessing.

"So be the end of this place. The sea that will be, will be home to our guidance, and we will lock away our knowledge until the time is meant for it to be restored. We will no longer ascend as have others. I say to you each, go upon the world at death and become part of it, waiting to give our knowledge to the ones marked by the storms. The gods work in ways beyond us, but we have all dreamed of storms and children. It is a sign of what is to come."

The group nodded to what their master said.

"In time we will have a purpose. When this path is walked again, it will be that time. We shall help those who cannot help themselves. We will do the will of the gods, but I fear it will be a time of great sorrow for those whose path we guide. For our path is never one of ease. May the faith of the Dwemhar always guide."

The vision ceased, and the room became dark again.

"What in the gods was that?" Fadis asked.

"I don't know," Edanos said. He stared at Valrin. "Vals, do you feel that they spoke of the Stormborn, of you and I?"

"They spoke of children and storms."

"We are on the right path, then," he said. "Let us return to our ship. We were meant to see this, but I feel we must get moving on our quest. We are near the end to what I have sought for my entire life. Vals, let us get to where we need to go."

"Dwemhar, strange," Braei said. "Maybe they aren't the myth I thought."

They exited the room, and Valrin felt something he had never felt before. He had more purpose than even standing before the sprite of Meredaas in Merea. He did not know much of this Dwemhar term or even what he had seen. He wasn't even sure of the name itself.

As they exited the structure, passing between the two statues, he asked Edanos of them. "Were they the sea people we hear of in rumor?"

"Vals, in all my days, I have never seen something like those. I would guess they were the sea people, and I feel we may see something like that again, in time. We must keep the path."

"Keep the path?" Fadis said. "Are you a priest?"

"No, Fadis, but you could use a path yourself. It seems you were a bit too zealous to join on a random adventure leading to death."

"Fair enough, I guess. I had myself a good time at the brothel in town. Death is okay for now. You should teach your son there about that."

Edanos grabbed him by the shoulder and spun him around. "You would mind your tongue. There are some in the world not tainted by your thinking. You are foul and unworthy. If we all survive this, I will be sure to give you pay and send you on your way once we make port. I do not care for you."

Edanos walked past him, beckoning Valrin to follow him.

Fadis shook his head as Braei walked past him.

"You did not tell him you're not my father?" Valrin asked.

"No, I care little to speak to him more than I need to. Let him assume."

They were nearly halfway across the walkway, and their ship was clearly ahead. Valrin was freezing. The expanse of the open ocean was frigid, and there was no warmth left in his body.

"No," Edanos said slowly.

Valrin looked up at him and noticed he was staring to the west. "What is it?"

Edanos didn't answer. "Let us move, quickly," he shouted.

The group made it to the ship in very quick time. Rortho bowed to Edanos.

"Captain, we have a good tide. We're ready to cast off."

Edanos was at the helm. "Then cast off now!"

"You heard the captain, raise the sails, get them up, quickly, quickly," Rortho ordered.

Fadis went to help the crew as Braei and Valrin joined Edanos at the helm.

"What is it?" Valrin asked.

"Dwarves. Behind us. Coming quickly."

Braei and Valrin looked behind them, seeing flames just visible in the veil of the fogs.

"How could they navigate and find us? How could they know where we were?"

"I have a guess," Edanos said. "There are such things that one can place and then follow through the works of magic. Not all aboard are crew who can be trusted, but it is too late to turn back now."

Valrin could tell they were talking about Fadis. He looked at the archer as he secured the sails. He wasn't sure what to make of him.

They pulled away from the ruins and came to an open expanse of ocean. The dwarven ships were drawing closer but still far behind them for the moment. There was a flat sea here. The twilight rim of an approaching dawn lit the sky in a purple hue, and at that moment, the water around them began to undulate and break.

Valrin went to the rail of the ship and looked over. Large creatures swam beside them.

"Whales," Braei told him. "Hundreds of them, maybe more. Edanos, look!"

But Edanos was looking behind him. The dwarven ship was not alone and the many vessels pursuing them were not slowing.

"I cannot believe they are moving at such a pace. It is unnatural."

"It is in unnatural waters we find ourselves, Captain," Rortho said.

The whales at either side of them were of every size and species. The water began to sparkle with a strange hue that led to a massive tower that appeared in the growing dawn sky.

"That wasn't there before," Rortho said.

"It was not." Edanos nodded. "Tighten sails, make

sure we have no more wind escaping than needed. We must get to the shoreline without fail."

Valrin went back to the helm with Edanos. He turned to see their pursuers and turned back to see Edanos looking at him.

"Do not worry about them. If what I believe is right, you will be safe, but I must get you there."

"We will get there, and we can discover whatever it is that is so guarded by Meredaas."

"Perhaps, but I may not be able to immediately follow. Nothing is certain for us."

A horn sounded. Not a dwarven horn nor an elven horn. In fact, it was no horn that any aboard had ever heard. It started deep, rumbling the ocean surface itself, and then, like a shift in the wind, it sounded again only with a higher pitch.

A sound came from beneath the ocean, and the water bubbled around them as large crags began to emerge, piercing through the surface of the clear expanse, turning it into what looked like several mountain ranges.

Edanos spun the wheel of the ship in an effort to move the ship from running aground.

"Hold your lines. We are in for rough sailing!" Rortho shouted out.

Edanos moved the wheel of the ship the opposite way as it seemed they now followed a strange road in the ocean made up of the stone fences of sudden obstacles.

The island drew closer, and as they snaked through

the strange pathway in the ocean, a deep fog rolled over them.

"Valrin! See to the crystal!"

Valrin ran to the front of the ship and checked the crystal. Passing his hand over it, the crystal spun to life, casting a bright flame toward the fogs. They receded, though much lower than before.

The rocky sailing passage began to recede as they came to the end of a line of jagged points.

"A bit of insurance?" asked Braei. "To assure those not worthy do not make it here?"

"I suppose," Edanos said to her. "We draw close to this place we have sought. Hopefully, the dwarves will not reach these waters."

The shoreline was ahead. A large pillar with a massive shell rose out of the water. The wind gusted, and the shell began to make a deep horn sound. They had made it.

As Valrin stood at the fore of the ship, Fadis came to his side.

"You believe in this strange journey to who knows, don't you?"

"I have no reason not to."

Fadis smirked. "I'd say that's true, but is it worth what we do? Heading to the far northern seas to nearly get killed for no reason in a rickety ship?"

"I'd say that you offered to come, and I'd argue that this was a, as you said, rickety ship."

"I was paid to come," he corrected, "but you are unlike me. You have some choice, do you not?"

"I do not."

"You were taken against your will?"

"No, but I have no one else and nothing else to do."

"A man always has a choice. It is simply if he has the courage to make it. I think you do, Valrin."

"A profound statement," Braei said from behind them.

"It is," Fadis said. "I will get back to cleaning the deck. I assume we will have a bit more ice building up, and it isn't going to scrape itself."

"Yes, it is good you find something of use to do."

As Fadis went back to ship duties, Braei stood with Valrin. The shoreline was ahead. It was bleak, with white sand and tall cliffs that reached up into the clouds. There was only one beach and two large white pillars off to one side of the beach.

As the ship drew close to shallows, Edanos ordered the sails lowered and passed the wheel to Rortho.

"I do not see our pursuers, but I expect them in time."

"We won't let them get close, Captain. I'll keep them from the shore."

Fadis strung his bow as the others prepared a small boat to row to shore.

"No," said Edanos.

"No?" the man asked. "Did I cause any trouble before?"

"Of course not, but I need you here. If the dwarves get close, you will be a useful asset."

Fadis was surprised and scanned the horizon. "No dwarves yet. I could just return and—"

"You will follow my orders. Rortho has command until I return."

Valrin got into the boat with Braei and several of the crew. Edanos joined them, and they were lowered into the water.

With a splash sending icy spray over Valrin's already windblown face, he looked around at the strange surroundings. Glowing plants grew up the side of the cliff face, and it seemed that though the presence of life was strangely strong here, he could see no other living animals. The whales from before had split off before the sudden eruption of rocks from the ocean floor.

As they drew close to the shore, a rogue current pushed them further to the shoreline, and in an instant, their small boat was left on the sands of the island's beach.

Valrin looked up the cliffs, immediately seeing what Meredaas had told him he would. A lone door marked with a star. As he and Valrin stepped out, the others of the crew drew their weapons.

"I see no reason for enemies here," Edanos cautioned, "but be mindful. This place is more unknown to my sense than the entirety of the ocean depths."

The door itself was up a small dune of sand and flatly placed into the cliffs. Valrin approached it with Braei at his side, and the door simply cracked open. He looked down at his amulet and noticed it was bright blue now.

As they entered into a dark chamber, the door shut

behind them to the sudden dismay of the crew. There were only ten others, but many of them were the new crew picked up at Merea before.

"Do not fear," Edanos told them. "If I am right and all I have studied is right, we are safe here."

The walls were splashed with torchlight that seemed to come to life with their presence in the long hall that reached out from them.

"Sea people?" asked Braei.

He nodded to her. "Perhaps, but I doubt any of them still exist. The vision at the tower before confirmed that; at least, I believe it did. We will find something else. Something we have searched for. Something I have searched for."

They progressed down the long hall. The light of the torches was nothing like the light coming from Valrin's amulet. He lifted it up, holding it as an additional light source until they came to another door. This one had the image of a large fish upon it. He pushed it open and felt a rush of warm, salty wind. They were in another chamber. A larger room of sorts, with a massive fire burning from a cylindrical pit that had no obvious fuel source. There were steps to their right, and after several paths that took them further and further down, they came to another gateway. This was bound by golden bars.

Valrin could hear the water on the other side. As he touched the bars, nothing happened.

"Your amulet, try it," Edanos said.

He took his amulet and did as Edanos said, placing

it against the bars. They began to glow and then slowly receded into the gateway.

He stepped in with Edanos at his heel. They were met by something neither of them expected. Braei immediately lifted her hands to summon spells, and the crew with them cowered.

4
VALRIN OF THE SEA

VALRIN GASPED as Edanos fell to his knees.

Before them was that which could only be described as a massive fish. Its head sat on the surface of the water, and on his head was a large crown of gold. Appearing suddenly, as if a veil was lifted, was elaborate stonework decorating the entire cave, reaching up above them and around the entire room.

"Meredaas of the many oceans. We are not worthy!"

The god of the sea was before them. The god many had spoken of in Valrin's life. Normally in curse or prayer but never as an actual sight to actually see in breathing form just as the whales from before.

"My eternal home quakes," Meredaas said. "Come, Valrin and Edanos, Stormborn, come to my depths."

The god-fish sank into the water as two figures emerged from the surface. They were like the sirens from before but much more beautiful. The females were nude except for long hair hanging down from their heads, just covering them.

As Valrin stepped forward, one of them handed him a large shell.

"Keep this upon your chest," she told him. "It will allow you to enter our grace's presence."

Valrin placed the shell on his chest, and suddenly it was difficult for him to breathe. He removed the shell.

"I can't breathe."

Edanos did as Valrin had and then jumped into the water.

"Your friend does not bear the amulet, but he has the idea that you must embrace. With the shell, you are not of the land but of the sea. Join the depths. You will find the water warm within this place."

Valrin placed the shell on his chest again and jumped in. At once, he felt himself floating downward, further down than ever possible without the shell. He took a deep breath, and he was able to breathe though he felt a strange tingle as he did. The shell suctioned to his chest, and he was able to put his hands out. He flapped his arms as he went, feeling the water float through his fingertips as Edanos looked up from below him and smiled.

Schools of fish floated between them. Sharks, octopuses, and even several more mermaids swam around them.

Valrin looked down further and could see glowing shells and hundreds of merpeople. He then looked into an area of coral along the bottom of the depths and saw the massive sea god, Meredaas, floating on the sea floor.

As his feet came to rest on the soft sand, he walked with Valrin to a large platform of archways and spinning spheres of coral. A white fire shot up and around them.

"You have unlocked the way to the future, dear Valrin and Edanos of the *Truest Bliss*. Captain of the surface realm, you have aided the young one along this path. You have the thanks of all for your efforts. You sacrifice much to complete this task."

"For the glory of the sea and your reign, Meredaas."

"My reign means little to those upon the oceans now, but I thank you. You are both of what you saw within the old tower of the sea peoples. How foolish were they to use my graceful and terrible ocean for their own destructive needs? Much like others who seek to plunder my home for their own advantage. It is souls like them who will derail that which has been set about in the world of the gods. I have found hope in you who come for that which was promised and foretold. You will have something that none else have. A tool, a treasure to some, but of something that requires the very life of one of you."

"We must die?" Valrin asked.

He didn't mean to sound so shocked or to speak so suddenly, but instead of some form of retribution or cruel words, the fish seemed to laugh, if it could be called laughter.

"No, my young one, but it will require something of a promise, a binding to your life. Remove your amulet so it may serve its true purpose for your life."

Valrin removed the amulet, and it floated away from him, resting in front of Meredaas.

"Those of the sea from before were wise to work to restore my faith in their race. So close they were to me in the beginning, it is horrid that they are all gone from the world; at least, as they are now. There will come a time when others are prepared, but not yet."

The amulet floated down and into the sand. There was a shock that Valrin felt in his feet, and then the sand began to rumble. The surface of the underwater expanse began to shift, and in a large plume of bubbling sand, something emerged and rose to the surface.

Meredaas spoke. "In time there will be much need of a captain of the seas. You are young, but you have the soul that is strong enough to do what you must in the coming years. Edanos of the *Truest Bliss*, long have you sought my seas for the chance to do what another will do instead. But I will bless you in time. You must protect this young one and his gift. You are not done in your life's quest. All will be known in time."

Valrin felt himself rising up, coming to the surface of the water. Hands came under him and Edanos. Mermaids propelled them up and out of the water. The shells that had helped them breathe fell off, and Valrin's eyes became huge as he looked down at the glowing golden object that the mermaids dropped him toward. He was nearly to whatever it was, and the mermaids released him. He floated down gracefully, standing on the strange glowing structure. As he stood there, the glowing subsided, and he noticed he was on a ship.

Edanos looked around and dropped to the deck of it. "So long I have awaited the chance to be on the deck of such a vessel as this. This is one of the Realm Vessels of the sea peoples. I had only read about them, but they have powers beyond any simple ship."

Valrin was not sure what to think. The vessel seemed like it had not sailed at all. The deck was of the purest wood and had not a single scratch. The sails were strange and did not have all the extra pulleys and ropes as did the *Truest Bliss*, and did not have weapons. He walked to one of the posts and saw his amulet in the wood. He reached out to take it when Meredaas bumped the side of the ship.

"Valrin of Travaa, you have made the journey of the Stormborn. You stand now on the vessel of your ancestors, a jewel of the sea, enchanted with the powers of old to uphold the sanctity of my oceans. You are of the sea. You are the sword of the sea. Your connection is like no other for you. If you choose to become the captain of the vessel, you will be connected to the ship. You will not need sleep as you do in your human form. You will be a stalwart beacon tied to my realm in living and in death. If you accept such a task, know only that you may never recant your vow. As Stormborn, you will accept your title and your fate in that time where you must give your life for those who will go forward."

There was a sudden deep silence unlike any Valrin had ever heard. He closed his eyes. He had spent so many days simply living on the island back home. He always listened to the stories of the sea, the captains, the bards, the drunken men spouting off about what they had seen. Aunt Tua was always there, protecting him, and in her final act of protection, she had given her life.

He looked to Edanos, and he saw tears running down his face.

"Vals, do not fret over me. Just to be within the presence of our mutual god is overwhelming for me. I wished, oh, how I wished to be in your boots and to take this on, but know I will be with you on your journey. I will protect you if you take this oath. You can do it, Vals."

Valrin took hold of the amulet. He wanted to simply pull it from its resting place in the ship. His heartbeat was in sync with the amulet. He was giving a part of himself for a calling that only a few days ago he knew nothing of. He closed his eyes and could feel the water against the bow of the boat. Further out, he could feel the oceans of the Glacial Seas and the ice moving in the great depths. He heard the songs of the whales as they spoke to one another and the scratching of the large octopuses moving along the deepest ravines beyond the reach of light.

He pushed the amulet into the wood of the ship and removed his hand.

"I, Valrin of Travaa, Stormborn, accept this ship

and the charge of Meredaas to protect his seas and to command this ship of old."

There was a flash of light, and the surroundings so glorious and dazzling faded away.

"Trust in me, Valrin," Meredaas said.

The ship moved along the shoreline. It rested against the stone docks as Braei and the others ran down toward them. The splendor they had seen before had vanished to the cave and only the golden gates shown.

"The ship! Edanos, the ship you always spoke of! The one you talked of from the old stories!"

Edanos wiped his eyes. "I have walked a righteous path in honor of the sea, and I know this path was what we should follow."

From the opposite side of the large cave system came the sounds of scratching stone. The rocky cave wall slid down, letting in a blistering wind from the outside seas. The torches around them went dark, and they once again were exposed to the frigid cold of the Glacial Seas.

Valrin went to the helm of the ship, and the sails seemed to react to just his touch on the wheel.

"Come aboard," Edanos told everyone. Braei jumped on, rubbing her fingers across the railings. The ship was no longer gold but instead was a deep red oak. There were several crystals at the helm, but Valrin had no idea what they did. As the crew joined them, it was strange for them to have no immediate need to do anything to help the ship go underway.

"Take us out, Valrin. We will meet up with the

Truest Bliss and decide what we must do next. The dwarves will no doubt be close. We must hope that we do not need to fight, but if we do, I will help you."

As he gave thought to the direction of the ship, it seemed to respond slightly with drifting that way but then more so as he actually turned the wheel. He had the strangest feelings as they began to depart.

He maneuvered the ship as it sliced through the water to the cave opening. It was agile, slender, and moved with such ease, there was no comparing it to even the *Truest Bliss*. As they went through the opening in the cave, they began out a long rocky crevice with only the sky above them. Valrin looked ahead at open sea and to clear waters. He would need to turn left as they exited, as best he could figure. As Edanos came to his side, he felt confident. He did not know what was to happen in the coming days, but he felt hope.

It was then several thuds struck the ship from above. Valrin looked up to see dwarves swinging down from rocks above. Braei shot several fiery spells at the intruders as the crew brandished their weapons.

Edanos drew his blade and pointed. "Get us to the *Truest Bliss*!"

Valrin gripped the wheel, keeping the ship moving forward but watching as more dwarves poured from above. Their crew fell to the deck, splashing blood as more dwarves swarmed the deck. One of them spotted Valrin and ran up the stairwell to him. Edanos parried his swinging ax, deflecting it away before slashing the man in the neck.

The ship made its way from its rocky birth to the

open sea. But the sea was not as open as he had thought. Eight black dwarven vessels were in a half circle, sealing the harbor. The *Truest Bliss* had been boarded.

Valrin heard a click, and a crossbow bolt struck Edanos in the shoulder. The captain of the *Truest Bliss* fell to the deck of Valrin's ship.

A dwarf began to laugh. There was another ship approaching. It was a large ship. It was the ship that before had been in the harbor at Travaa.

"Well, well, well, it seems the ole' dwarf captain had his suspicions, and they turned out just as he suspected," the dwarf shouted from afar.

Several clawed chains were thrown into the deck but could not grasp the wood. They simply slid and fell off the side.

"So it is nigh uncatchable!" The dwarf laughed. "But it is the ship."

"Stop the hollering, Rugag. It is me you want," Edanos shouted.

"Oh, Edanos, it was you once, but it is the wee lad now. He has my ship, the ship my king deserves. The ship that my king's desire for resulted in some of your own poor crew being left on a deserted island just to be picked up, for the righteous Edanos couldn't leave poor saps just to die."

The ship had slowly drifted toward the *Truest Bliss*, and the ship of Rugag had gone with it. The current was very strong, so Valrin assumed it was actually partially his thought that moved the ship.

As they drew closer, Valrin and Braei, who were being held at spear point, noticed the dwarves on the ship holding the crew hostage were the same ones that Edanos had saved.

Rortho looked out, and Fadis was at his side.

"They betrayed us, Edanos!" Rortho shouted. "The bastards gave us up. They had some type of dwarven device in their jewelry. We've been sold out by your kindness."

"You cannot take the boy," Edanos said. "He isn't yours; he isn't mine. He is his own. He is of the great god Meredaas."

The dwarf laughed again with a boisterous tone. "Meredaas, the giant fish? I no longer believe in the fallacies of the weak. If the one of the seas wants to do something about me, let the bastard squid lover!"

Edanos crawled to Valrin. "You must live, no matter what. You must escape this place with the ship. The fate of the Stormborn, the fate of our futures, rest with you, Valrin."

One of the dwarves who was nearest walked over to Edanos and kicked him.

"Shut up, you damn fool! No more rattlin'!" The dwarf then went toward Valrin.

"Take the boy, and then we will take the ship. We will kill the rest and feed them to the sharks, and then when the sharks are done, we'll take the sharks. Can't have good trading supplies go to waste!"

The dwarf stomped toward him. Valrin grimaced. Drawing his sword, he held it out toward his foe.

"Now, little boy, we don't want you to hurt yourself. Give me the blade, and it will be enough. You don't want to kill, and we do not want you to."

He held the blade up, but he was shaking. He knew very little, save a few sword fights back at home that were all for play. There was that one swordsman—it was an elf. He knew a lot and said his sons were like Valrin's age in appearance and already as proficient as any man. It was hard for Valrin to believe that. He turned his thought to his adversary. He was breathing heavily, and he made steps back as the dwarf approached. He closed his eyes.

Meredaas, help.

The ship shook and rocked beneath his feet. The dwarf lost balance and fell. The other dwarves still hanging on from above struggled to hold on as the ship began to toss in the water. There was a blast of water to their right, and several of the whales from before struck Rugag's ship. Meredaas heard him.

Braei took the moment to cast a stormy barrage of lightning into different dwarves on the ship. The dwarf who had stumbled now grabbed his foot. Valrin stabbed him with the point of his blade, severing the dwarf's fingers. He then slashed it across the back of the exposed hairy neck, sending a splatter of blood on either side of the man.

He ran to Edanos, helping his friend up. The bolt was in his chest, and Edanos struggled to breathe.

Rugag had been distracted by the onslaught of sea creatures attacking his boat. Several large octopuses climbed up the side, and the whales kept his ship from being steadied.

Over on the *Truest Bliss*, the few remaining loyal crew fought to take back the ship. The outer line of dwarven ships began to fire their bolts, sending massive chained hooks hurling through the air.

Rortho shouted over, "Get to our ship. We are clear of breathing dwarves, 'cept myself."

Fadis jumped to the ship with Valrin and ran toward where Edanos was. As he came up, he drew his bow, aiming toward Valrin. Valrin dropped as the bolt passed just to his side, taking down the dwarf who had tried to capture him.

"If you're going to have a sword, best actually use it to kill the dwarves," Fadis told him.

Fadis and Braei took hold of Edanos. "Get me to my ship and then stay with Valrin. He needs your help. He is your captain."

Braei shook her head. "Get Edanos to the *Truest Bliss*! We will need both ships to break through the dwarven fleet! You're not dying, Edanos! We will all get out of this!"

Valrin followed behind them as they went to the front of the vessel. Rortho was waiting, and though the ships bounced precariously close to one another, they did not strike, and they were able to move Edanos to his ship. A bolt flew into the side of the *Truest Bliss*, sending wood splintering into the air.

"Follow us!" Rortho shouted.

Edanos was struggling to stand aboard his ship, but

was staring at Valrin. "Follow me out, Vals. I will show you the way."

"And I will show you how to send their ships to the bottom of the sea!" Rortho shouted.

The dwarf, first mate of the damaged vessel *Truest Bliss*, ran to man the crossbows. Most of the crew remained aboard the ship, but none had the zeal of the dwarf.

Fadis drew his bow, firing at several dwarves already aiming at them. Valrin watched as he drew arrow after arrow, releasing in quick succession. He then ran to the railings and fired a set of two arrows, striking more dwarves aboard the enemy vessel. "Come, Valrin. You must get to the helm!"

He ran to the wheel. Taking it in hand, he turned away from the *Truest Bliss*, running his ship against the vessel of Rugag.

"Bastard boy!" he heard the dwarf shouting.

The *Truest Bliss* pulled in front of them. Edanos was at the helm, and Rortho ran along the crossbows, sending bolts into the vessels that were approaching them. It took great strength for the dwarf, firing the massive bolts and then pulling back on the twined chains by himself. Many of the crew were falling to arrow fire from the dwarven vessels. There wasn't any more of the crew on Valrin's vessel. None except Fadis and Braei, at least.

Edanos made an obvious pointing motion that Valrin followed. His ship moved quickly, almost overtaking whom he was following, and the dwarves were closing in.

It was a narrow passage that they were sailing toward, a spot where there was only one dwarven vessel and then open sea. It wasn't an opening before, but when the ocean creatures began attacking, the other ships had moved to help Rugag.

"Fire!" he heard from behind him. He turned to see several streaks of fiery arrows fly over his ship and strike the *Truest Bliss*. It was a moment later when another wave came, this one sending a bolt over Valrin's head. Braei went to the side of the ship and cast a blast of fire into the ocean, creating a large veil of steam rising up into the air. It did a good job of shrouding their vessels.

Edanos was moving the ship to the left again, taking a path around the towering island. If they could get distance between them and the other ships, they had a chance.

Another line of bolts came flying toward them, but due to the Rusis' distraction, their bolts missed.

Valrin felt confident. He felt relaxed to some point. They had somehow escaped the clutches of Rugag, and through no real understanding himself, Meredaas had answered his short and sudden prayer.

A horn called. This one he had heard before. Braei jerked her glance toward the *Truest Bliss*. Several more dwarven ships appeared in a line, running a passage to block them in. These had been hidden. Waiting. It was like it was all part of Rugag's game.

Valrin looked behind and saw the rest of the dwarven fleet bringing in the net of ships. There was a narrow opening to open ocean, but there was a dwarven vessel running parallel to them, attempting to cut them off.

The *Truest Bliss* changed course. Its sails were at full. It ran a path almost directly with Valrin, but Rortho was no longer at the crossbows. His ax was out, and he stood at the front of the ship. He was holding the ropes and bracing himself.

As Valrin kept his course, aiming for the ever-closing opening, Edanos rammed the *Truest Bliss* into the dwarven vessel. Edanos then drew his blade and ran with Rortho, jumping onto the dwarven vessel that they had thrown off course, leaving the way open for Valrin. He moved his ship around the floating wreckage and to open sea. As he twisted the wheel back to the left, he noticed Edanos and Rortho fighting multiple dwarves.

Fadis fired several arrows, striking dwarves all along the opposite deck.

Valrin had taken the wrong path. He now ran along the line of dwarven vessels instead of out and further away. A barrage of bolts came screaming over the top of the deck, just nearly missing the masts and the small crew Valrin had to start with.

Braei was on the railing. She appeared extremely weak, but she was still casting spells. The Rusis' strength was failing her. Fadis held strong.

"We need to get out of here, Captain," Fadis said.

He was the captain. The captain of the Stormborn vessel. But he had a choice, and though he didn't know what he was doing, he had to try. He wheeled the ship into the dwarven line.

"Valrin! That is not what I had in mind!" Fadis shouted.

He did not know what would happen, but he looked to the crystals at the helm. Twisting the first one, the masts began to shine brightly, and a blast of fire shot out of the side of the ship. A moment later, the hull of the ship struck the dwarven vessel. The ships tore at one another, leaving chunks of the dwarven vessel in the water.

Fadis angled his bow, loosing into the dwarves one after another as they attempted to board. Braei sat on the deck, hyperventilating but trying to still look over the railings and cast whatever she could.

Valrin had his plan. He was new to sailing, but this was his ship. Ordained to him by birth in a storm upon the sea that cast him into the care of his aunt, Tua. He had taken the step forward in faith, and now he had to save the one who had done so much for him in the short time he was in his life. He had to save Edanos.

As he ran his ship beside the dwarven vessels, he twisted the crystals, sending blasts of arcane fire toward the ships. The dwarves who had been manning the crossbows fell back to avoid the searing stream. As he went ship to ship, he noticed the blasts weakening, but he had still done catastrophic damage to the other vessels.

The other dwarven ships, including Rugag's, were closing on them.

"Fadis, retrieve our friends. Do what you can, please."

"I will do so, Captain!"

As they came along the last ship, Valrin spotted Edanos was on the ground, but the first mate was still up, and though covered in blood, he had not stopped killing those of his kind. Fadis jumped to the enemy ship, and Valrin turned the wheel, forcing his ship into the dwarven one. The dwarves on the vessel had seen what had happened to the other ships and fled as Edanos and Rortho came aboard his ship. The mast of the *Truest Bliss* was still just visible, but the ship of Edanos was falling into the depths. That was not the fate of the remaining crew today. Fadis had retrieved Edanos, and Rortho followed.

"Valrin! Get us out of here! Toward OPEN sea this time!" Fadis shouted.

Valrin turned the ship away from the dwarven one and made for the open sea. As the other vessels of Rugag came near, he twisted the same crystal again and a blast of fire shot out again, this time toward the other vessels. The dwarven vessels did not pursue them and instead went to their other crippled ships. They had escaped and Valrin guided them into the bleak expanse. Safer waters, at least for now.

Fadis had taken the helm as Valrin went to Edanos.

"Vals, you should have left me. You were reckless. You could've gotten yourself and this ship destroyed."

He stared at him, seeing the anger in his eyes and the anguish of the pain he was in. He smiled. "Seems I need a captain to teach me still."

Edanos smiled back. "It does seem so."

Rortho knelt down, pushing a strange herbal mixture into the many wounds Edanos had. The bolt from the dwarven attackers was still in place.

"He will need healing, something beyond our skill set. We had supplies on the other ship, but this ship does not quite seem seaworthy beyond having some flashy powers, if you can call 'em that."

Valrin looked around. He did not yet understand the vessel they were on, but there had to be something. It was then a blast of water sprayed the deck. He went to the edge and noticed a whale pushing a wooden box.

As he tried to reach for it, he found it just out of reach. Rortho used his ax to pull it closer and then reached down to pull it out of the water.

The chest itself had the same emblem as the door before the place where they had gotten the ship. It was the image of Meredaas. He opened the chest to find several golden items, none of which he knew what were for.

There was a single parchment within, and it was addressed to Valrin directly.

He opened the letter and began to read.

Valrin, Stormborn. You have escaped from near death, saved one who believed in you, and now sail upon the seas of uncertainty. You have a vessel unlike any other, and you must learn it and unlock its true powers. There is much for you to discover, but I do say for you to take these devices I have included. Set them upon the aft deck and watch as the powers of the seafarers awaken.

From there, you will be led in time to where you must go. There is much more for the Stormborn to do.

The message said nothing else. He carried the box to the rear of the ship and took the golden items. Each were a different prism. They were made of gold but were near opaque. He set each of them on the ship's deck, and they began to spin before floating together and moving into the wood itself. On the lower deck, a stone and metallic altar of sorts formed out of the very wood of the ship. A massive image of what Valrin could only describe as a floating map made of air appeared before them.

"A map of the sea," Fadis said. "I do not recognize most of this, but to the far south is where we met up, Merea. I can tell from the outline. But whatever this is, it is moving. Like it is the actual sea itself."

Valrin stared at the map, seeing a dense cloud cover moving over the image that matched the clouds above. As he stared, he saw an island. He turned the ship, and it seemed the map he stared at changed as well.

"We will try here," he told the others. He wasn't sure where they were going, but considering they were so far north and none of them knew where exactly to go, it seemed like the best idea. He did not know how much time Edanos had, and as his friend seemed to be breathing faster and in more pain, he assumed not too long at all.

. . .

In time, they came upon the island seen on the map. Though it was abandoned itself, Rortho was able to find supplies good enough to remove the barb from Edanos.

He started a fire and got a small knife red hot.

"This is going to hurt, but you know I must," the dwarf warned.

Edanos fell unconscious and was struggling to breathe. At the last moment, and to their surprise, a fairy floated down and moved over Edanos' wounds. Rortho quickly removed the barb. Edanos opened his eyes for a moment, and his breathing returned to normal. The fairy crisscrossed over his body and it seemed that after being healed by the power of the fairy, Edanos fell into a deep sleep.

"Look! He's better!" Braei said.

But even though he seem to have improved, a dark red mark appeared where the injury had been. Edanos shivered and his breathing was erratic.

"Better but not perfect," Fadis said.

"We'll watch him," Rortho said, "We need to get back to sea. There are other places we can go. I'll tend to Edanos for now."

They departed the island, sailing south for a time as Valrin tried to prepare for what it meant to be a Stormborn. The dwarves of Rugag were not going to simply allow him to escape, but he had beaten them once. In his young mind, for at least now, that was enough. The moon rose, and he did not feel tired as the others were. Though Fadis and Braei both questioned him, he gave them his reasoning, which they didn't believe but were too tired to argue.

As he glanced up at the night sky and millions of stars, the polar lights shined a bright green. He closed his eyes. He was Valrin of Travaa. Stormborn.

His true quest had just begun.

MAGE SOUL

BOOK TWO

1
SHADOWS OF OLD

Valrin sat beside Edanos. It had been three days since his wounds were healed. The fairy magic had sealed the wound, and though at the time Rortho was confident he was improving, his sureness had begun to fade. The once captain of the *Truest Bliss* had not awoken, and his breathing had changed again. The redness they noticed before had gotten worse and was spreading around the original site of the injury.

"Storm is coming," he heard Braei say from behind him.

The Rusis touched him on the shoulder.

"I will stay with him for now. You have spent every night at his side, and you could use the rest."

Valrin glanced at her. "I told you that I no longer need sleep."

"Perhaps not, but you are the captain of this vessel. A captain should be on deck. I will stay with him for now."

The chambers within the ship were well lit but empty. There were barren shelves and netting for supplies, but very little else. He went back up the stairwell and opened the wooden hatch at the top.

He emerged on the deck to find Fadis and Rortho both at the helm.

"Storm is coming, Captain," the dwarf said.

A long line of black thunderclouds were moving toward them, and the gusts of southern air were as salty as they were relentless.

Valrin went to the pedestal and moved his hand over the crystal. The map showed vast seas around them and no obvious places to take shelter.

"We've moved south for the last two days, but we cannot seem to get there. The current and winds are wrong. It is like the gods bid us stay in this region."

Fadis went to the edge of the ship. "The gods can bid all they want, but this storm might have other plans of its own. I haven't seen one so big in quite a few years. Besides, the swells are really picking up. Perhaps we should head back north? It might be safer."

Valrin shook his head. "Rortho, you've sailed on these waters for much longer than any of us. What do you think?"

The dwarf grunted and looked up at the clouds. "Keep us angled to the storm. We should move east and try to go around. We have few answers right now. If we can find a place to hide, it might be best."

"Are we too far from Merea?"

"Yes and we could have a fight on our hands just to get that way," he replied solemnly. "There are many islands in the far north of the glacial seas, some not so friendly, and some flat abandoned. The ethereal qualities of the far north are a mystery to many. You have places like Merea and, a bit to the southeast of that, Corson. But most places are frozen ruins and realms of beasts long forgotten. We are lucky we haven't been swallowed up by some monster to be honest. There are a few of those in the deep depths or so the old ice dwarf stories say."

"Great. Stories," Fadis joked.

Rortho gave him a sharp glance. "A man of archery is uncommon in these waters. What is your true story . . . archer?"

"My story matters little, but I aim to make my past better. In current company, since I have little to hide, know I am from Taria and have been gone from there for six years."

"Criminal?"

"In a way, to some. I let those I love slip away."

The dwarf laughed. "Then please, good archer, do not love us."

Though it was meant in good humor, Fadis just looked down and then walked to the rear railings and stared out.

Valrin could tell he was upset, and even Rortho seemed surprised by Fadis' abrupt actions. Valrin wondered of where he came from, but did not go to him. It seemed best, at this point, to just let him be alone with his thoughts.

. . .

The ship was cutting through the water at a now wondrous pace, but the storm seemed to be turning. That, or its grand expanse, was too much for them to outrun, and they were simply losing any hope of having enough time to escape it.

"You thought of a name for this ship yet, Valrin?" Rortho questioned.

He hadn't, and he really hadn't thought to name it at all.

"All ships of the sea must have a name," he continued. "This one is no different. It may have powers and be a so-called realm ship, but it is a law of the sea that all ships must have a name."

"A law?"

"Well, more of a preference really, a good luck type . . . er . . . thing."

Valrin thought a bit and then looked out across the waters. He had nothing that came to mind in the short time he had actually been thinking of a name.

"Well," Rortho said, "it is no matter. But you need to be thinking of something."

As Valrin stared out across the water, he saw a haziness appear in the distance. The winds shifted, and Fadis ran down to the lower deck.

"This storm is drawing upon us. I will tell Braei to prepare herself."

Rortho shifted the wheel in his hands. The ship seemed to jerk against him.

"The rudder is giving me a bit of a stubborn pull. Valrin, over here. Come help me."

Valrin went to the helm and tried to work with him

to guide the ship. The waves were increasing in size, and the storm had turned the sky black.

"This ship can cast fire from its sails. I don't guess you have any other tricks?"

Valrin grimaced as he pulled the wheel. "I wouldn't know where to start!"

The ship was overtaken with a showering rain. They began to lurch from side to side in the winds, and the sails began to glow before lowering completely.

"What in the god Throka was that?" the dwarf said. "Where are our sails?"

Valrin looked down at the crystals. He hadn't touched them. In his moment of distraction, a massive wave struck the ship, throwing him away from the helm. He rolled into the railings, and a large wave of icy water shot across the deck. He sat up and looked out to a series of flashing lightning. There was suddenly an island coming into view. Rortho had seen it too. He turned the wheel hard in an attempt to guide the ship, but it was no good. The ocean tossed them further, moving the ship with haste toward massive rocky cliffs. It was then, in the shroud of the storms, a water cyclone twisted out of the clouds and moved toward them.

"Hold on to something!" Rortho shouted.

The blast of icy air and water moved right up to the edge of the ship and spun them in a rapid motion. The island passed around them in a blur as they were tossed into a rocky cove crowned with black cliffs and snow-covered ruins.

The cyclone moved away from the cove, and the

swell of the storms seemed to subside now that they were in the natural protection of the island.

"I have never seen any of this sort! This storm has a mind of its own!" Rortho shouted, coughing and soaking wet. Valrin got to his feet and looked around.

"Dwarven ruins?" he asked.

The towers of rock were capped with many structures with stark domes and many broken towers.

The dwarf shook his head. "No, the architecture is not dwarven. I am not sure what this is."

Braei and Fadis both emerged from below deck.

"Is Edanos okay?" Valrin asked.

"He is, but we were tossed around really good," Braei said. "Where are we?"

Fadis glanced around and made a pointing motion. "I have seen ruins like this. But it was in the south. They are not dwarven or elven. Something else."

He strung his bow.

"What are you doing?" Rortho asked.

"The dear sickly captain needs out of the cold and for good rest. I will scout ahead. See if I can find something or somewhere for us to take shelter."

The ship had come to rest against a large outcropping of rocks. Though Valrin thought to move the ship closer to shore and perhaps a better spot to disembark, Fadis jumped ahead.

Rortho made his way to the edge.

"I'll go with him. Make sure he doesn't cause any trouble."

As the two of them trudged up a rocky path, Valrin

looked to Braei and smiled. "I think I might survive my first few days as a captain, after all."

She laughed. "It is strange. You are young to be a captain."

"Not too much younger than you."

"Well, you don't see me as a captain, now do you?"

They both smiled again, and then Valrin looked toward where Edanos was. "I just don't understand. He won't wake up."

Braei made a motion with her eyebrows. "Well . . . I'm not sure." She sighed. "I always heard fairy magic was the most powerful of healing magics. Perhaps he needs a bit more? The only reason he was to his feet and fighting as he was, was his determination to help us escape. Which turning your ship towards the other vessels, well. . . that was really brave of you."

"I have to protect my crew. Even if it might cost me."

She went to the edge of the deck and looked down into the water. "Meredaas, I guess, has hope in you as a 'Stormborn' or whatever it is called, and this ship, I can't seem to explain it. How does it have magical powers?"

"Dwemhar or sea peoples? I am not sure the difference at this point, but I am guessing it has something to do with that."

"I don't know. Us Rusis never cared for those of other races. I talk a lot of my superiority to most, but that is exactly why my race is nearly extinct."

"You have never seen another Rusis?"

"No, not breathing anyway. I have memory of my

mother and father, a mere fragment of a picture. I see her, and above her is my father. His hands are alight in fire, and my mother's body is badly burned. I don't remember too much else. Be happy, Valrin, that you do not know your parents. It is not always a memory that you will be able to remember fondly."

He was shocked at her words. His thoughts of who his parents could have been were always fond. A warm feeling, or more so a fictitious story in his mind, from many nights wondering where he had really come from. Now, he wondered if his orphaning was a blessing.

It was only a few more minutes when Rortho and Fadis returned in a confident stride.

"There is a good place for us up the hill a bit," Rortho said. "It has shelter from the wind and rain and only had a few cave spiders to deal with."

"Eight cave spiders, dwarf, eight, and three of them nearly shot wads of web on you."

"Well, he is right." The dwarf nodded. "But he is good with that bow. Got off three arrows before I removed my ax from the first carcass!"

Valrin dropped the anchors. He had forgotten about that before, and while it was strange to leave the ship where it was, it was better than the ground he thought they could get to. The tides were shifting, and the ground which was covered in water just a bit before were now sands and jagged spikes of rock.

Working together, they moved Edanos and carried him up the rocky path. It was a road of some kind, and without concentrating too much on the random cracks and broken steps, Valrin could tell it was well made. He wondered if it had been here since before the great flooding that destroyed the sea peoples. If so, the place would have been on a mountain, at least so he assumed.

They reached the edge of a large platform, and the wind cut through them with a bitter chill. Valrin looked up to see the storm in all of its rage. More of the cyclones spun in the distance. The sea was terrifying in the magnificence of its uproar. He looked back to his ship and saw that strangely, the water remained very calm even though the water outside of the cove was still churning.

Rortho and Fadis carried Edanos. The captain's hand fell flaccid from his body, and Valrin lifted it up to put back on his stomach.

Braei ran ahead of them and to the obvious towering structure they were heading toward. It was like a temple of some kind. A large dome with arches and columns that ran down either side of it. A center double door was slightly ajar but seemed to move with the winds whistling around its edges. Valrin ran ahead and joined Braei in holding it open. They moved Edanos in and then shut the doors. The Rusis quickly created flames for light, and Valrin jumped, spotting the corpses of the massive spiders.

"I thought they were smaller!" he yelled.

"No, no, dear lad. They are quite large," Rortho teased.

The spiders' remains were near the size of a bear. He had seen bear pelts come in his island home in the past, but seeing these monsters was something else entirely.

Braei walked to several basins that lined the room and lit them with her magic. Though the coals were long dormant and cold, they came to life with relative ease.

It seemed that while this place was long abandoned, that perhaps the spiders had only recently taken up residence, though he had no idea where such creatures would come from in this desolate region of the sea.

They had a few items from the ship to makes pallets, and a small fire gave off some warmth. Above them, an opening in the dome let in a gleam of moonlight wrapped in the occasional storm cloud.

Edanos still slept, and Braei fell asleep as Valrin looked at her. Fadis leaned against the wall of the room and carved a mark in his bow as Rortho stared into the fire.

"What are you doing?" Valrin asked the archer.

He finished the straight mark and returned his knife to its sheath.

"Marks. Marks for good deeds."

"Good deeds?"

He set the bow down and leaned back, closing his eyes.

"Deeds. When your life has culminated with the product of bad choices, you start trying to do a bit better." He opened his eyes and stared at the fire before glancing toward Valrin. "To be more worthy."

Valrin wondered exactly what kind of life Fadis had

come from. What bad deeds he had committed and what he was trying to be worthy of, but he didn't push it. The howling wind outside and the dank smell of the room was enough to upset anyone without further questioning.

The dwarf lay back against a rock and began to sing.

"Troubled waters
Beyond the coldest reach.
I dream of love
And mountains high
But ahead I have
Many ocean nights.

A long voyage home,
A long voyage home.

Ax head dulled
From many broken bones,
From fearless man
And coward elf.
I stand upon,
The rocks of Harrodarr

Where ancestors roam,
In the stony home.

I cannot weep
For those gone away,
But I will sing my song
A lonely dwarven song."

Valrin listened to his words. They were lonesome and sad. He seemed to sniffle and then quickly shuffled his hand away from his eyes as he noticed Valrin was watching.

"I'm not too great at songs. Its been a long time I've been away from the halls I have called home. Being within these stone walls reminds me of those places. Eventually, perhaps we will come across old dwarven ruins. You will see the grandeur of my people and perhaps put from memory the horror you have seen of us so far."

"I don't really see all dwarves as bad. Just some of them. I am sure there are many dwarves who are giving and open."

Rortho laughed. "Well, just because we're all not bad doesn't mean we're pushovers. Dwarves are a conceited lot. We are proud, and we keep to ourselves. That as it is, once you are our friend, that bond is stronger than hammered dragon ore."

"Better than elves," Fadis said.

Rortho coughed. "Yes, well, elves are their own sort."

"You do not like elves?" Valrin asked Fadis.

"I guess you could say that. I have my own issues with them. Where I'm from, back in Taria, I spent a good amount of years fighting elves."

"I always heard elves were the greatest with bows."

Fadis smirked. "Yes, well, they bleed all the same. Practice can take you a long way, but shadows can hide any that does not wish to be seen."

"You know," Rortho said, "I knew a Ranger once. A rough man but a good friend for our short time together. He said something like that, well, er, before he died."

"All Rangers die, my dwarf. I just hope to have some say in where my own death takes place."

"So you were this Ranger, whatever that is?" Valrin asked.

"A long time ago. When you were likely a newborn. Ranger's protect their lands and the lands of their neighbors. They hold to a mutual respect of one another and generally take the most risks to protect what they love. Kings have been protected and slayed by Ranger's in my lands. But yes, it was quite a few years ago, it was about that time I did away with that part of my life. I came up north. There's less to deal with up here, but there is always some kind of trouble and a bit of coin to be made…"

There was a sudden scratching outside of the door. Valrin jumped, drawing his blade nearly out. Rortho was at his feet, and Fadis moved his hand to his bow and worked to get an arrow to string.

"Braei!" Rortho shouted in a whispered tone.

She sat up and glanced around.

The scratching came again and this time was louder.

Rortho motioned to Valrin. "Back up!"

Valrin stumbled back but held his sword out. He bit his lip and stood over Edanos.

The scratching came again, and the door swung open with a gust of bitter sea air. The fire went out, and a spray of something flew in.

"Spider acid!" Rortho shouted. "Braei!"

The Rusis cast a bright flash of orange flame toward the doorway and engulfed a massive spider. It screamed and crackled as it shrunk to a broken form. Its flesh was orange with melting carapace turning it into a gelatinous mass.

Rortho stepped forward into the doorway. His glare shifted to either side, and he sniffed the air as he took slow steps. There was a loud hiss, and he jerked right before slashing his ax into the attacker. Another spider came from behind him, and Fadis released an arrow, bringing the creature down.

Valrin then looked beyond his friends and saw several red eyes in multiple spots in the distance.

"More of them!" he shouted.

Another volley of venom flew their way, striking the ground near Edanos and splashing the wall next to Fadis.

The archer fired another two arrows at the

approaching beasts. Two fell, while a third hissed and jumped. Rortho blocked with his ax, but the spider knocked him down. The creature stabbed its legs in a forward motion, trying to move over the dwarf and inject its venom. Braei rushed forward and placed her hands over the creature, letting out a brilliant burst of electricity that stunned the beast. Rortho pushed it off of him and smashed his ax into it. It squealed a strange sound and then died.

"Are you okay?" Braei asked as she pulled Rortho to his feet.

The dwarf rotated his shoulder and grimaced. "Yes, I am fine. I just smell of spider now."

Valrin ran to the doorway to look at the dead creature. It was larger than the largest bear pelt he had ever seen. It had multiple eyes and hairy but frost-colored skin.

"Perhaps we disturbed their nests?" Fadis asked as he motioned to the room they were in.

"I guess," Rortho said, "but these beasts could not live in this desolate place. There is no food."

"Except us," Braei suggested.

A sudden series of flashes appeared in the distance. Valrin looked up to see several bright flames heading toward them.

"Get back!" Rortho shouted.

The flames struck around them, shattering the rocks and causing the stone to partially glow.

Fadis had his bow bent but did not release.

"I do not see anything or anyone!" he said to the others.

A few seconds passed. They all hugged the interior of their shelter. Valrin peeked around the corner, and he saw another flash, this time blue, before several blasts of ice struck at random around them. Then fire came again, this time striking near Edanos. The stones around him began to melt.

Rortho and Valrin ran over and pulled him out of the direct fire as another blast came in.

Fadis leaned out and released an arrow. As soon as he was in cover again, another series of blasts of both ice and fire struck just near him.

"Damn these things!" Braei shouted.

The Rusis emerged from the opening with a shimmering ward to block the incoming attacks. There were two bright flashes as the blasts struck her shield. Fadis filed out behind her and loosed an arrow around her side, striking a figure in the shadows. Valrin went to the door, but Rortho held him back.

"We have no magic shield or bow in which to fight with. This is their fight," he told him.

Another blast struck the shield, and then Braei dissolved her ward. Spinning, she sent several blasts out to multiple figures on the platform. They each summoned wards and then immediately dropped them.

A voice from their right shouted out, "You fight as a Rusis, young one. Your hands are alight with arcane power and your battle zeal is unmatched."

"We want no trouble upon this dark night!" Braei shouted out. "We have an injured man, and we just wished to wait out the storm. We will be gone by morning, we swear."

Fadis still had his bow bent. "You don't have to back down from these sprites."

Braei was shaking but not from fear. There was almost excitement in her voice. "They're not elves, and they are much more powerful than I."

The one figure who spoke before approached. Fadis immediately stepped forward, his arrow at his cheek.

"Stay back!"

The figure stopped, and Valrin noticed he simply lifted a finger. The arrow Fadis held at draw disintegrated into embers, and his bow string twanged empty.

He went to draw another arrow, when the figure lifted his hand, summoning a large ball of flame.

Fadis lowered his bow.

"You are Rusis!" Braei exclaimed.

The figured paused, lowering his spell. He threw back his hood to reveal a gray-haired man with a scraggly beard.

"Some of the last," he replied. "Though we do not go by that name anymore. We are the keepers of songs. Priests upon this lonely rock. While in deep meditation, we felt the stirring of the seas. A Stormborn has emerged, and the realm ship has a master."

Valrin and Rortho moved out of the shelter and crept up to where Fadis and Braei stood. The man who was speaking immediately bowed.

"They had said it would be a child. We all felt it as

such. You are young, but long shall be your time upon the seas."

The man then stood back up straight.

"I am Lorlaam. My brothers, these fellow monks, have taken a vow of silence since your arrival, but know each of them meditate on your future and we have our ways of providing insight to one another."

"I am Valrin of Travaa, Stormborn."

"Ah yes, Stormborn. A child made in part from the souls of sea peoples. That cult broke away from the Dwemhar long ago. Indeed, there is much mystery to them. It is our place to help you, or so it seems the waters of the Glacial Seas have told us."

"My friend Edanos, he is back in the shelter." Valrin motioned. "He is not well."

Two of the Rusis monks went toward the shelter.

"We will see for your friend," Lorlaam said. "For now, you should all come out of this cold."

Valrin saw Fadis looking around.

"Are these spiders some magical creation of your magic, or . . . ?" he asked, waiting for an answer.

"Oh, they were our friends," Lorlaam said with a slight disgust to his tone. "You took one of the few places they seemed to enjoy sleeping. They came to us around two weeks ago, floating on a block of ice and nearly dead. We cared for them and were allowing them a place to live for the time being. It was quite a miracle to bring them back to full life from nearly dead."

Fadis shrugged, "Well, they aren't nearly dead now."

Rortho laughed and slapped Fadis on the back.

"Did you not have injured?" Valrin asked Lorlaam. "I saw an arrow strike one of you."

"A mirage, a spell on the mind. We were unharmed in our engagement."

They both walked with Braei as she followed the other Rusis. Edanos was carried in the arms of the monks, leaving Lorlaam and Valrin to walk at the very back.

"How young are you, Captain?"

"How did you know that I was the captain?"

"Well, the realm ship has a captain bound to it. Since you are the Stormborn, that would make you a captain. The ship has many powers beyond that of a simple vessel. I assume you know of some of them already?"

They followed a pathway that took them back past the realm ship and to a large arched dome that made the previous one look like a small closet. There was a massive column in its center, and as they walked around, Valrin saw large torch basins and a hallway. At the end of this hall was a large door.

"I do know of some of the ship's power. We dealt with the Barb King's dwarves and Rugag."

Lorlaam nodded. "I have heard the cries of the ocean and know of the dwarves. Is that who has cursed Edanos here?"

"He isn't cursed," Valrin corrected him. "He was hit with a poisoned barb, perhaps, but not cursed."

"I see. Well, poisons work on the body in a way that

a curse does not, but there is truth in the other way of things too."

Reaching the doors, they noticed large dark circular metal handles with a slight sheen of ice on them. Rortho opened the door and they entered. There was a rush of warm air that Valrin was relieved to feel. The room they entered was a cathedral of sorts. There were candles along all the walls and a massive library of books as far as Valrin could see.

"Much of the knowledge of the old world that we could find has been gathered here. We each spent over one hundred years searching the lands for texts and manuscripts to collect and guard and study. This is the complete sowing of our works."

Rortho and Braei immediately picked up one of the books.

"It is a dwarvish metal book!" the dwarf said. "I have not seen one of these since I was a child!"

Lorlaam snickered. "Some are simple. A mere textbook for schooling as the dwarf has found, but once we see to your friend, I will show you something that you as a captain will find most useful no matter what you think you already know of the sea."

The massive room where all the books were also had offshoots of small open-air chambers with sleeping quarters, a kitchen of sorts, and a large fire pit that billowed a faint smoke into the upper portions of the cathedral and out to the night sky.

They proceeded to a large altar, and Valrin joined his crew to observe what the Keepers of Songs were to do next.

Lorlaam went to Edanos' forehead as the others circled around. In total, there were eight of them. At this point Lorlaam revealed a large staff with a crystal orb that he moved over Edanos in a circular motion.

"I have never thought I would ever get to see another Rusis!" Braei said. "We were just talking of this, weren't we?"

"Yes. Now I just hope they can help him," Valrin told her. "I thought your powers were of elemental magic?"

Rortho touched him on the shoulder. "These men may have been Rusis, but I think they have moved past the simple knowledge of their race. We shall see."

The monks placed their hands on Edanos and closed their eyes. It was the most silent time Valrin had ever experienced. Somehow, though there was no actual sound or light, there was a near palpable power alive in the room that had numbed them all to any noise except a faint rushing sensation that they could fully feel throughout their bodies. It was like something filled Valrin's ears, but he didn't feel the need to remove it or try to clear his ears. They then could hear as normal again. A hum filled the air that was just audible over the crackling of the nearby fire pit. There was undulating sound and then a high-pitched ringing. Slowly, their hearing returned, and the monks remained in a bowed position. Lorlaam approached them and rested on his staff.

"There is something about what has stricken your friend that baffles even our knowledge. We must take more time than I expected. I can only bid you rest, here among the books and comforts that we have here. There are beds in the distant lofts."

He pointed behind them.

"Please know that we will work to help your friend, but we do now wonder what it is he is stricken with. We see the evidence of the spear and we can feel the presence of fairy magic, but it wasn't enough."

He then turned and returned to the others around Edanos.

"I worry of our dear captain," Rortho said, "But these monks seem to know a bit more than us. Sleep without the threat of spiders? I will take it,"

As the others went to lie down, Valrin followed them but did not feel the need for sleep.

"That is so very strange," Braei told him.

"I know. I do not even feel sleepy."

She lay down and covered herself. The others were in nearby beds, and from the loud snoring coming from that direction, it seemed Rortho took no time in taking Lorlaam's offer to heart.

"There are things for me to see here, I am sure," Valrin told her. "You all need your rest. Enjoy it."

She smiled and turned over.

He left the area they were in and stood back near the entryway of the halls. The Keepers of Songs were still around Edanos and did not seem to notice him. He walked back up to the large doors at the entryway and went back outside.

The sun was on the horizon. A soft orange glow

just over the edge of the sea. The ruins they were in the night before dotted the upper cliffs in a circle around them, though there were periodic breaks where he could see the expanse of the sea. He followed a stairwell up and around the side of the structure they were in. There was an overhang and a tiny crystal sitting in a notch. He climbed up to it and noticed there was a humming sound coming from the pinkish rock.

He had never seen a place like this. Following around to another platform, he could see the back of the island and a large beach here. There seemed to be glowing crystals all along the perimeter. The wind on this side of the structure was much colder. The light of the sun gave him no warmth, and he shivered. He then heard the sound of a lock sliding to his right. He turned to find an opening door. He stepped back at first, afraid of what he had disturbed in this strange place. But to his relieved surprise, it was Lorlaam.

"No sleep for the captain of the realm ship?"

"No, I am not tired."

"When you are at port and it is safe, you should at least try." The old man smiled and then shut the door behind him. "You are a curious boy, Valrin. What drew you to come outside?"

He hadn't really been drawn outside, in his opinion.

"Nothing really. I guess I just wanted to see. I had thought Rusis were much rarer, and to find so many of you in a place like this, I had to see what else was here."

"An adventurous spirit. Something needed in the Glacial Seas. This place was built by the Dwemhar, our sworn enemies, if you can call them that. Most of the intricacies of such a building have faded away. There are places beneath that still hold secrets, but having my blood prevents it. I have pierced the veil of magic and seen crystals within. No doubt something your ship uses?"

"I don't really know. It uses crystals for its powers, but I just do not know too much else."

Lorlaam smiled. "Well, first I bid you bring your ship around the edge of the island into the cove below. I believe I can help you in at least a small way. The area below has a port of the ones who built your ship. There is a place I wish to show you, but I want your ship to be in a safer place."

"Is it not already?" he asked.

"Dwarven vessels could still find it there. Although I find the chance small, I deem you bring it into the protected port. There is a veil upon it that from the outside waters makes this region invisible, save massive cliffs. Follow the cliffs around and you will see the path open to you. Do not worry, the storm from before is well gone and I may have had a hand in guiding your vessel here."

Valrin peered at the man. "You? You created the storm?"

"Not quite the storm but the forces of the water that drew you toward me. It is no matter now; just bring your ship this way."

. . .

Valrin returned to his ship. It was a good but careful run to make it back to the vessel. He felt strange leaving the others, even though it was only for a moment. He had never been alone upon the sea, and pulling the plank up that led from his ship to the shore was a strange moment for him. It was hard for him to imagine ever being alone on the sea.

As he went to the helm, he thought of what Lorlaam had said. It was odd the Rusis had actually pulled them toward the island, but it did not seem he had any negative intentions by it, and thus far, he and his fellow monks were helping them beyond what just about anyone else could.

He steered the ship away from the shoreline with only a bit of sail up. The crystals below the helm glowed brightly. The water was calm outside of the cove. He turned to the right and began sailing around the edge of the island. The cliffs to his side were massive and dark. With the pale gray morning sky above him and the whistling winds cutting from behind, he felt alone but was strangely at peace.

As the ship rocked forward and back as he steered around jagged rocks coming up from the sea, he kept along the cliffs until it seemed the rocks moved away from one another and a passage appeared. As he crossed into the path, he gasped as now he was within the port. He looked behind him to find that there were no cliffs at all, though they had been real enough just a moment ago. It was a powerful mirage created by magic.

As he guided the ship into a massive cave underneath the structure that before he and Lorlaam were standing above, he saw that Lorlaam was waiting for him. The ship began to move on its own, and Valrin tried to fight the wheel but could not. The vessel drifted against a long black stone to the right, and with a strange click, the ship was set against the wall. Glowing runes appeared on the ground by the ship.

He stepped off and noticed Lorlaam was staring up at the walls. The entire structure seemed to be glowing.

"For so long I have awaited this day. It is a strange finding to see it all as it was foretold."

"I still question exactly what this all means. The events a few days ago happened very quickly."

"In time, you will understand it more clearly. Now, let me show you something."

He led Valrin further into the cave and to the massive doorway covered in ice. There were effigies covering it.

The Rusis placed his hands on the door and used flames to melt the ice.

"Through many translations found across the oceans, I have determined that this was at one time a shipwright's quarters. Though I dare say it, the markings of Vankou are upon the outside, etched on the floor."

Valrin noticed the runes and what appeared to be an image of a ship. Though he couldn't read it, he did see the sharp slashes, almost cruel marks, on the ground.

"Vankou?"

"Composer of the songs of eternity. A god of

death. The god of death if death could be a god. He is far from here, far from you. You must not fear that which is sealed away. Your fate is beyond his reach. But this place is marked as a tomb. I deem you to be careful."

"You want me to go in there?"

He nodded. "You must know more of your ship, and I have felt the power within this place but have not been able to go there. Your friend Edanos will need more than I have here, Valrin. I have an elixir maker that can do much more than craft simple potions, but I will need something from the South. Go into here and seek out what you can find. When you are done, simply return to the halls above. I will prepare the others for your journey."

Valrin pulled open the door, and a strange smell struck his nostrils.

"This passage has not been opened since it was sealed." Lorlaam went to reach into the doorway, and the air shifted, suddenly pushing against him, "And it's one you will have to go into alone."

Valrin drew his blade and stepped in. He looked back to Lorlaam, who pulled an unlit torch from his robes. He lit the tip with his powers and handed it to him.

"Good luck, Stormborn."

Valrin stepped forward, and the doorway shut behind him. He looked ahead to see a long hall with strewn objects all over the floor and archways well above his head spaced out every few feet. There was ice along the walls and no sense of warmth to be found. He began forward. His every step echoed down the halls. He looked around to large open expanses on either side, seeing what he thought was movement only to see tattered cloth blowing from slight gusts in the bowels of the caves.

It appeared as if the mountain rock itself had grown into the structure. The rock piercing through the ornate panels of the hall was sheer and pointy. There were several broken pillars littering the path, and torn manuscript pages.

He continued on, spotting several doorways but finding them all blocked. He wasn't sure what to make of this place overall. He came to a large circular room and found the skeleton of a ship on a raised platform. There were crystals and ore lying about. A large smelter, long, cold, and barren, took up the wall to the right, and large doorways flanked one another where the completed ship could be moved out. There was a single pedestal and a metal protrusion sticking up.

Valrin sheathed his sword for the moment. There were no other rooms he could see, and so far, the sealed passage had simply been empty. He went to the switch on the pedestal and took hold of it. Looking around as if someone was actually going to see him touch it, he took a deep breath and twisted it.

There was a rumble beneath his feet. The smelter to his right roared to life, and bright crystals in the corners of the room began to spin in place giving off a radiant glow to the surroundings. A series of panels to his right opened along the wall, and he saw several manuscripts and crystals, like the ones on his ship, upon a large shelf made into the wall.

He smiled and went over to the wall. He took one of the four books and thumbed through it. The language was that of the dwarves; he could tell that but nothing else.

But Rortho said the dwarves didn't build this place.

He tucked the books away one by one. He did not know their significance, but he knew Rortho would be able to read them. He then went to the crystals. Lorlaam told him these somehow helped power his ship. He would need them at some point. But as he grabbed the crystals, he heard a lever fall behind him. He turned, spotting something glowing gold on the opposite side of the room.

He set the crystals down and drew his sword. At this moment, he wished to have someone else with him. Rortho, Fadis, Braei, any or all of them really. There came a strange scratching sound. He noticed that several golden lights moved toward him in an erratic way. There were four in total. As they drew closer, he noticed they were like small turtles, except metallic. One by one, they came to rest in front of him. They were mechanical. They had small gears atop their backs with blue crystals atop their heads. One of them was flashing, and in a sudden flash of lightning, the turtle changed forms and became a small golden tower.

A voice then came.

"*If this room has been awoken, I will know the plans set forth before have come to pass. We were deemed evil by our* masters; we of the sea were the last of the sect who believed ourselves truly different. We could not escape the flooding of old. We were the dissenters. We seek redemption, and through my work here, I will have done my part. Stormborn, you have awoken. Your path will lead to our salvation, and if the gods will it, my work here will be enough.

"I was Arnea, shipwright of the once grand Dwemhar. I bestow upon you not only the texts to teach you of the old realm ships written in a language I believe will survive the true tests of time, but moon crystals to keep your ship well powered.

"With you, I bid you take my assistants. They are as sea turtles, but you will find that even on land they work quickly. They can repair your vessel and will work to assure it stays floating beyond the days of the Stormborn. But to most, they will never be seen, and that is as it should be. Only another such as yourself can truly use the powers you possess. I bid you one last request. Retrieve my body and return me to the sea. I would much rather rest outside of what has become my prison."

The golden tower became three turtles again before each of them turned into small golden balls. Valrin picked them each up, noting them to be no larger than his hand. He noticed a small brown sack near the shelves where he found the crystals, and worked to put the assistants and the crystals in the bag.

He thought of how Arnea had left him the strange message and his last request. He gave thought to ignore it but then noticed the doorway in the direction the assistants had come from. It was open now, no doubt from the assistants, but he hadn't noticed it. He guessed it must have been another veiling spell, like the one outside the island.

He proceeded forward to enter a room adorned in hasty markings and covered in red splashes. He noticed a strange smell in the air. Not of rotting corpses or a foulness of that sort, but of something else. Something like some kind of food.

He walked toward a glowing light on the wall and noticed that it was a small fire. He then looked to see a frail man lying on the ground. He jumped at first but then cautiously knelt down and found the man was still warm. Blood pooled around him. His eyes were open and his mouth was agape. The man could not have been dead for very long, yet this place was sealed. He wondered if someone was in here with him. He scanned the room but did not see anyone or anything. Valrin then noticed a dagger lying on the ground just under the man. He reached down to touch it, and in his mind's eye, there was a flash of memory. He saw the sealing of the room. The frail figure before him was a proud man but was deeply saddened as the doors to the outside were sealed and he sat alone, surrounded by his assistants.

I have eternity to wait. I will wait within this room until eternity comes to pass. Alone, I am always alone. Tormented by the songs of Vankou, the deceiver, I cannot escape. Once the time comes. When I feel the Stormborn open the way, I will have death at last. Though I will no doubt try to obtain it before then.

Valrin then saw the image of the old man aging over many, many years until at last, he sees the man smile before driving the dagger into his stomach over and over. The man collapses.

The cold bite of the air took Valrin, and his hand

seemed stuck to the dagger. He saw the image of the man again and then the dagger fell from his hand with a clang. At this point, he realized the man had been trapped in this place until his arrival a few minutes ago. There was a small window to the outside world that Valrin noticed in the corner of his eye. That was this man's only way to see out for however long he had been sealed here. He had not been as lucky as the Dwemhar in the place Edanos and the others had stumbled upon a few nights ago. This man had been cursed, and he felt a strange pulling in his mind that he wasn't the only one who was cursed to live as such.

Valrin, though small, was able to lift the man still dripping in blood and carry him back out. There was something sweet of the notion. The act of returning one of the ones he somehow could almost call family to their resting place. The feeling of death was heavy upon him, but as he reached the outside again, he went down past his ship to the edge of the docking platform and tossed the body into the seas.

"Goodbye, Arnea."

He knew from the visions he had seen before with the others that those who preceded the creation of the Stormborn were a separate cult of the Dwemhar. They regretted what they had become, and they sought redemption. At least this one had found it, in some form.

2
MYSTERIOUS FRIEND

VALRIN WAS COVERED IN BLOOD. As the body of the now-dead ancient one disappeared into the black, cold waters of the sea, he looked around for the path that Lorlaam had taken to get to this place. He found a stairwell that led back up, and began up the spiraling path to the peak where before he had stood with the Rusis.

He looked down at the blood smears on his arms. He had never had the blood of another person on him like this. As discomforting as it was to him, he saw the honor in carrying out the final act wished of him. He felt the bag containing the crystals and the assistants, along with the books written in the dwarven language. Arnea must have thought much of the dwarves to assume they would survive the unknown amount of time that would pass waiting for the Stormborn.

He went back down to the doorways to the halls where the others were. The sun was up higher in the sky now, and he wondered what Lorlaam would actually tell them of Edanos.

As he entered and began down the stairwell, Braei immediately saw him, and her eyes grew large.

"Valrin, you are hurt!"

Rortho and Fadis quickly joined her, followed by Lorlaam.

"I am not hurt," he told them. "Bloody, but not hurt."

"What happened?" Fadis asked.

"The blood is not mine. There was a man, an ancient man. I don't really understand it, but he has been alive since well before now. The place was empty and cold, but slowly, I was able to determine some secrets."

He handed the books to Rortho. "Written in your language, and from what I can guess, they will guide us with the realm ship. I also found crystals," he said, looking at Lorlaam.

"The power I had meditated on and found beneath us was more than simply these trinkets. There was a man beneath us?"

"I don't understand it myself," Valrin said, "but he was there. A few days ago, we witnessed a vision within ruins to the west. There we saw the sea peoples and their talk of the coming floods. They spoke of going out to the world and awaiting the Stormborn. I had thought this was meant as a more spiritual sense, not literal."

"Did the man say anything else?" Braei asked.

"He spoke of Vankou and hearing his songs."

"A tormented one?" Rortho questioned.

"A what?"

"There is belief that some who owe the god of death will not be allowed death. Perhaps this ancient one was one of them."

"Or perhaps he is a key to the old prophecy of the North. Of the one who will release death, or so it was spoken." Lorlaam said

"That is an elven prophecy," Rortho stated.

"That was a prophecy of the far northern Glacial Seas, spoken by Vankou himself when he was sealed away. But we digress, this is not of the Stormborn's concern. That man is dead. But I do worry of what more will be uncovered."

He turned from them and went back toward Edanos.

There was now a single monk standing over him, and the others moved around the halls in silence.

"The Glacial Seas are a dangerous place. Though where you must go, the danger will not be magical in nature but dwarven. You must go south of here, to a city called Corson. It is there you will seek out Trilsa, a man who calls that place home. He knows of the dwarven potion trades and how to find one who makes them."

Lorlaam went to a large stone circle with several cups arranged atop a platform.

"This is an elixir enchanter of the sea peoples. I can use this to determine what any poison is made of and, in that, determine a cure. Your friend was not simply poisoned as like one who is struck by the barb of a stingray or the slap of a jellyfish of the South. This was a poison that went deeper and was blessed with a dark magic. This is beyond my skills, and I fear if more of this exists. Your friend will remain here safe with us, but you must seek out Trilsa. He is a friend of mine; just do not use my name as you know it. He knew me as the Mage of Ice. Tell him this, and he will help you."

"Corson? I have a cousin who runs an inn there. It has been a good while since I was there, but I will be happy to see him. Be happy we are not elves. They do not like elves there at all!"

"Sounds like a fine place," said Fadis.

Valrin went to Edanos as the others prepared to head to the ship. He knelt at him and put his hand on his chest.

"We will return. Rest, friend."

He stepped back and into Lorlaam, who was standing behind him.

"We will watch over him. Keep faith in your crew and your ship, and may Meredaas watch over you."

They exited the halls and hurried their way up the stairwell leading back around to the ship.

"You moved the ship?" Braei asked.

"Yes, an enchanted cove of sorts."

Fadis shook his head. "Why is everything enchanted, cursed, or somehow not just good wood and iron?"

"Coming from a man with an elvish bow?" Rortho asked.

"It is only elven wood. I made it myself. I've learned to avoid elven weapons. They're not worth the trouble."

Rortho shook his head with a grin. "One day we will sit down and you will tell me about your adventure before here. I have to assume it is quite a tale."

Valrin led them down to the ship, and Rortho stared at the docked vessel.

"How is this ship tied to the dock? It is like it is locked in or something."

"You seem quite disturbed by this," Braei teased.

"It's just I have never seen such a thing. I have seen many dwarven mechanics, and this is beyond all of that."

"These docks were built by the same people who built the ship," Valrin told him. "The doors ahead took me down to the shipwright's room where a partially constructed ship was abandoned at some point in the past. Though I wonder if it was before the floods, how did the ship get to the water? I assume they lowered it?"

"You ask questions that make my head hurt thinking of answers," Rortho said. "I will look in these books. Perhaps we will find answers to your questions and mine. Oh, and next time you're going on an adventure, wake us all up!"

"I agree," Braei said.

"It wasn't really an adventure, more like a small journey into a long sealed place."

"An adventure," Rortho stated again. "That is what you had."

As Valrin touched the wheel of the ship, whatever hold was on the ship released and the sails came up slightly as they moved away from the docks. They made quick speed leaving the harbor, and Valrin brought up the map in the center of the ship. He looked across the vast seas and noted Travaa. "Corson would be to the west of your home island, lad," Rortho told him.

He looked over and saw an island. "There?" He pointed.

"Yes."

As he adjusted the ship, the map shifted with them, and he could tell they were moving in the right direction.

He manipulated the crystal near the map, and he was able to see a much greater expanse of the oceans, but most of it was unknown to all upon the boat.

"We have been to many of the islands of the lower Glacial Seas," Braei said, "but the far north is known to be both icier and more dangerous. Edanos always was wary of going that way. The island we were on before was still in that region, and it is my guess that is why the Keepers of Songs have been left alone."

"They also don't cause the dwarves trouble," Rortho suggested. "I could see the dwarves seeking to add that place to their kingdom at the first notice of trouble."

"Then we must protect them and assure no dwarf, save you, ever finds out about them," Valrin said.

. . .

The island became a mere outline behind them, and several new islands appeared in front of them. Each had its own look, character, and likely story hidden to the common passerby. There were penguins on one, and at least twice a seal emerged to watch them as they sailed by.

The sunlight was a welcome sight, but it was nearing the time of the year where it would not be out as long.

As they traveled for a few hours, it became clear that they would make it to their destination sometime at night. Valrin had handed the wheel over to Braei, as it seemed that Rortho had learned something from his reading.

"Let me see the crystals you retrieved," he said excitedly.

Valrin pulled them from his bag and handed them to him.

"It seems that these use moonlight to recharge the other crystals of the ship. I have told you of how the further northern regions of the sea have many secrets?"

Valrin nodded.

"Well, these crystals have properties that allow them to pull radiant magic from the air itself, at least, when you are sailing in these waters. It takes in lunar magic in the air and somehow stores it as energy. Now, I assume if you were to go south of the waters, this effect would lessen and eventually fail. But that is what these are for."

Rortho went to the back of the ship and moved his

finger along the wood. A switch flipped down, and with a flick, he opened several compartments on the back of the ship. Taking each crystal, he placed them in literal holders that then closed around the crystals, securing them.

"Now, I have found a bit about the helm crystals. The translations are rough, but I can tell that of the four main ones you have. The top one engages the weapon we saw before, the arcane flames, while the one at the bottom can raise a ward, similar to what Braei can do. There also is a lockdown for the ship. A type of security. The ship will only be accessible by you in this case, and it will be surrounded by an impregnable shield until you come near it."

"That is strange. How can this ship have this kind of power?"

"The best I can see, the sea peoples were using a mix of Dwemhar crystal magic with that of Rusis magic and a bit of dwarven mechanics. I'm just now touching the surface, but at one time, these ships could do magnificent things, even fly, if you can believe it."

"Now come, dwarf," Braei shouted, "no ship like this can fly."

Rortho thumbed through one of the books and revealed a picture of several realm ships at flight against a cloudy sky.

Braei shook her head. "Well, if that is something this ship can do, then you might as well figure it out so we can get on to Corson before dark."

"That seems the problem, though," Rortho added.

"The magic that powers the ship will go dark over time. I assume small actions would use less magic, but large actions, such as flying, if the vessel can do it, would take a significant time to recharge. We should keep to the sea and to normal sailing actions as much as possible."

"We don't need a fight," Valrin said.

"But we should always expect one," Fadis said, suddenly standing and looking out. "A dwarven vessel is to our left."

Valrin and Rortho both turned to see a ship traveling west along the same path as them.

Rortho took the wheel. "We need to keep our distance." The dwarf reached to where the crystals were and twisted a knob on the right side. "You can control the sails here," he told Valrin.

The ship slowed its pace, and the dwarven vessel drifted further away. He turned them further north.

"We will approach Corson from the north. I would rather arrive late than be captured by dwarves. A nasty lot, damn sea pirates."

"Don't we go toward a place where your own cousin is?"

"Yes, and we should be fine there. If we run into any trouble I can easily take on a few angry dwarves but I don't want to risk alerting the entire dwarven navy to our presence. They are no doubt looking for this ship, in whatever form they remember it."

"Do you think Rugag would have regrouped that quickly?" Fadis asked.

"Oh yes. He went back crying to the Barb King,

and from there, they will search these seas for us. They may send Rugag and his groups, or perhaps they will have him hit up a few traveling pods of whales while another bastard comes after us."

"Where is the Barb King at?" Valrin asked.

"He has an island chain to the east. They call the place Gurundothrak. It is a long mountainous region where his floating palace is suspended above the great open ocean, and it keeps him from being attacked. It is a marvel to see, to be honest. Massive towers scale up the mountains, and chains stretch down to hold the abomination above an arcane-enhanced stirring sea that makes short work of any approaching sea vessel. It is of the same design as the magics that protect Mereaa, but his is always active and none who came against him ever made it to the palace of thorns. He is protected by countless dwarves and even more foul creatures. So if you had any thought of going after him, I say keep it from mind."

Valrin had a thought of it, but now he didn't know if he should even say it.

Fadis chuckled. "I can tell that the boy seeks blood. A good way to deal with your problems is to head straight for it, but even better, wait until you can make your enemy hurt in the worst way possible."

Valrin stared at him. "I do not want war with them. That is not my charge as a Stormborn."

"Well, what is?"

"Stop troubling the boy or you can find yourself a new ship in Corson," Braei snapped.

"I do not mean to trouble him, but once Edanos is

healed, we will need to move forward in a way that makes sense. We're not just going to float around and see what dwarf finds us and how we might escape again."

"No," Braei said, "once Edanos is better, we will seek out the ones of wisdom who hid within the world. We will trust Valrin. That will be with or without you."

Fadis walked away from them.

Valrin smirked to Braei, who did the same back. She was constantly standing up for him, but since they had first met, it seemed like she was a bit more playful toward him. He kind of liked it.

As Fadis went to the front of the ship, Valrin followed him.

"Thank you," he said.

"Thanks for what? It seems like I'm causing you more trouble than good."

"You are a faithful person. You have more than done your part protecting and helping the others. They might not like what you say, but you're trying to help. Before I was on the *Truest Bliss*, I only had a handful of people who actually cared about me, and only one of those I can say never took advantage of me. My Aunt Tua. She was a vampire and an elf, but she protected all of us in the end. I would hope that if I was to die, that I would do so in an action that protects others."

"So you're telling me you're already planning your death?"

"Well, no."

"Listen, Valrin, I have seen enough death for the both of us. There is no honor in death. It is bloody.

Messy. It smells. My actions before heading north a few years ago resulted in many unnecessary deaths. I had thought to revoke my vows as a Ranger, but I didn't. I did as honor would have me do. It didn't get me too far." Fadis paused for a moment. He took a deep breath as he closed his eyes, and then looked directly at Valrin. "I see a zeal in you. That king of Barbs is not liked, but the people are too scared to rise up against him. I'm not saying start a war, but if you have an arrow drawn and your enemy is in front of you, there is no harm in letting your bolt do the dirty work."

Valrin nodded. "I am happy to have you in the crew, Fadis. Just . . . well . . . watch it with the others."

"Strange coming from a child, but I will do so."

"You know I'm not that young."

"Young to me, little guy, young to me."

They shared a smile, and Valrin went back toward the helm.

Their journey had continued with little issue at all. The moon was high in the sky when Rortho pointed and nodded. "Land-ho," he said in a less-than-exuberant voice.

Corson was ahead. Its dark outline had a few specks of light, and fresh snowfall covered the island.

"How long has it been since you've been here?" Fadis asked.

"Ten years, four months, and fourteen days."

"Specific," Braei said.

"My kin and I had a bit of a falling out."

"Perhaps we should avoid him, then," Valrin suggested.

"No, no. He is one of the few I trust. He has a nice inn, too."

As they moved the ship around the west side of the island, they came to several wooden docks. Valrin looked up to the actual city and noticed a series of elevated wooden platforms and large houses.

"There is another area to dock. Right by the inn. We will go there."

Rortho guided the ship around the edge of the island to a separate inlet with a few small sailing ships and mostly empty docks.

"Generally this is only for ships in repair, but my good cousin will not care."

They pulled up along the docks and threw ropes to tie off. Fadis jumped off first, followed by Braei. Once the ship was secure, Valrin and Rortho joined them. Rortho pushed himself to the front of the line.

"Come on," he said, making a motion with his hand.

Valrin looked around at the black sand beaches and dark rocks that were sheen in the moonlight. The ocean had washed away the snowfall, revealing the volcanic rock that made up the island.

"Be happy it isn't yet winter. During the dead winter, this place is under so much snow, you can barely walk the paths!"

There was a large two-story house ahead. It was red in color and had a sign hanging in front of the door that was in need of some paint but could still be made out. Valrin took a moment to make out the blocky, runic letters but read it to himself: *Spitting Crab Fish*.

Rortho pushed open the door, and they entered. Valrin immediately smelled the aroma of an odd-smelling stew.

"RORTHO!" a man bellowed out.

Valrin pushed his way past Fadis to see another dwarf approaching Rortho.

"You stay away for many years, but yet now you come on the eve of the christening of my new bar! I just received this beautiful dwarven-made top for the bar. The same bar you helped me build for the inn you left me with to join in the misadventures of some captain."

There was no one else in the inn at this hour, and Valrin was actually happy about that. He was looking around when Rortho's cousin walked toward him and knelt down. Fadis immediately drew a dagger, and the dwarf looked up.

"Some rougher types, my lost cousin, and a child."

"He's my captain, Uris."

"Aye! Truly? Such a young captain."

"The name is Valrin," he told him. "We are looking for a man named Trilsa."

The dwarf stared at him. "He has a hovel in the far north of the island. But he also killed my most recent spice runner. Not the greatest thing to happen. I've been making a point to cook more for the locals, and well, fish becomes bland in time. I will need to find another to go south."

"We're not here to run spices for you," Rortho said. "I have to . . . I need to speak with you. We've had trouble with Rugag. Has he been here recently?"

The dwarf looked outside and then back to an obviously stern Rortho.

"No, not in some time. Most dwarves have stayed away. Most elves too. Ever since that ordeal with the elf who killed all of those poor fishers, elves haven't dared stepped foot on this island."

"Though that was well over what, one hundred years?"

"Well, he didn't die, and those bastard sprites will outlive us all. Damn them, Rortho. Come on and sit down."

The dwarf went to the door of the inn and locked it.

"I will get you all something to eat. Just a moment."

Uris went behind the bar and retrieved bowls before serving them all a bit of stew. Valrin ate it, and the warm broth was soothing to his throat. The taste was of artic fish, but it also had the most fragrant herbs.

"Ha," the dwarf said. "It must be good. No one is talking."

There was a sudden knock at the door, and they each jumped, turning around.

"Calm down, calm down," the dwarf said.

He went to the door and shooed them off. "My good cousin is here. We'll be open tomorrow. Go on, go to bed, you sea cucumbers." He shut the door back. "Pesky drunks."

"You really shouldn't tell them I am here. Rugag knows of me."

He leaned onto the table. "I do not know what trouble you're in, but it doesn't need to find its way here. I may not agree with them, but they are dwarves. Our people."

Rortho finished his stew and stood.

"My cousin, you and I will have a drink and talk of our people. They will go to Trilsa. We are pressed for time, and we'll depart tonight."

The others stood as he did.

"Very well, take the road outside and head east. It will dead end and you will find a rocky recess high atop the hill. There you will find Trilsa. Beware, he is a testy man."

Rortho looked at them. "Find him. Get what we need and get back here. If Rugag gets any sense that we are here, he will be on top of us quicker than I like."

Braei and Valrin immediately went to the door, and Fadis sheathed his knife he had kept out since entering the inn. As the door shut behind them, Valrin shivered at the cold of the outside compared to the inn.

"That was a bit abrasive," Braei commented.

But none of them had anything else to say of Uris.

"This way," Fadis said.

The road away from the inn was desolate and dark. There were many houses, much like the fishing houses that Valrin had grown up seeing on Travaa, but no one was out at this hour. Unlike Mereaa, the land was generally flat and most all of the structures looked identical.

"A dark place," Valrin said.

"Soon it will be dark all the time in these regions. I kind of look forward to it," Braei said. "At least we will be able to hide easier."

The way out of town became less and less a path and more of just open rocky ground. The city was now behind them, and ahead there was a hilly region from where they could observe the sea clearly in all directions. For the longest while, they just walked, expecting to find something but only finding more rocks and uneven ground that made even careful walking difficult and dangerous. They continued up, avoiding drop-offs and following narrow pathways until at last, they began into a small inlet with a beach of volcanic glass. Here, just visible in a rocky house, was a man sitting outside smoking.

"Who are you to come this way?" the man asked before they had even got close enough to warrant saying hello.

They continued walking at first, but the man stood. "Who are you?" he shouted up at them.

"Friends of the Ice Mage," Valrin said.

There was silence, and the man set his pipe down before hobbling toward them. "You know the Ice Mage?" he asked them.

"Yes, and he needs your help."

The man quickly turned away and went into his house.

They paused for a moment, unsure of what they should do.

"So what now?" Braei asked.

Valrin went forward, leaving the two of them, and headed directly for the house. They ran to catch up with him, when just before the house, the sand gave way and they fell straight down, landing in a shallow cave just over their heads.

"What in the—?" Fadis began as he pushed himself up.

But the man came to the opening. "You fell for a simple trap and I'm supposed to believe you are friends with the Ice Mage?"

"We are," Valrin said. "We need help with something. Our friend was struck by a strange poison."

The ground began to move beneath their feet.

"I know some things about poison, but have you ever heard of a seaweed trap?"

The ground began to upturn. Pieces of sand and shell churned in the bubbling water around their feet.

"No, we haven't, but this is hardly something we are curious about," Braei said.

The man above them laughed. "You will soon learn what it is."

"Trilsa, we did nothing to you. What are you doing?"

"I have seen assassins before," he said. "I have hid here for so long, the dwarves know I am here, but after I killed the first twenty they sent for me, they agreed to leave me alone. Now you seem to know more about me than I care, so I assume they sent you masquerading as my friend's friend to let me allow you close. But no, that will not happen."

Several twisting arms of seaweed came up. Braei attempted to burn it away, but her flames did nothing to the enchanted plants.

Fadis pointed at Trilsa. "You are making a mistake. If we wanted you dead, you'd be dead."

"Charming words from someone in a trap."

Valrin drew his sword, but the seaweed grabbed hold of his arms, pulling them down. "I am Stormborn, and I demand you release me from this trap."

"Stormborn, and why would I care of that?"

"Because this poison does not just poison one, it curses them too. The Ice Mage, your friend, told me you were the only one who could help us. He said you could be trusted, and if we do not return to him, he will search us out and determine what happened!"

The seaweed suddenly stopped.

"Sharp words from a young one. Perhaps you are not assassins."

A single rope came down to them. The seaweed receded.

"Come, now."

They climbed back out to see that Trilsa was again smoking his pipe.

Fadis sneered at the man, and Braei let a spark of electricity streak off her fingertips.

"Good thing I did not kill a Rusis. The Ice Mage always had an affinity for those. We once went on a quest to retrieve his staff. He had to avoid a poisonous beast, and I needed a rare ingredient to make a salve to protect him from its venom. It was a fun adventure and one of a few we partook in."

"Why treat us like this if we know the name of your friend?" Braei asked.

He took a long draw from his pipe and exhaled. "I wasn't going to kill you, but many have died in my sandpits. The deal is that most assassins are cheap, particularly the ones the Barb King sends. Most plea with me, curse me, say the glory of the Barb King will endure. I am used to that. You three were different. Using words like 'Stormborn' and such. I am curious of that. I do not know that term."

"It doesn't matter the words," Fadis said. "The boy told you of a poison. How can you help us?"

"You were sent for Evurn, in truth, dear man."

"Evurn?" Valrin asked.

"Yes, another poor man, err . . . elf. He is from the far south. Narisond, I believe the city is called. He lives further south than this. You will draw close to dwarven places going that way, but if you are friends of the Ice Mage, you no doubt will be fine. Evurn deals in the more odd poisons. I know a good deal and am an expert if ever there was one, but Evurn is a true master of plants, poisons, and the like."

"How do we find this elf Evurn?" Braei asked.

"Just head south from Corson. You will see an oddity in the sea. A mushroom, green in color, dots the island, giving it a strange appearance to the stark white and black of the Glacial Seas. I do challenge you not to eat them either . . . I had a friend do that once."

"And?" Valrin asked.

"I said I *had* a friend do that once."

Valrin wasn't sure if this was an attempt at humor or the man was serious. "Thank you, Trilsa, for your time."

The man nodded and lifted his pipe. "Tell the Ice Mage his old friend misses him. Another adventure would be a fun excursion."

"We will," Valrin said.

As they left the man to his pipe, they made a hurried walk back to the village.

"Did Lorlaam actually say he would hunt the man down?" Braei asked.

"No, but I wouldn't want to anger the Ice Mage myself. I figured it would work."

"Lying now?" Fadis asked. "Now don't go telling Edanos I taught you that. I assure you he will assume it was me no matter what I say."

They made it back to the inn to find Rortho and Uris standing outside.

Rortho approached them. "So?"

"We must go south," Valrin said.

"South?"

"We have to find an elf, a man named Evurn."

Rortho looked over to Uris.

"There will be dwarven vessels that way," Uris said.

"We have to do as we must," he replied.

"Good tidings to you, cousin," Uris told him. "Perhaps when you get done with what your doing we can head south for a bit. To Harrodarr or Michranok? It would be a glorious good time." They embraced before Uris looked at the others, "Anyway, good luck to all of you. Know this is a safe place if you need to hide. I will do what I can for you."

The dwarf went back into the inn, and they headed for the ship.

"Did you have a good conversation with him?" Braei asked.

"An enlightening one. The dwarves are searching for us. They had already been here looking for a child captain. It seems our adventures to the far north have indeed spread out in rumor and talk among the dwarves."

"So they are hunting us and they know to watch for Valrin?" Fadis asked.

"Yes, I hope in going south we do not need to go to any other city."

"No," Valrin said, "only to an island and an elf."

"Some would say that is a bad idea as well," Fadis said. "You all know I'm not a fan of sprites."

As they pulled away from Corson, they sailed with haste in a southerly direction. They spotted torchlights in the far east.

Rortho pointed. "Dwarves, likely. Those are large ships."

"Should we sail further west?" Fadis asked.

"No, in the dark they cannot see us. We would be good to continue south as is. Hopefully, our next meeting will not take us any closer to the dwarves than is needed."

The others had lain down, and Valrin guided the ship south. He had seen no other islands, and he kept a keen eye out for the strangely green-covered island he expected to see at some point. He looked up to the stars, trying to remember the passage of time and the constellations that Edanos had taught him. He was a captain, but he felt almost lost at the task. To him, it didn't help that he was looked at as special to some degree by the others, but yet also still a child. He knew he was young, but he had to set himself from the boyish image he had. Perhaps in time, that chance would come.

It was still just before dawn. The clouds had shifted away, and a purple hue struck the horizon. The water had become calmer, and for a good while, Valrin had moved the ship toward a trio of high-reaching islands. These were the first he had seen since they left Corson, and he had worked to assure he continually headed south.

The first of the two islands was obviously not green at all. There was red algae that grew around the base of the tall island. As he moved the ship around it, he noticed it was actually very small in width and seemed to have a rocky extension that connected to another island. This one was larger, but it, too, lacked the green mushrooms he was told would make a blatant finding of Evurn's home obvious. At last, he circled around the third island. It was of sheer rock and the largest of the three. He could see no plants, no animals, not even holes carved out by the sea. He made it around the edge of this one when just before he turned to move away, he saw a small beach and mushrooms with green tops growing on it.

"Yes, this is it!"

He turned the ship and twisted the knob to lower the sails. As he did this, the ship ran aground and tossed from one side to the next. Without any prompting or activation, the assistants Valrin had retrieved from the shipwright before came to life and rolled across the deck with a slight hum to their movement. They turned to the four legged form and scurried over the edge of the boat that had ran aground. He dropped the anchor as his disheveled crew stumbled atop the deck.

"Sounds like you tore the outside of the ship," Rortho said. "What happened?"

"We're here." Valrin pointed out.

Rortho turned and looked at the island. "So we are, but Throka be blessed, don't tear apart the deck of the vessel. I don't know a shipwright who could actually fix this kind of ship!"

Fadis strung his bow. "An island with green mushrooms and an elf. Those sound like the perfect ingredients for a fun time."

The front of the ship was still resting on the sands. They leaped from the ship to the sand and formed a line as they walked toward a shadowy overgrown beach. Valrin looked behind and didn't noticed any damage or any signs of the assistants. They were quick at their work and were most definitely out of sight.

As they walked up the beach, a white snake fled from beneath the sand and disappeared into the underbrush ahead.

Fadis put an arrow to string and moved ahead of them. As he got to just about the spot the snake had disappeared he turned around to wait for the others. A moment later, a spear from the trees struck between them and Fadis. A white smoke billowed from the shaft, and Valrin felt his strength drained. He fell to the ground and looked at the others, who had been stricken the same way. He was unable to see clearly, and his arms and legs did not want to work.

He felt himself being dragged. The ground went from sand to that of hard rock, and then he could only see darkness.

He heard ringing in his ears. He tried to talk but couldn't even hear himself. He felt sick but was too weak to even move. He was lying against something hard. He could do nothing but listen to the ringing.

3
UNDERREALMS

It was a good while, but the annoying ringing eventually stopped, and then his vision cleared at nearly the same time. The others were with him, but they were all bound.

"Valrin!" Braei said.

"What happened?" he asked.

Rortho grunted. "Elven trickery. Some type of poison, short-acting, or so it seems."

"Yes," a voice hissed from the shadows. "Short-acting but with purpose."

Valrin saw the white snake from before. It slithered between them, hissing as it did. It returned to the shadows.

"It is a strange group to have on my lonely island. I do not expect visitors. I rather like to eat them."

Valrin looked around and was shocked to see skeletal remains of either human, elf, or dwarf hanging above them.

"You have found the lair of Evurn, and I must question why?"

The snake returned, slithering over Valrin's boots before twisting quickly back to the shadows.

"We seek you for your assistance. We were sent by one known as the Ice Mage to a man named Trilsa. Trilsa told us that you were an elf who could help us with poisons," Valrin told him.

The snake emerged again, but this time on the shoulder of a strangely opaque elf. Aside from blackened curved nails, his pointed ears were so long, they twisted toward his neck. The elf wore the skin of some animal and had crab claws hanging off his shoulders.

"So you come here not as an offering or a mere shipwreck but to ask me about poison?"

"Yes, but we'd appreciate if you would let us go so we could talk as decent people," Rortho said.

"But I am not what you call 'decent people.' I am not welcome at 'decent places,' but my friend here Rasi likes me."

The snake twisted around his neck and down his body. The snake then went to Valrin's hands, and he could feel it nipping at the rope.

"Rasi likes you all, but I still think you would be better roasted. The bones of dwarves are a hardy compound for a lethal poison."

Valrin's hands were freed, and he stood. Rasi slithered over to Braei next and began to bite at the rope holding her.

"I free you," Evurn said, "but I do so out of happy hopes you will not kill me. I am no mere elf, as they call me; I am a shadow elf. We are known to be dangerous."

"I've never heard of a shadow elf," Fadis said.

"It is good, then. We were assassins once, a typical profession for the name, but most of The Shadows never live as other elves in trees of the blessed Etha or in 'decent places.'"

They were all free now, and though Fadis made a motion for weapons, Rortho dissuaded him. If Evurn had wanted to kill them, he would have done it. There was no reason to provoke him.

"Come with me," Evurn beckoned.

They followed the elf deeper into the cave system. Luminescent bugs scurried along the walls around them, and the elf lit their path with a staff that glowed an orange color. The cave opened up into a cavern with a wooden bridge that was flanked by trickling waterfalls.

Valrin looked over the edge of the bridge and saw multiple glowing plants at the bottom of the cave.

"I grow many things," Evurn told them. "Most you cannot get in any other place than here. I have traveled far and long to obtain such rare flora."

"So you are into alchemy?" Rortho questioned.

He ignored Rortho for a moment. Leading them up a narrow stairwell, they ascended to a tower of sorts where the ocean winds cut through the stones.

"I take you to my home so we may sit and speak in more comfort than the caves."

In the darkness, it was hard to actually see the elf himself. He was simply a hooded figure leading them on. They walked across a stone walkway, and Valrin paused to look out of a hole in the passage. The sea was beneath them.

"Are we leaving the island?"

"Yes," Evurn replied. "That is but one of three. My home is in the one we go to; although, it is not as simple as that."

Reaching the other island, they came to a room of vines with large leaves that wrapped up into a small opening of sunlight.

"Follow me to more comfortable places, dear friends."

The elf stepped into the vines and smiled at them as he descended into the undergrowth.

"I think I will wait here," Fadis said.

"Come now, archer. Let's not get scared!" Rortho said.

They each stood on the vines, though Fadis was still reluctant, and slowly began to descend.

Valrin felt his feet tugged on at first, but then a snaking trio of vines twisted over him, and he took a deep breath as his head was covered. He couldn't see anything. He felt for a few moments that he was falling. The sensation came several times, but each time, the vines grabbed hold of him again.

"This is not the most comfortable situation I have ever been in," Fadis said in a garbled speech.

It was a few more moments before Valrin felt his feet released. A second later and he found himself falling a few feet and standing in fresh sod. They were in a large cavern. Mushrooms grew in every spot they could see.

Evurn stood above them just up a small stairwell, his staff shining orange light upon them. Valrin noticed that his staff had the carvings of flowers of differing kinds and a skull at its head. Atop it was the glowing crystal. It looked very similar to the staff Lorlaam used when attempting to heal Edanos.

"I heard your question, dwarf, and of course I am into alchemy, herbology, and every other named science of growing herbs and plants, in general, to otherwise shape the world. You were the fools to search me out about a poison, after all. This way."

They followed a large stairwell that narrowed to a circular passage. As they walked down the passage, Valrin stopped to look out of the windows. He saw a fish.

"What in the gods is this?" Fadis said.

"You're religious?" Rortho said.

"I may become it if this place begins filling with water."

Valrin touched the glass and noticed one of the fish came toward him and stared. It reminded him when he was near Meredaas with Edanos. They were actually underwater right now. He peered a bit longer and then went to join Evurn in the next cavern.

There wasn't much of the traditional sense in the elf's quiet abode. There was a shelf with several books. A simple bed and a few foods on a bare table. However, on the back wall of the cavern, there were several instruments and bubbling concoctions. There were heads of multiple animals in glass jars, along with what appeared to be at least a few human skulls.

"You admire my sciences?" Evurn asked him.

"I . . . I . . . Just have never seen something like this."

"I studied in the college in Fadabrin when I was a young boy. Earth magic. I was a most studious student, but I knew even then that I had a knack for the more unpleasant sciences. Tell me, why have you sought me?"

Valrin looked to the others and then back to the elf. "Our friend was struck by a dwarven bolt. He fell unconscious, and we used what we could to remove the barb. We were fortunate to have fairies that healed him further, and we thought he would just sleep it off, but then he hasn't awoken."

"You were sent to me, then?"

"Yes, the Ice Mage mentioned that the poison has a curse attached to it in some form. He is poisoned, yes, but is also cursed."

The elf looked down and rubbed his head.

"A strange poison to have these qualities, but you are in luck. I happen to know of a place. It is where the dwarves once gathered their poisons. An island to the east. There are dwarves that way, but if we are quick, we can get what you need. I take it that is what you want? A sample?"

"The Ice Mage says he can create an elixir from it."

Evurn snickered. "Your friend must have access to a great piece of magic to do that."

Valrin remained silent.

"Keep your secrets, then. It is no matter to me."

"So, are you going to tell us where to go?" Fadis asked.

"Dear man, I had said that *we* can get what you need. *We* implies I am going too. There are many poisons crafted in the dwarven isles."

"You mean to take us near the actual capital city?" Rortho asked.

"Yes, but just near it. If you want to source the poison they are using, we must go to where they obtain it. I know of this because for a time, I created their poisons. You must trust me, dwarf. I know what these bastards of the sea do to those who come against them. I had questions of your allegiances, but now I know you wish to avoid them as well."

Evurn let his snake curl up and around his staff.

"My home will be well without me. The fungus needs to grow. They need their time alone and to be without my constant tinkering."

Evurn said little else. He gathered a few trinkets into a bag and donned a robe before pushing them back through the passage toward the vines.

"Who built this place?" Rortho asked.

"Who else? Me. It is not dwarves alone who can craft. I sometimes close off my home and my mushroom cavern and take to the sea to find rare shells and maybe a fish for dinner. It is not often I get the unlucky dwarf or elf who is marooned on my island."

Evurn chuckled and stood beneath the vines. Valrin and the others joined him, and they were pulled back up.

Valrin couldn't decide if going up or down was actually worse, but it was actually faster the second time. They made it back out through the cave and across the miniature jungle-like region of the larger island.

"You do realize it is too cold for anything you have here to make sense?" Braei asked the elf.

"Finally, the quiet one speaks. If I had known you would ask such a foolish question, I would not have desired you to open your mouth."

Evurn pointed up to the edges of the cavernous expanse that covered the actual trees.

"I have spells in place that feed the trees and provide a way to regulate the careful climate I need, along with a ward to protect it from the cruel cold winds. Have you four not noticed that it is not cold in most of my happy home?"

Valrin nodded. "I had—"

"Nope, you didn't notice. And people wonder why I disappeared. I cannot stand people."

Evurn boarded the ship on his own with the others following.

"A nice ship you have. A strange ship too. Perhaps there is more mystery here than has been revealed. You mentioned Trilsa, a man in Corson, but you also mentioned an Ice Mage. I do think there is much more than has been spoken of."

He stared at Valrin with a questioning glare.

"Perhaps," Valrin told him.

. . .

Once they had boarded, Valrin pulled the anchor and allowed the ship to be pulled away from the shallow docking he had performed. Rortho was on the bow of the ship and looked over the edge.

"No damage that I can see, and I didn't see any before, so I guess your little crash was okay for the ship."

"Little crash?" Evurn said. "Rasi was nearly crushed by your behemoth smashing into the sand!"

The snake appeared out of one of his sleeves and slid across the deck of the ship.

"Did the snake have to come?" Fadis questioned.

"The snake is more valuable to me than any of you. If you want my help, you will be blessed to have Rasi with you. She is an albino arctic water snake, but she has been with me for so long, she is beyond a simple snake. Pray you do not need to see that."

Valrin guided the ship to the east. He went to actually switch on the map, but Rortho shook his head.

"He is a stranger, and I would prefer he not know every secret."

Evurn was sitting cross-legged on the front of the ship and humming as his snake circled around him. Braei stood somewhat behind him and actually knelt down to try to pet Rasi.

"Don't encourage it," Fadis said.

Rasi slithered toward her and brushed her hand before returning to her master.

"Captain," Evurn said, "keep your ship heading east until the evening. We will come to a large island with the ruins of a dwarven tower. It is there; I worked for many years gathering herbs and developing poisons for the Barb King."

"How close were you to the man?" Valrin asked.

"Very, so close I could have attempted to poison him and might have poisoned his wife."

"That is why you are hiding!" Rortho exclaimed. "You tried to kill him."

"I did not try, I did. Just because his body is alive does not mean his heart is. I struck him harder than the hand of death upon his own self. He never knew it was me. I set fire to my home upon the island and dragged a corpse into it to make my disappearance easier.

"Dwarves are a superstitious lot, especially these dwarves. The Barb King became obsessed with finding rare artifacts. He once poisoned an entire island of men just to convince the patriarch of the island to unlock a door."

"You mean you poisoned an entire island," Fadis stated.

"Indeed." Evurn looked at him with a discerning eye. "You make many statements, man. I sense you do not like Evurn and Rasi."

"Your snake is fine. I have issues with elves."

"As do I. It is why I eat them. Have you ever tasted the blood of those otherwise eternal?"

Fadis became silent after that.

They made swift time. Spotting an island ahead, Valrin pointed it out to Rortho. "It seems we have found it," he told him.

Rortho walked to the bow and seemed confused as they drew closer. "Evurn, you said it was a dwarven ruin?"

"I did," he said, still sitting on the deck.

"There is a large construct, and I do not believe it ruins any longer."

Evurn stood and looked out toward the island. "They delved into the mountain!" he said.

"Not surprising," Braei commented. "Dwarves tend to do that."

"Not *that* mountain. There was a darkness upon it. It kept them away. They didn't even like visiting my lab back then. Indeed, this has become more difficult. Valrin, take us south. There is another place we can hide until dark. I dare not approach that place while any light is still upon the sea."

Valrin turned the wheel hard, taking them south and toward an outcropping of rocks.

If they had been spotted, it wasn't obvious yet, but he guided the ship into the towering formations. As the ship slowed they began to be tossed by the rolling waves of the ocean.

"Cast off anchors," Evurn commanded.

The shadow elf had a much more serious demeanor now. He tapped his staff on the deck of the ship, and Rasi curled up it.

"We will wait, and then we will need to figure out our next path. I cannot stress now the importance of your work, Stormborn."

Valrin looked at Braei and Rortho. He walked toward Evurn, "How did you know?"

"Really, you question me? A realm ship with a boy captain? I may be a bit eccentric by some standards, but I know the prophecy of the Stormborn. The Barb King was obsessed with it. My concern now is that his obsession has driven him to something else. If he has delved into that place," he said, pointing toward the other island, "than he is willing to risk much. The Barb King thinks he is as you. He believes he is a Stormborn. But he believes, too, that he is meant to rule.

"Boy, I do not care for your purpose, but I know what terror was within that place. Many islands of the Glacial Seas hold secrets. That one was a coven of witches. Witches from the south, the far south. Itsu magic, or so they say."

"Itsu?" Rortho asked. "They have been gone from our world for some time."

"They can still be felt, still be learned of, and still be reached if one tries hard enough. The magic within that rock, the souls of the damned trapped beneath, that is what powered the crucible for my poisons. I had no desire to seek out that power, but if the dwarves have, we must be on guard."

Evurn went to the edge of the ship. "We must wait for darkness. Then we will determine our path."

As they waited for the sun to go down, Rortho studied the dwarven books Valrin had found while the others went down below to make a bite to eat. It was a simple enough dinner, but cold. A rolled mash of minced fish and a dash of spice. Braei had started to make some hot tea, but a passing-by fishing vessel scared them into dousing the fire and instead remaining still.

Darkness fell, and Evurn pointed to the island. "Now, Valrin, I bid us go."

They pulled up the anchors and began back toward the island. They could tell from even afar that there were many watchtowers and high walls. Though made of wood, they still would prove enough to keep them from easily scaling them. A patrolling ship made its way around the isle.

Valrin made a careful turn to avoid it.

"The old port is walled in," Evurn said, "but I have an option for us. There are caves that they do not know of. We can go that way. Though there are still risks, it will have to be enough."

"Where is this cave?" Rortho questioned.

"Beyond the overlooking reach of the walls on the east side."

Valrin looked toward where Evurn directed, seeing a bluff and sheer cliffs.

He guided the ship that way.

"The caves will work," Evurn continued. "There is a passage within that leads up to my old lab and the source of the poison. It is an effigy of a demigod of the Itsu. Has anyone heard of Vearika?"

"That is a word for spider, at least in dwarven," Rortho said.

"Close enough, for her poison is of the most potent. I would dilute it with less than harmful ingredients. I dare not use the most potent and pure for a poison. It can capture your very soul. Once you drain the victim of blood, you could enchant powerful objects by bathing said objects in the blood. Or as a vampire, you could drink it and gain their knowledge. A useful skill for some."

"Where is this cave?" Fadis questioned. "I see no break in the rocks."

Valrin moved the ship along the sheer side of the bluff.

"Drop your anchor, Stormborn."

Valrin did so.

Evurn shed his robes and secured a satchel around his neck. His skinny form was pale, but though his face was rough and his hair scraggly, his elven blood kept his body as pure as a child. He took his staff and went to the edge of the ship.

"Breath of Gills, come!"

He struck the water, and several strands of a greenish plant wrapped around his staff.

"The cave is here but under the surface."

"That water is freezing!" Braei said "How will you be able to find some underwater cave and deal with the cold? How do you know the enemy is not waiting for you on the other side?"

Evurn laughed. "It is a cave and none know of it save me. I sealed it when I left. Trust this shadow elf that he knows more than you in this matter."

He went to Valrin and handed him some of the plants he retrieved from the water and then also gave him a small stone.

"Ember Rock. Place it against your body and the

cold will flee from you. Once we are in the water, place the plant in your mouth and breathe."

"Where is mine?" Fadis said. "You are not going alone with the boy."

"Your bow is cheap; I will take the girl. She wields no weapons but yet is in your company. Rusis, I suspect. You did not happen to just be with the Stormborn. If you knew of the Ice Mage, then each of you have purpose. But for now your purpose is here on the ship."

He handed Braei the same things he had just handed Valrin.

"Be watchful," he told Rortho and Fadis. "I cannot promise an easy escape."

As they went to the edge of the ship, Valrin looked over to see the patrolling ship coming toward them.

"I will have to move further out and hope the moon stays hidden," Rortho said. "Braei, take care of them."

She nodded. Both of them placed the ember stones against their skin. Evurn jumped in, and they followed after him.

Valrin expected cold, but he didn't feel it. He knew he was in the water, but it didn't even seem wet. He just felt sensations around his body.

"Now, under," Evurn commanded.

Valrin placed the strange grass in his mouth and sunk down. He suddenly felt the plant come to life. It went down his throat, and it felt like he choked, followed by a sensation of something in his nose. He was able to breathe suddenly. It was almost like back with Meredaas but much more uncomfortable.

Evurn signaled for him and Braei to follow him toward the darkness of the rocks.

He kicked and did a wide breaststroke, moving quicker than Braei but barely able to keep up with Evurn, whose long legs seemed to propel him at a speed beyond what was capable of them. They dove deeper, pausing before they got to the actual rock and letting themselves fall downward. Darkness surrounded them.

Valrin looked up. He could see the waves striking the rocks above him and feel the power of the currents changing. At least, he thought it was a current. He jumped when something touched his back. He jerked around to see a large squid moving past. Braei's eyes became huge, and she kicked like crazy to get next to Evurn. The squid moved off, and Evurn seemed to be laughing at them. He made a motion with his staff, and they continued to follow him, though Braei was now literally right next to him.

They made it to the underwater rock, and Evurn moved his staff along the rocks until its light illuminated a large silver handle. Moss hanging and shifting from the handle nearly hid it completely. Evurn took hold of it and pulled. It didn't budge at first. He took his staff and placed it on the metal. There was a flash, and it fell open before breaking from its hinge and floating down into the depths. Evurn disappeared inside the small cave.

Braei motioned for him, and they debated who

would go in first. Braei eventually won, and he pulled himself into the opening. He couldn't see anything at all, but he kicked and reached upward. His fingertips broke the surface, and as his mouth hit the air, the plant that helped him breathe fell off. He didn't see Evurn.

Braei came up next and glanced around. "There is a way up," she said.

He followed her to a ledge and pulled himself up to another platform. It was there, now a bit higher, they saw Evurn sitting on the body of a dead dwarf.

"Um, what happened?" Braei asked.

"Well, that is an unintelligent question. I swear, do you ever say anything with thought? The dwarf died. Might as well use him as a seat."

"Did he call for help or anything?" Valrin asked, grasping his sword.

"Call? He can't even move. He's as stiff as a brick." Evurn tapped the dwarf's head with his staff. "This bastard probably came down here to rest and never went back up. That is why you don't go into other people's things."

"Well, it is a passage in a place they occupy," Braei said. "You can't expect them to stay out."

"Are we done, Rusis? I have dealt with your kind before. They did not talk nearly as much." Evurn tapped his staff again and stood. "Come now, we don't want to overstay our welcome in my old home."

He gave Braei a swift shake of his head and then lifted his staff. Rasi had come with them. The snake dropped down to the ground and slithered ahead.

"Rasi will watch out for us. Dwarves can be crafty with traps. There may not be any, but Rasi will search nonetheless!"

They followed the elf through a large passage and then up a series of stairs that made an angular ascent toward another large door. The door itself was already blasted open. Evidence of fire marks and smoke surrounded it.

"This was locked and sealed," he muttered. "Dwarves delve too deep into places they shouldn't."

Walking in, they found a ransacked room that seemed to greatly disturb the elf. He made long strides, shifting through tattered books and kicking broken furniture out of his way.

"This way to my old lab," he told them.

As they followed him down a narrow hallway, they came to a large room with rubble everywhere. There was an image of part of a spider in the wall, but the statue in front of it had been broken.

"Dear Vearika, they have really messed up your sacred place."

Evurn, they tempt me with a most delectable temptation.

Valrin and Braei both jumped. Valrin drew his sword and Braei had a spell of flame in hand.

"She speaks to us freely," Evurn said. The shadow elf seemed at awe of this. Clearly he did not expect it. "Dear Vearika, long have I prayed to you. Now, I hear of a poison and curse."

They have tainted me. They have fed me delights. I serve their needs in the place known as The Black.

4
THE BLACK

"What is that?" Valrin asked.

"It was the edge of the old ruins," Evurn said. "If you look at this statue as the top of a grand cathedral, my dear Vearika speaks of her altar beneath her feet."

He lifted his hands. "Dear Vearika, what do you wish from me to obtain a piece of your venom?"

Claim it from the intruders. Spill their blood within my chasms!

The room shook, and Valrin felt his heart thudding in his chest.

"Well, this seems easy enough!" Evurn said light-heartedly as he now had a quick step to his walk.

"We can't attack them," Braei said. "We do not have the power to do such a thing. There are just three of us."

"Four," he corrected.

"Um, no. Three."

He motioned for them to follow him and began to

walk. "I am sorry, dear Rasi. To Braei, you are not a person. Do you see why we avoid people now, my fair snake? Do you see why we feed on them when they happen upon our happy island?"

He led them out of the room and to a large balcony that was partially broken. They moved quickly in the shadows and crossed a narrow path that was open to the outside. Valrin spotted the constructed woodworks and the dwarves patrolling them.

"There is no way we can go out that way," Braei said. "Let us hope he has a plan."

She pointed for him to follow after Evurn. The elf had already made it to another passage, and his staff glowed brighter as he peered into the passage before he dimmed it.

He knelt and waited for them. Rasi climbed back into his robes to hide.

"We go this way, into The Black. Watch yourself, this place is home to the pets of Vearika. I did my best to avoid this place then. Even Rasi did not care for those."

Valrin drew his blade and nodded to Evurn. The elf turned and began to feel his way down into the darkness. The stairwell twisted downward for some time, and then there was a large opening with a single torch burning on the left side.

"They have defiled this place. I dare to wonder how much they have delved into," Evurn said with annoyance.

There was a rank smell and a thick musty film in the air.

"I have come here on many, many occasions. The pets of Vearika will know my scent, but strangers may prove troubling. If they show their fangs, I say step back slowly and do not proceed."

Valrin heard Evurn whisper something after his last word, and his staff began to glow. A pale orange light revealed a horror before them.

There were massive spiders; at least, they looked like spiders at first. Much larger and more grotesque than even the ones they had dealt with a few nights ago. It looked that they were actually kin of spiders. They had fewer legs and thicker bodies, and the best part was that they weren't moving. Valrin stared at the creatures. There were no glistening fangs and no sounds of claws scraping the floor.

There were several more of the creatures a bit further down, but most of them were broken to the point their legs were cracked and riddled with marks. Evurn knelt to one of them and brought his staff close to its head.

"Dear friend of Vearika, the dwarves must've done a number on your souls." He looked up at Valrin and Braei. "They took their poison and defaced the poor creatures."

"A dead creature is better than one threatening us," Braei said.

Evurn stood up and jerked back toward their path. "There was a time, dear Rusis, that I would had turned you into a plant for such a comment, but I do fear this development." His glare turned to a smirk, and he pointed to the beasts. "These creatures were not dead for too long before now. Something has moved the dwarves to push into The Black. I do not dare guess what horror they have teased Vearika with. She is not easily pleased."

They continued forward, passing more of the dead creatures. Valrin stepped around the massive legs of one that had died in the center of the path, and was happy that the creature was dead. He dared to wonder how they would have gotten away from such creatures had they, as Evurn mentioned, showed their fangs.

The path came to two large doors. They were very dark regardless of the staff light that Evurn moved from side to side. He pushed open the door carefully, peeking in and dimming his staff further. He pushed the door open and motioned for them to follow.

There was another stairwell and a strange blue light shining on the walls. A chant was in the air, but Valrin could not distinguish the words.

"Dwarven magic," Evurn hissed. "Mind your ears of this sea vomit!"

They made their way down the stairs and came to metal gates that were two times the height of the elf but slightly ajar.

There were large statues of the creatures from before on either side of the gates.

"The holy entrance, defiled," Evurn stated.

He motioned for them to stay, and put his staff out in front of him, slowly creeping through the gate. Valrin went to peek around the corner, but Braei put her hand on his shoulder.

"Wait, let Evurn tell us to proceed."

He shrugged off her hand, and they both peered around. The elf was already a good few paces away and was also peering around the edge of a second threshold. He turned to see them and signaled for them to proceed but put a hushing finger to his lips.

Valrin went through with Braei just behind him and went to the other side of the threshold. Evurn pointed, and Valrin looked into the room ahead.

He spotted a massive blue fire hovering above the protracted legs of a spider on its back. The spider was actually some kind of statue, a place for vile incantations. There were bodies of bleeding elves lying all over the actual altar built into the center of the spider. They had been prisoners, or perhaps, it just seemed that due to their appearance. Their skin was sallow and tight, and their eyes moved slowly but with blank gazes. Their blood was thick and bubbled out of their bodies like it was old.

A dwarf appeared and lifted a large bony staff into the fire. He brought it down toward the bodies, and there was a screech from many of them. Their eyes widened and became a bright white, and from their mouths poured a white smoke.

"Brothers!" the dwarf said, turning toward them.

Valrin and Braei both jumped, and the dwarf continued to speak.

"Brothers, arise, stand from your silent praise!"

Valrin looked around the corner to see that the dwarf wasn't talking to them but to many dwarves in black hoods who were now standing up. Their forms had blended into the shadows, and now he wondered how many dwarves were actually in the sanctuary of The Black.

"We feed the creature Vearika the blood of eternals. Through my powers we have kept them alive, to tease the beast, and allow it the flavors to come. We call forth the great one from the realm of gods. May she bless us with more of what the mountain had hidden from us. We serve our Barb King, for he is wise. He has foreseen the forces of the sea to play a part in a great undoing of a shrouding darkness, when beasts of old will come from the realm of that deemed evil by the world. Our king will slay them and in so creep toward the great god Throka in power! The gods of the North know not the strength of the Barb King.

"He is great. He sends our fleets to claim the treasures of the prophesied Stormborn. He will claim what is his, and I will command legions in time. A prophecy speaks of elves from the shadows who will undo this prophecy. They will close the gates so that the world will never have the trials of the coming darkness, elves from the very seas that surround us, brothers. They will destroy us, but our king intends to poison all who live within these seas. Be it men, creatures of the sea, or anything that comes against us, but especially the elves. He will not be stopped, but he must have more of the blood of Vearika!"

Evurn crossed the threshold and touched Braei on the shoulder. "This is a mad dwarf. He speaks of that which he does not know. He speaks of the one who will awaken what has long been silent. He speaks of a prophecy of the Glacial Seas so old to even myself that I am surprised even this Barb King knows of it."

"What are we going to do?" Valrin asked.

"We must do as Vearika has told us. Prepare yourselves."

The dwarf spoke again, lifting his hands into the sky with his back to them.

"I give you the full flavor of the eternals. Know you have this offering from Irikow, servant of the Shrouds, last church of the dead one in these icy waters! Bless us with more of your essence and know we will fill this altar with many of the eternal blood!"

The dwarf stepped back, and the legs of the statue came to life. With a red glow to the stone, it began to move inward, squeezing the bodies and taking what last bit of life they had. The blue fire below sucked into the center of the glowing red, and from the edges of the statue came a bright, glowing green substance.

Irikow reached up into the air. From his hooded form, Valrin saw only his grayish hands reaching over the pouring green fluid.

"Thank you. We embrace your darkness. Forgive us of slaying your guardians. Do forgive us dwarves for not earning our way into your sanctum before now."

A scratchy voice spoke within whispers of wind pouring in all around them. *Poison is words spoken at guilt to embrace the betrayed. I give more of my essence, but it is for who claims it.*

Evurn stepped into the void and sent a blast of yellow energy from his staff. The dwarves closest to him flew forward and began to shake violently. Valrin stepped out with Braei and stood behind Evurn, who sent a second bolt of yellow energy into the one called Irikow. The dwarf fell to the ground, shaking.

The dwarves spun, drawing staves of their own just to fall to a blast of the poisonous earth magic wielded by Evurn. Rasi slid forward. She jumped onto the neck of one of the dwarves before biting into his face. The dwarf screamed and fell to the ground as the spot Rasi had bitten began to rot immediately.

Valrin stabbed one of them in the throat, but he discovered the spell of the elf had already begun to cause blood to pour from their eyes and noses. Valrin's blade was mere mercy. Braei shot a blast of electricity into a group who tried to flee to the other side of the room, dropping them to the ground. Evurn then blasted another shot of his staff toward them. All of the dwarves who had been standing were now dying on the floor.

"Praise be to Vearika. Dear Vearika, I now take some of your essence."

Evurn took out several glass bottles and sampled the glowing substance from the statue. "This is all that is needed. Enough for the need you have, Valrin Stormborn."

Valrin rubbed his blade against his boot and sheathed it. Evurn handed him one of the vials. He held it up, looking at the strange fluid. "Now, we can return," he said to Braei with a smile. "We have what we need."

"Do you have what you need?" a voice grumbled from their side.

Braei pulled Valrin back as Evurn flipped his staff toward the mound of dwarves.

The one called Irikow stood up. His eyes glowed red. "You cannot throw down a servant of the Shrouds with mere earth magic. I am of death; I command the earth to split and pour forth those to serve me as needed! Dwarves are more than mere iron and hot metals!" Irikow lifted his staff toward Evurn. "Elven waste, you cannot kill what is dead!"

Irikow threw back his hood in an arcane wind of purple magic that enveloped him.

"It is a lich!" Evurn cried. "Stormborn, flee from this place. Flee now!"

Braei grabbed Valrin. "Now, we must go!"

A blast of green magic struck Evurn, and he cowered under a growing ward of gold he used to push back at the lich's attack.

The lich shouted, "None will escape! None will leave this rock!" A shrill scream pierced the air as Valrin turned to run with Braei. He felt horrible leaving Evurn, but the elf was the only one who stood a chance against the power of the lich.

As they climbed up the stairwell, they jumped the steps before pushing open the black doors. There was a loud horn call that bellowed through the ruins.

"They know we're here! We must get to the sea!"

Sprinting through the hall of the dead spider creatures, they came to the stairwell and Valrin remembered the outside path. As they reached the top of the stairwell, they took to the open air path and made their way down the side of the mountain to a platform. The water was below them, but they would have to follow the ruins to get lower.

Dwarves were behind them. They could hear their gruff voices and the shuffling of their heavy boots.

Braei hugged the wall, and Valrin hid behind crumbling ruins just a few paces from the opening that led toward the stairwell to The Black. Several dwarves stopped at the stairwell.

"The Master Irikow shouted. He must be in trouble," one said.

"I am not going into that place, no matter the pay, and you could tell the Barb King that yourself!" another said.

A larger dwarf arrived with several other dwarves behind him. "Get down there now! Or I will give you to the lich to do what he wishes!"

Without further debate, the dwarves began to move down, and the large one stopped at the opening and peered out. Valrin was well hidden. Lying on his stomach and looking through a crack in the rock, he was impossible to see.

The other dwarves descended, but this other one stepped outside. Though Valrin was well hidden, Braei was much more visible. She clung frozen along the wall and attempted to make herself as flat as possible. The dwarf stepped toward the ruins where Valrin hid. He sniffed the air.

"Damn dark magic," he said to himself. The dwarf spat just near Valrin and then turned to walk when he paused. He was looking toward Braei.

Valrin looked up, and she stared directly at the

dwarf. He wasn't sure if the old dwarf's vision was bad or if he was pausing to make his finding shudder in fear before he announced himself.

He unslung a large hammer and stepped forward. "Come, you little rat. You've been messing where you shouldn't."

Valrin noticed now that Braei had tried to move further away from the dwarf and now her hands were holding her on the rocks she clung to.

"No weapon, even?" the dwarf said.

Valrin had to do something. But he doubted his skill. He had fought a dwarf once, but this one was much better armored, beyond that of the mere sea pirate he had fought before.

The dwarf smashed his ax into the side of the ruins. The rocks forced Braei to jump further up. She had no leverage to get back to the platform and possibly attack the dwarf, and there was nowhere for her to run. The dwarf was at the edge.

"Come on, little lady. I'm not much into weaker species, but you'd fetch me a bit at the gambling hall back home!"

Valrin gripped his sword. His hands were sweating, and he struggled to control his breathing. In a quick jump, he pushed up and ran for the dwarf, thrusting his blade into his back. It didn't pierce the armor, and the tip got stuck before he jerked it back. The dwarf stumbled as he turned. With a yell, he stomped forward, swinging at him. Valrin jumped back, the head of the hammer just missing him. He had to choose fast. Either run further back or attack his adversary.

He had to do it, and as the dwarf recovered from his swing, Valrin moved quickly forward, slashing the dwarf's hand and piercing the dwarf's unguarded hand. He then pushed on again, further taking advantage of his opponent and shoving the dwarf with his shoulder. The dwarf fell backward, hobbling on the edge of the precipice for a moment. Valrin steadied his footing as he grabbed the edge of the ruins to keep himself from falling. In a moment of unexpected shock, he watched as the dwarf tumbled down the rocky ruins into the depths of the sea below.

Braei had already begun to climb back over and now managed to climb to a better spot and jump down to Valrin.

"That was . . . that was . . . amazing! You did better than I hoped. I am sorry; I tried to get up above him, and well, I didn't do it. You saved me."

He took a moment to think about what had happened. It was the first time he had actually done it. He looked down over the edge again. He had killed that dwarf to save his friend. It felt strange to him and he still didn't believe he had actually done it.

Valrin nodded at her and twirled his sword, "Let's go and get away from this place."

Braei looked back toward the opening and saw no other dwarves. Further away, they could see large torches coming alight along the battlements. She went to the opposite edge where the earlier event had unfolded, and pointed.

"There is a ledge, and it looks to be another stairwell. We may have to jump, but we can get to the sea."

"Once we get there, we can't swim to them without the stones that Evurn gave us and their magic is gone. How are we going to signal them to get us?"

"We can do it, just watch. You know I can figure out something."

She gave him a quick grin. They climbed down a section of rock to a barely visible ledge that ran toward the platform Braei pointed out before. Once on the platform, she looked above them and scanned the area.

"Okay, the rocks we were hiding behind are that way."

She summoned a large flame between her hands. "I just hope they are there and watching."

She sent a blast of fire at an angle across the ocean. It began to trace upward and then exploded into a bright orange flash.

"Now, we go down the stairs. The dwarves are so dense, they will take time to figure out what that was, and by then, we will be gone."

They went down the stairwell and went to another long pathway. This one seemed to be straight and run directly out and away from the island. Hopefully it would work to get them lower to the water. There were rocky arches overhead, and at least twice Valrin thought he spotted movement above them.

As they came to an open area where the water was just below, they found themselves very close to the wooden battlements that were blocking the original entrance when they came in. Braei looked out from them and saw a shadow moving across the water.

"That is them; they are coming," she said.

It was as perfect as they could get to. The area had deep water and an open spot where the ship could come in fairly close.

"We will need to go to them. They can only come so close to the walls," Braei told him.

Valrin scanned the battlements above him. There were a few lone dwarves on watch, but he guessed many of them had gone to the lich. He thought of Evurn. He had liked the elf. Though he was a bit strange, he had a passion for his work. Valrin reached and touched the vial of Vearika's essence. This was the only hope they had for Edanos. They just had to get back to the island.

"Valrin, into the water. They are nearing shore."

He slipped into the icy water. His feet slid in the gravel shore. They were in a cove, so the waves of the seas were not so much a concern, but as he slipped into neck-deep water, he felt the feeling of daggers shooting through his body. He kicked, seeing his ship drawing close.

"Hey! Alarm! Ring the bells! ALARM! ALARM!" a voice shouted behind them. Valrin turned and glanced behind him. A dwarf was on the edge of the wall, pointing. He seemed confused, as if no one had heard him. He looked back out just as an arrow caught him in the head. Fadis was on the railing of the ship and already had another arrow already to cheek.

Valrin began to swim harder. The ship turned and

slid in the water. Fadis was now above him. Valrin looked up as a rope splashed near him. He gripped it as he was pulled into the boat.

"Where is the elf?" Fadis asked.

"We ran into trouble. He stayed behind so we could escape."

"Braei!" Fadis shouted.

The Rusis began into the water.

Valrin was shivering uncontrollably. Rortho came to him and set him down before going to the edge with Fadis.

Valrin tried to control the chatter of his teeth. He checked that he still had the vial and it was unbroken. Thankfully, it was intact.

There was a sudden shudder to the sea and a loud crashing sound.

He stood up, stumbling forward as he did, and gripped the center pillar of the ship.

The fortress was burning with a green fire, and a large section had been destroyed. Dwarves were strewn about the wreckage, and a single figure with a glowing orange staff ran upon the battlements.

"Evurn!" Valrin said.

There were many dwarves emerging from the ruins. Fadis drew another arrow and took down the one closest to the elf.

"Rortho," Valrin said, "once we get Braei, we will move to assist the elf."

Rortho nodded and then looked down to the water. "Braei! What are you doing?"

Valrin went to the railings and looked for Braei.

She had returned to shore and was making her way toward the battlements.

"Damn Rusis!" Rortho growled.

Fadis ran along the deck of the ship. He released several arrows as Rortho moved the ship alongside the walls.

"Valrin, I have been doing a bit of reading and have a good hand at this ship now. You will need to catch up if this works right!"

Valrin watched as the dwarf manipulated the crystals. The sails of the ship shifted in the wind, and the wooden poles of the ship began to glow red. A moment later, a blast of electrical bolts shot up and over the edge of the walls, sending dwarves flying over the side. Braei made it to the walls just after that, pulling herself up and joining Evurn.

The Rusis and the elf sent blasts of magic into the dwarves, throwing them to their deaths. Valrin watched as Braei summoned a massive ball of fire and then sent the blast in a brilliant flash toward the ruins. It split off and streaked before battering the dwarves still clamoring up through the burning wreckage.

The ship was now just next to them, and Evurn stepped onto the railings. Braei was still moving forward on the battlements casting her spells.

From the glowing arcane ruins came a scream, a ghostly shrill unlike any Valrin had ever heard before. In the flames of the broken down tower emerged the dwarven lich Irikow. He floated just above the ground, moving his staff in a circle as the many dwarves were brought back to the realm of the living.

"You will not escape, Stormborn! You were foolish not to flee while you could!"

Braei sent an arcing bolt of lightning toward him, and he met the attack with a greenish bolt of his own. The whips of electrical bolts twisted and rippled in all directions, but Braei was not backing down.

Evurn sent a blast of his own, but the magic already in the air caused his attack to dissipate. He had spent too much of his energy as it was. He was too weak.

The undead dwarves were swarming around the lich and slowly began to creep toward Braei. Fadis released several arrows, taking them down one after another.

"To the ship!" Evurn cried.

Braei tried to step back, but she couldn't. Her feet wouldn't move, and her attack was beginning to fail. In her distraction defending against the main spells from the lich, she had not noticed several miniature wisping spells, like shadowy hands, creeping toward her legs. The spells wrapped around and began pulling her toward the lich.

"He has entrapped her!" Evurn said.

Fadis fired an arrow, but it was deflected by the arcane winds now rushing over the area. "Damn magic!" he cursed.

Valrin looked behind their ship and saw the dwarven patrol vessel advancing on them around the edge of the island. Evurn stood with his staff out. "Ranger, draw an arrow!"

Fadis drew back an arrow and looked back at the elf.

Evurn's staff began to glow a bright red. Energy swarmed from his staff to Fadis's bow.

"Take down that lich!" Evurn said.

Fadis released the arrow, and this time the lightning couldn't deflect it. The lich turned toward them for a moment and sent a blast of magic into the air, but the arrow flew straight into his side.

"A dwarf can never defeat an elf, you rock-scraping fool!"

Braei pushed herself up, now free from the lich's grasp. Irikow fell backward, grasping at his wound as the arrow began to disintegrate, leaving a large festering hole near his ribs.

The Rusis ran toward the ship and leaped. As soon as Fadis grabbed hold of her, Rortho turned the ship and raised the sails. The patrol vessel moved to pursue, but Rortho made a quick adjustment to the weapons of the vessel and sent a blast of fire at the sails of the dwarven ship. They pulled away from the burning fortress and vessel of the dwarves, catching swift winds speeding them north.

Evurn ran to the back of the ship, and Valrin joined him. In the distance, the lich was standing again, and a green and purple smoke rose from the side of his body. Fadis drew back another arrow, but Evurn tapped his bow down.

"He is powerful. Very powerful. I have killed more of him with my enchantment on your bolt, but being a lich, he is mostly dead already. I have no spell to turn him to dust, and it will take great magic to defeat him. Save your arrows. If you're a vampire, well, you could bite him, but we are fresh out of vampires among our companions, I assume."

Evurn exhaled and collapsed to the deck.

Braei, too, was lying down, and Valrin went to her.

"I had to help him. He helped us, and well, you helped me, so I did what I did," Braei explained.

Valrin hugged her. "I know Edanos would not be too happy with a move like that."

"Ha, he'll never know, and now we have what we need."

They moved quickly north. Valrin brought up the star map for a moment to confirm their heading and took the wheel from Rortho. The shadow elf had proved his loyalty to them. Braei went to Evurn, who was now meditating just behind Valrin. He opened his eyes before she spoke, smiling at her. He stood up and took her hands.

"I have been harsh with my words to you, but I'd be dead if it were not for your skill and your courage. I will not think of you as lesser, but I still might find your words a bit unintelligent."

Braei gave him a peculiar look. "I guess I will take that as a friendly insult?"

Evurn chuckled. "That is fine. You go find rest in the lower quarters. I will speak with our friend here for a while."

As Braei went below deck, Evurn sat down next to Valrin. Fadis abruptly walked up at the same time.

"Evurn, how did you know?"

"How did I know what? That you wish to hide that you're a Ranger?"

Fadis stared, dumbfounded. "Well . . . yes, I told them at one point, but not you."

"No man can shoot a bow as you. You use elven wood and, from what I saw, release arrows with the skill of my distant kin. I care little for titles, but you are a Ranger."

"Fair enough, elf. It seems my past is suddenly just showing up in my present." He began to walk away.

Evurn nodded even though Fadis didn't see. "Yes, how many years will it take for you to return to who you left?"

Fadis stopped walking for a moment, looked back with just a glance, and kept walking away.

Valrin looked to Evurn. "Fadis hasn't been with us for very long, but he has been a great help."

"I am sure of that. Rangers are loyal to what they believe in. To push someone to run from what he knows to come to the Glacial Seas is significant. That man is stricken with grief. But it does not concern us now. To have peace, he will have to deal with what he pushes down deep within himself. Enough of him. So is it true that Stormborn do not sleep once upon their vessel?"

"So far," Valrin said, "but I do think I sleep sometimes. I'm not sure how it works."

"It will take time. This vessel is a marvel of the sea

peoples. I knew of them back in the South, but it was more of a rumor to be true. In Fadabrin, we had many books from the North. It was a marvel to know of what was here before the ice moved in with the torrential waters. It is said the land itself sunk, creating the seas. A horrible but wondrous marvel if you think of it. The islands are the tops of massive mountains. If only we could explore them all."

Valrin nodded. "Perhaps it would be great, but at the same time, delving into that island back there had its own trouble. Can any really be trusted to not cause evil with what they find?"

"No," he replied plainly. "No man nor elf nor Rusis, not even the mermaids of the oceans, can be trusted with that. But that is not our choice. We cannot control everyone. That is where the empires of the world fail. You cannot control what you do not understand, even if you think you have any degree of actual knowledge of it. There are wondrous powers and horrid curses; we cannot restrict their use, but we can do what is right. Look at me—I eat any who come upon my island. I do it to survive. I do not leave my island except on extreme need. I left to embrace the one called 'Stormborn.' That is what I have determined is right. I know we must travel with haste to save your friend," he paused for a moment, "and I am undecided of my path afterward."

Rasi the snake slithered away from him and went up the wheel of the ship, crossing over Valrin's hands before wrapping up on his arm.

"Oh, dear Rasi, you found yourself a friend?"

The snake's cold skin gave a further chill to Valrin's arm, and he stroked the snake before it uncurled and returned to Evurn.

"Perhaps we will stay a bit longer, then."

They had been traveling for a few hours. Evurn had fallen asleep just behind him. The sun crossed over the horizon, and gray clouds rolled over them. The sea was chaotic, and he felt a deeper dread than he had felt before. He kept his eyes on the horizon and held the wheel steady. He felt a haste to their actions beyond just Edanos' condition, and he did not know why.

The others awoke after some time and made quick work to prepare a meal and a bit of coffee. He gave the wheel to Rortho and ate and drank with the others.

They did not seem to sense the feeling that he felt. They were happy, joking. Even Fadis, who seemed to have a sadness upon him at most times, was more relaxed.

Valrin went to Rortho, who was holding the wheel and reading one of the dwarven books on the realm ships.

"This vessel is so complex. I seem to have found a mention of it having the ability to move into the places of the gods with ease. I do not understand this. The gods are not in the same world as us."

"So a different realm? This is a realm ship, as we call it."

"Well, yes," Rortho agreed, though he was a bit perturbed being called out on the obvious answer. "I just can't fathom such a thing. I also do not see a crystal or a way to activate it."

"You will," Valrin said. "I am in no hurry to meet more of the gods. The one was life-changing enough."

"Well, well, the Great Poet will deem your death in many, many years from now, I'm sure. You can see them then. Be happy you are not a mere man. They say they do not transcend to an afterlife when they die. Something of them being too curious of their own world to believe that another exists. Some even say this will lead to their own destruction. They were never meant to last. The dwarves have no need of them anyway."

Fadis had overheard their conversation. "Talking of men, are we? The dwarves I know of have plenty need for us. Lots of traders in the Taria regions."

"Well, there is that little trade thing. But well, fine." Rortho just shook his head. "Some men are useful. Some men, like Fadis here, a bit more than a simple man. It is those who stand out in their short lifespans that the songs are about. They are rare."

"I assure you there are no songs of me, dwarf."

"Not yet," Valrin suggested.

"Don't go getting too much faith in me. I will likely let you down."

Fadis went to the rear of the ship and peered out over the water before looking down.

Valrin shifted the wheels in his hands and again felt a deep dread. Now it seemed the others felt it too. The relaxed conversations had ceased. The air had dropped to a deeper cold, and it was not just the sun beginning to sink again below the horizon.

"Fadis," Rortho said, "due west, on the horizon. Do my dwarf eyes deceive me?"

Fadis walked over to the dwarf and squinted.

"Ships, many ships."

Braei and Evurn both looked out.

"Do they pursue us?" Braei asked.

"No, there are too many of them for that," Rortho replied. "They already were coming this way before. I'm not sure why. The island of the Keeper of Songs is hidden."

"Perhaps no more," Evurn said. "Perhaps the Barb King chases the Stormborn? He has many spies, many rocks that have eyes and birds that are loyal to who holds their feed."

Valrin spotted the island of the Keepers of Songs ahead.

"Valrin, we may not have too long here," Rortho warned. "We must hope the favor of Meredaas is with us."

He was even more unsettled now. He guided the ship to the east. As they crossed around the side of the island and entered the veiled harbor, Evurn jumped, thinking they were going to strike the rocks that made up the hidden way. The ship seemed to guide itself through the passage as they approached, and as they reached the dock, the ship secured itself once again.

Valrin jumped off ahead of the rest and made his way quickly to the inner hall. Their time was running out.

5

SACRED BONDING

VALRIN PUSHED OPEN the door of the hall and made his way toward Edanos. He could see the captain lying where they had left him, but something was wrong. The monks surrounded him and held their hands out, summoning small flames. Lorlaam looked up as Valrin ran up to them.

"I have it! I have the poison!"

Lorlaam walked around the others and took the vial from him.

"I had worried that they had caught you. We have seen dark omens in the stars." He glanced down at the poison. "This is pure. Beyond pure. Was Trilsa doing well?"

"He was, and he mentioned that he wishes to go on an adventure with the Ice Mage."

Lorlaam turned from him. "Now that was a fun little foray."

As the others finally made it to the hall, Lorlaam

went to a large white altar. His staff began to glow with a red hue and he moved it over the altar causing the runes to glow. He set the vial of poison down as he made marks with his fingertips on the stones.

"The captain looks worse," Braei said.

Lorlaam nodded. "He has fallen closer to the realm of death. We have chased away the coldness of Vankou with our powers, but his time is short."

Lorlaam took the poison and poured it over a crystal in the center of the altar. The crystal became cloudy with black smoke and then began to vibrate in place. A few moments later, a green hue poured forth, rolling off the altar.

"It will take time," he said. "If this is what has stricken Edanos, I will be able to mix a potion to heal him."

"You have little time," Rortho said. "A fleet of dwarves approach. We must hope the stormy waters from before can keep them from reaching the island and not propel them into it as what happened to us."

"We guided the waters to bring you here," Lorlaam announced to them. "It was fate for you to come here and a fate we have long awaited. Much is changing. The dwarves will come, but I have hope in this place." He turned to the other old Rusis men standing around Edanos. "Brothers, long have we hidden here. Though we have left many times to search out more knowledge and keep all that we guard secure, we must do what our ancestors did not. We must guard this island and not allow ourselves deceived."

"What can we do? Ambush?" Fadis asked.

"That may stop a few," Braei said, "but we are too few for it to matter. Valrin, we should take everyone and leave. We can sneak from this place before they get here!"

"That cannot happen," Lorlaam said. "We must remain here to heal your friend. I will try to prevent their searching of this place. Their ships will prove troublesome, but I believe you four can do something of it. There are two towers on either edge of the island. One stands on the northernmost peak; the other is on the south."

He pulled two crystals from his robes.

"Place these in the pedestals of those towers and we will gain favor from the gods, at least for a while."

Rortho and Valrin took the crystals.

"Shadow elf," Lorlaam said, "I see you standing near the back. You come with them after so many years in hiding?"

"It isn't like I had much a choice. We didn't leave the dwarves in the best manner. Plus, there is a lich working with the dwarves. The beast holds exceptional power. But not too much for a Rusis, if I can still call you that."

"You know each other?" Braei asked.

"From long ago," Evurn said with a smile. "I had thought the old Ice Mage dead. I would have you know this young girl saved my life." He pointed to Braei. "She is a fine Rusis, and I would indeed be dead without her aid."

"I am not yet, but even if it becomes so"—Lorlaam

took a deep breath—"you know what must be guarded."

There was a moment of silence. Evurn stared in disbelief at Lorlaam.

"Truly, still within the North?"

"Yes, I could not risk it any place else."

"With the coming of the Stormborn and the Barb King's wrath, you still think it wise to—"

"Tell me what choice I had, elf. South to your kind?"

Evurn gripped his staff and then walked forward.

"Very well, Rusis. We will see what comes of such news."

Evurn walked out of the hall, and all of the Keepers of Songs followed him.

"What was that about?" Valrin asked.

"If it becomes necessary, you shall know, but for now I await the way to heal your friend. Go quickly to the towers. The shadow elf and my brothers will speak with those who approach our cove. Perhaps they will manage to deal with our incursion."

Lorlaam turned away and went to Edanos. He knelt down and then began to recite verses to a song Valrin didn't know.

"Well, I and the archer will go to the southern tower. You and Braei can go to the northern," Rortho said. "I have little faith that these dwarves mean to talk. The Barb King knows more than we do of our moves. We were betrayed by the crew last time. I do not know how the dwarves have learned of this place, but we must do all we can to survive."

They hurried out of the hall and made it to the outside world. Fadis and Rortho went south, and Braei and Valrin went toward the other tower. Though, Valrin couldn't see exactly where they were going.

They followed a path back to the structure they had stayed in the first night they arrived and moved past it along a rocky path that reached up into a higher region of the island. From this height, they could see to the cove and noted the assembly of the monks along with Evurn.

"Who do you think betrayed us? How did they know to come to this island?" Valrin asked.

Braei pulled herself up on a ledge and then helped Valrin do the same. It was a narrow path, but it was the only way to continue going up.

"I don't know. I wonder if we were betrayed to start with. This Barb King does have many spies, but it must be more than that. I will be happy when we are on the water again and far from land where dwarves can easily surround us."

As they reached an area of more ruins, Valrin could see the sea and the many ships approaching. There were at least twenty, and with their massive lanterns and boisterous crews, they were in no way trying to sneak up on the island.

They reached a tower with a large round rock at its center. The tower reached high above the island and had a large orb at its top. As Braei moved into the tower itself, Valrin looked behind them to see the other tower to the far south of them. It looked like Rortho and Fadis were moving just beside it.

Braei leaned over the large round rock and noticed there were carvings in the rock. There was a small hole that she could feel on top of the monolith.

"This must be it," she said. "I don't see any way into the tower itself, and this seems like a place for the crystal."

Valrin reached to where she pointed and placed the crystal in the hole. There was a sudden humming that filled the air, and above them, a bright flash lit the orb in a brilliant white fire. To the south, the same thing happened with the other tower.

"Good," Braei said. "Let us get back toward the main hall."

They made the careful trek back the way they had come, and Valrin noticed that several of the dwarven vessels had turned into the cove. Though Braei led him back toward the hall and the others, he wanted to go see what words the dwarves sought to have with Evurn and the Keepers of Songs.

"This isn't a good idea," Braei said.

"I want to know why they've come here. Especially if we're the reason they're here."

As they made their way back down the pathway that led to the cove, Valrin noticed that the dwarves were already disembarking and rowing toward the island itself.

The monks stood as tall statues along the edges of the cove. Evurn stood on a rock with his staff crossed in his arms and Rasi at his feet. As the dwarven vessel made landfall, Valrin noticed the dwarf who jumped onto the sand with several other dwarves with him. It was Rugag, the one from before.

"Happy island of the North. We dwarves come to claim what is ours. A ship came here, a special ship. I do not believe you could have missed it."

Rugag was shouting to all of the monks, but they did not move or show a response. Their hands were at their sides, and Rugag looked up to Evurn, who was shaking his head.

"Great," the dwarf moaned, "an elf. This place is a whole trove of lost knowledge and people. Wasted forms of life. I have you know that we have worked for a long time to give your people something very special. Perhaps I should give you some?"

Another dwarf shuffling behind him grabbed Rugag by the shoulder. "The Barb King said no. Not before it is ready. If you do not kill him with it, they will learn what the poison is and work on an antidote."

"Oh, for a poison acquired in the South from the Spider Queen?" Evurn asked.

Rugag looked at the dwarf who had spoken and then glared at Evurn.

"Your people are beaten, elf. These ruins are now the property of our king. All of you monks," he shouted, "will come with us or be burned where you stand. My king seeks your knowledge. The gods have spoken to the Barb King and bestowed upon us your location. My kin will take what is ours. Every rock and hewed stone is ordained by the highest as ours. You will surrender it to us."

The line of monks did not agree. Their hands

suddenly erupted in magical light. Their elemental spells ready.

"They already know," Rugag said. "This elf said the words exactly. Use the poison, end this before it costs us too much."

The dwarves on the beach reached at their belts, grasping tiny glass stars with a substance inside.

"Now!" Evurn shouted.

An arcane blast of lightning, fire, and ice erupted from the beach, striking the dwarves on approach to the shoreline, along with the ones already standing there.

Rugag grabbed one of his dwarves and blocked the monks' blast before throwing several vials against the rocks nearest to him. The monk nearest to them fell to the ground, coughing, and began to shake violently.

Evurn jumped down, slamming his staff in the sand and sending up a tangling vine of seaweed that wrapped up Rugag and brought the dwarf down into the sand.

He ran forward just as the dwarf had freed himself, and smacked Rugag on the head. Other dwarves made it to the beach, and the entire shoreline was suddenly engaged in battle.

Valrin went to stand when Braei pulled him back. "We must get to the hall and Edanos. There are too many here."

Evurn was now engaged in a duel with Rugag. The dwarf wielded a large staff with the bones of some sea creature as his weapon of choice.

"Fire upon the island! Kill all who are not

dwarves!" he shouted. The dwarf then turned to the closest ships and made a motion with his hand.

Evurn stammered back, keeping his distance as the dwarf brought forth another vial of the poison.

"It is made to kill your kind, but it will work on any. These monks are nothing. Perhaps you should just give up."

A moment later, Valrin watched as several flaming rocks came flying from the ships and struck all over the ruins of the island. A gaseous haze poured out of the stones.

Braei covered her nose and pulled Valrin up, this time not letting Valrin keep them there. They ran for the doorway to the halls. He turned to see Evurn and noticed the elf running from the dwarves and not too far behind them. Ahead they could see Rortho and Fadis at the hall. Fadis loosed several arrows over their heads.

Another volley of the burning rocks struck behind Evurn, and looking back, they could only see a hazy fog of cursed death covering the island. They made it to the hall and barreled through the door.

"Poison!" Rortho shouted, struggling to catch his breath.

"Likely the same as what was used on Edanos," Fadis said, "only a different form."

Evurn made it through the door next with Rasi squirming up and down his body.

Braei shut the door and put down a latch to lock it, at least for the time being.

"The others, the other Rusis, are dead," he said.

"How did you escape it?" Valrin asked.

"This stuff cannot hurt me. I have embraced the kiss of Vearika before, but dwarven steel is a different issue." He revealed that his hand was cut with a deep wound. "I worry little of wounds such as this. It will heal," he said. "I managed to strike the one called Rugag really well before I fled. They were dragging him back to the ship the last I saw."

They made their way back to the actual hall to see Edanos floating above the stone altar. Lorlaam was chanting as a greenish hue floated around both of them. The others stood silently as Lorlaam continued his spell. Edanos' body floated down and then back up. The green smoke flowed into his body through his nose and mouth and then back out and dispelling into the air. This happened several more times before his body floated back down to the stone.

Valrin noticed that many wares of herbs and bottled substances had been dumped out and scattered around Edanos. Lorlaam stopped chanting and opened his eyes.

"This poison is horrid but not impossible to heal at least some. I have stopped its process within your friend. It is weakened. The poison loses its potency with the mix of herbs from all corners of the world. But I fear more of this poison."

"The poison covers the island," Evurn said, "and your brothers have fallen to its effects."

"So it shall be and so it is." He looked to Valrin. "I

am happy to have met you, Stormborn, but it seems my fate is tied to that of the Dwemhar beneath this place. But you will leave here. You will embrace that which I have not in some time. Evurn, do not fail me, old friend."

There came loud smacking sounds from the doorway.

"They come," Lorlaam said. "You must take your friend and take a secret passage out of this place. Come, I will show you."

He began to walk away, and Rortho and Fadis went to Edanos.

"Lorlaam," Valrin said, "I do not understand. We activated the towers as you wished, but it did not stop the dwarves and Edanos is not any better."

"Your eyes deceive you. Look at your friend."

Valrin went to Edanos, and he noticed that the captain's eyes stared at him.

Rortho and Fadis lifted him up, and he seemed to reach out to Valrin.

"He heals, but I am afraid the curse will remain in part. Your friend will be troubled, but he will be alive. Now come, come quickly this way!"

Valrin could hear the pounding on the doors. Evidently, they were stronger than they looked.

Lorlaam took them down a side hallway they hadn't seen before. It was a dark path that was colder and began to wind around a center column and further into the mountain. As they came to a lower level, Evurn lit his staff with arcane fire and painted the dark corridor in orange.

Lorlaam stared at each of them, "This is where I leave you. Follow the pathway as far as it goes and then press on the stones marked in ruins. That will take you to your ship. Be from this place and go to the one other I love in this world. The one I die for now."

"What do you mean?" Valrin asked. "Come with us!"

"You cannot save everyone, Valrin, and most of me is already dead."

His face became extremely pale, and green wisps of smoke rose off his skin.

"I have long waited here, alone, and while I gave the appearance of many, my brother monks were not as you would think. They were all but pieces of my own spirit, they were parts of me. It was old magic, Valrin, something you had heard of before. My kin died below us, and I die now." Tears fell from his eyes, "I was Rusis and I was Dwemhar, and then I failed and became as the cult you know as sea peoples. None must know the secret of the Dwemhar folly. You must never admit you know the link between the ascended and the lost. I go to finish what you began upon this holy island, and I will take as many as I can of that dwarven filth with me."

Lorlaam began to glow in a golden hue. He lifted his staff and in a flash both he and the staff disintegrated. His poisoned body became then as green mist on the floor. A moment later there was another flash and a brilliant light ascended back up the stairs.

"He learned to ascend as the old ones, though I

wonder what he does. I do fear I know." Evurn paused and looked at the others. "We must hurry!"

The group moved with haste down the hallway, coming to the dead end and the runic stone. Valrin pushed the stone, and the passage opened up. They could see night sky ahead, and a roaring wind met them as they emerged into the cold. Valrin could see his ship ahead of them moored in the harbor. They made their way down several stairwells and around the edge of the cave near the doors to the lower levels.

Valrin got to the ship first and went to the helm. The others quickly boarded, and the lock that held the ship released.

The cave began to rumble, and it seemed the entire structure of the island was faltering. Cracks formed in the walls and the water churned as the monolithic stones in the harbor began to quake.

"What is happening?" Braei asked.

"It does not matter," Fadis cried. "Get us out of here, Valrin!"

He moved the crystals at the helm, and the sails lifted, engorged with the wind. They fled the harbor as the very mountains that made up the ring of the protected area turned to dust and fell. The winds blew over them, pushing the ship away from the island. Valrin turned to see if any dwarven ships were following, and he could not make out anything but a brilliant light shining over the island. The two towers they had activated were electrified and shooting bolts of lightning all over the ruins. He checked the heading of the ship and then looked back again. There was a flash of light, and a blast of wind and water propelled them east in a hastening pace. The outline of the island began to fade as the ship was pushed further and further away.

Suddenly it felt as if the wind stopped and the ocean moved backward under the ship. They were jerked across the water. The ship began to spin, and the front of the ship now faced the direction they had come from. Another flash came, and a massive explosion of water and rock shot up into the sky, sending a dazzling light in all directions. The night became as day for a moment, and then all they could hear was the sounds of the ocean tossing the ship back and forth.

Valrin's eyes burned, and it seemed everyone else was having the same issue.

"What was that?" Rortho asked.

"I have never seen such a thing," Evurn said. "Not in my entire life. That was beyond what I thought he was to do but no less terrifying."

"He was one of the awaiting souls of the sea peoples. Everything we saw was because of him. It was always just him, and he kept his secret as long as he could," Valrin said.

"What magic was that?" Fadis asked.

"No mere magic," Evurn said, "but I have to imagine our problems with the dwarves is done. At least for a while."

"Then Rugag is dead?" Valrin questioned.

"Valrin," a familiar voice said.

He looked down to see Edanos staring at him. "It really worked!" Valrin said. "You're healed!"

Edanos began to sit up but faltered and fell backward. Rortho knelt down and lifted him up.

"It is okay, Captain. We have you."

Edanos stared at Valrin. "I dreamed I had died. I dreamed I was choked by a spider. I saw blackness and a frigid icy wasteland. I heard songs and then felt the warmth of life again. I saw myself high above the sea. I saw the Barb King. I killed him. I then saw a place, a place familiar to me, but yet a place I have never seen."

His head fell backward, and he seemed to no longer be conscious.

"Edanos!" Braei said.

He slowly opened his eyes. "I am so tired . . . I feel . . . weak."

"The poison was strong," Evurn told him. "Whatever cure you were given will take time to fully nourish your body."

Edanos nodded to Evurn, seemingly not caring that he had no clue who the shadow elf was. Edanos then turned to Valrin.

"Valrin, we must go to the place I saw. It is a place of old, a place of spirits, a place where our fates wait for us."

"Okay, does it have a name? Or do you know which way to go?"

Though he wished to answer and he opened his mouth to do so, he fell unconscious again. This time, he remained that way.

"We will take him below deck," Rortho said. "At least this time I have better faith in him getting better.

He hasn't looked this good since before he was injured by the dwarven bolt."

As Fadis, Rortho, and Braei took Edanos below deck, Evurn went to Valrin.

"We must honor the one called Lorlaam and do his bidding. Until your friend knows of where he seeks us to go, it is pointless to wander. We must go to where Lorlaam spoke. He had a child with a human woman long ago."

"A child?" Valrin asked.

"Yes, the Ice Mage had his fun, but it was too risky for him to take his love and his child to where he was. It was long ago when he nearly let that regret destroy him, but I have made my trips to check on her. I must admit that I had stopped for a while. I had actually thought Lorlaam had since taken her. She is of age to leave that place.

"I can say that at least she grows strong and in a sanctuary surrounded by those loyal to the gods of the North. It is not too far away. A shrine to Dimn, the god of winds. One of many temples in the Glacial Seas. But it is not mere chance that she is there. It is time for her to be released from her sacred vows to the god and embrace the call of the Stormborn as her father did."

Valrin chuckled. "So easy a vow to break? What if she doesn't want to come?"

Evurn looked down to his staff and smiled as Rasi curled out of his robes and over his hand.

"Then I must kill her."

. . .

If you'd like to read a standalone story that reveals the adventure of Evurn and Lorlaam as mentioned here, please search for Wizard Trials on Amazon or tap this link.

My Book

ELF BANE

BOOK THREE

1
WIND TEMPLE OF SWIA

The winds of the north blew against Valrin's face. While the others slept beneath deck, he held the wheel of the ship. Evurn had told him to keep his current heading. As the moon trekked over and behind them, he expected to see the light of the sun soon. He didn't know how long this journey would take to this temple of the god Dimn, but the sea was not going to give them an easy journey.

The events from the days before were still fresh in his mind. Evurn seemed to know much of the Stormborn and even Lorlaam's past, though Valrin had thought they didn't know one another that well. Evurn had said that either Lorlaam's daughter would come with them or he would kill her. Valrin wondered what would actually transpire once they got to their destination. Wherever that was.

The morning lights of the twinkling stars nestled by the purples of the early dawn skies gave him comfort. He knew the others would awaken before too long, and he was hoping to speak to Edanos.

In time, the way below decks opened and Rortho emerged. He stumbled his way around and looked about, bracing his arms to the cold winds. "Valrin, do we keep the eastern trek? It feels much colder this way."

"The winds have been harsh, but I have kept our path."

A moment later, another emerged from below. Rortho took the wheel. "Go, Valrin."

It was Edanos. He looked around with a bit of confusion and then spotted Valrin running toward him. They embraced.

"It worked," Valrin said.

"It did," Edanos confirmed. "Though I spoke with Rortho before I came up. You are taking well to being a captain. Traveling to a dwarven fortress, meeting a living shadow elf? I had thought they were all dead."

Valrin laughed. "No, he is very much alive. He has a snake, too—Rasi."

"A snake?" Edanos gave him a peculiar look. "Well, ships need a crew, and I see you have managed well enough without a very large one."

"The ship helps a good deal. On the island we were at before, I found a shipwright of the ancient ships. He was a man whom the god of death had forbidden to die. He finally killed himself a few moments prior to when I discovered him in a hidden room. It seems that my mere presence was enough to free him from the bonds prohibiting his death. It was just before discovering his body that I was given these strange mechanical turtles capable of repairing the ship and. . ."

Valrin suddenly felt dizzy and stumbled backward.

Edanos gripped him. "What is wrong?"

"I don't know. I feel—I feel like my mind is leaving me for a moment."

The ship tossed from a rogue current and then spun to the side.

"Whoa," Rortho said. "There are no currents like this in open sea."

Edanos felt his head. "You do not feel as if you are sick."

Valrin laid back and began to breathe hard. As he looked up, he saw flashes and felt as if he rode just below the waves. The ship was all around him, and he could feel his chest thumping.

"Have you had any rest?" he heard Edanos ask.

He shook his head but couldn't speak.

"Stop the ship!" Edanos said.

"Aye, Captain!"

Rortho dropped the anchors. As the ship slowed to a stop, Valrin could feel his breathing getting easier. At this point, Braei, Evurn, and Fadis joined them on deck.

"What is wrong with him?" Braei asked.

"He is too tired," Edanos said. "The ship has given him power, but he is still new to it. You shouldn't have pushed him to do what he did. You"—he pointed to Rortho and Braei—"should have stopped him!"

Valrin shook his head, but Edanos didn't see him. Rortho pointed back at Edanos. "The boy insisted, and he was my captain. You were in no place to give any wisdom, and Valrin wouldn't have had it, anyway. I did not know what danger there was to him not sleeping. I thought it was part of this ship."

Edanos randomly let out a scream and then shook his arm and head.

"The effects of the curse," Evurn said. "You are not well."

"I am fine!" he shouted back. He then collapsed, grabbing his head. Braei went to embrace him, and his hand jerked up to stop her.

"I am fine; I am fine," he said, out of breath. "I just felt so angry and cold. Like before when I was sick."

"Your soul drew near to the eternal choirs of Vankou," Evurn said. "Lorlaam dragged you back to this life by the power of Vearika's venom. Strange happenings can be expected, however unfortunate they are."

Valrin began to feel better himself and managed to sit up. Edanos looked at him and shook his head as he uneasily stood up.

"I may have been out of reach while I was unwell, but you must know that if your ship is at dock, you can rest. You may have to force yourself, but no magic can take away the functions of your body. You must give yourself rest in order to survive. At least for now, the binding of yourself with this ship is very new. We will continue on now that you are better, but I bid you at least sit and have some coffee."

As Braei made them a few cups of dark coffee and

they went through what little supplies they had for a scrap of food, the ship began heading east again.

The winds still blew against them, but as the sun began its lowly trek along the horizon, Evurn went to the edge of the railing and pointed outward.

"We draw near to the temple," he told them.

Valrin looked out. He could see a strange mountainous island ahead. It had a large wisp of clouds surrounding its peak, and even from a distance, he could make out the sheen stone of a structure that stretched across the island itself. He was curious about this place they were going to and what further mysteries they would find.

"So what kind of isle is this, Evurn?" Fadis asked.

"A monastery to the wind god Dimn and a place of peace and meditation that has a ward of magic to protect its inhabitants from darker things." Evurn let the last few words trail off.

"I assume this ward was placed by her father?" Fadis asked.

Evurn stared at Fadis. "In a way, yes. He did send me to acquire what was needed, but do not trouble yourself about it, Ranger. She is mine to deal with. I am the closest she has to family, and frankly, she doesn't need any distractions. So keep your thoughts to yourself."

"Well I don't like your assumption elf but I will be sure to mind my words," Fadis rolled his eyes in annoyance.

The shadow elf walked toward the front of the ship, leaving the others near Valrin at the helm.

"A daughter locked away from the world. I think I have heard this story," Braei said.

"If she is anything like Lorlaam, she will be in no need of assistance," Rortho stated. "If Evurn has threatened to end her life if she does not come with us, I worry about what exactly she is."

"With the poison that the dwarves have, we have to hope she is willing to help us. From there, we need to figure out what place Edanos speaks of. He said it was an old place, with spirits," Valrin said.

"Good luck figuring out our destination from those hints," Braei said.

As they came closer to the island, Valrin could see the temple much better now. It was a large tower with pipes near the top of it. They heard a humming sound, especially as they drew closer. There was a dock ahead and, from what they could see, nothing like guards or defenses.

"Approach the docks," Evurn said. "I depart first, alone. Otherwise, you will be picking this ship off the bottom of the ocean floor."

Fadis put an arrow to string as they approached the docks. As Valrin directed the ship into the moorings, Evurn jumped to the docks. Rortho threw him lines, but the elf ignored them.

"Do not tie off in a place you are not sure about. I thought you all were the sailors, dwarf."

He stomped away, his staff slightly glowing as Rasi jumped onto the ground before him and slithered ahead. He disappeared beyond a wall.

A gust of wind blew upon them. The massive

horns of the island sounded, and several tips of the towers began to glow a bright gold.

"A temple to Dimn," Braei said. "I know little of the wind god."

"I've never understood the gods," Fadis stated. "I mean, why must everything have a god? The winds? The mountains? The sea? Can't they just be their own substance without a holy recognition?"

"Hmph," Rortho said. "You are but a man, Fadis. Your substance was made to teach those of the other races and no more. Do not question the gods or their ways, for they are beyond you. The Great Poet created us all to feel his world under the mother sun. Thoughts like yours led to great loss of life in the ages before."

"I get your words, Rortho, but there is so much loss of life just from these supposed gods. When have they ever actually helped us?"

"The ship," Valrin said. "From Meredaas."

"That was you," he pointed out, "You had the amulet, and Edanos made his way to your island with a crew on a ship that went further north than I had ever gone without any gods to help you. Not to mention this ship, something created by a lost race and again not a god."

"But it was a god that blessed us with the tools to burn away the fogs, to tell us the path to take to actually reach this ship which was underwater. Meredaas raised it from the sea floor to the surface, and then when Rugag captured us just after, Meredaas sent his creatures to assist us. How else do you explain our escape?"

"A bit of luck and a daring captain, two of them, actually. Not to mention a Rusis, a dwarf, and a man with a bow."

Valrin nodded. "I would not be a captain without the gods."

Fadis shook his head, "Perhaps, but it wasn't the gods who led me here, nor was it the source of the courage you had to turn the ship and save Edanos and Rortho here. The gods care little for us, and any holy types who say otherwise should be drowned."

About that time, Evurn returned with a man wearing a bright blue robe.

"Good people," Evurn began, "we are welcome to come inside and attend to what we need."

The man in the blue robe bowed as he reached the edge of the ship. "I am Sautoa, Priest of Dimn and Wind Culler of this temple. I welcome you to our remote sanctuary."

The winds suddenly gusted and blew through those on the ship.

"Our god welcomes you, as well."

As they tied off the ship, Edanos stood, albeit shakily, as Rortho helped him off. Fadis returned his arrow to his quiver and motioned for Valrin to go.

As Valrin exited the ship, Sautoa bowed again. "Stormborn. I had heard of you in whispers of the wind and know some of your plights. You are safe here for the time you grace our presence. You will all be as honorary guests."

Fadis nodded with an uncertain glare as Evurn shook his head.

"I doubt I will be deemed honorary by all," Evurn said.

"Take no worry," Sautoa told him, "She has grown stronger and has found peace in your utter abandonment of her." They began to walk, and Sautoa continued. "It has been several years since you were near this place, and in that time, she has learned meditation to increase her influence, telepathy, along with spirit convergence, and of course, the elemental magics."

As they made their way around the corner, they came to a large silver door with the emblem of a cyclone on it. Sautoa motioned toward the door and winds from above twisted down and the passage opened, revealing a long marble-stone corridor with white fire glowing from torches. The walls themselves were inscribed with writings, unlike anything Valrin had ever seen.

"So from your words, she has both of her parents' powers and a bit more of the Ice Mage's blood," Evurn said.

"It would seem as such is true. Lorlaam was a powerful man, and his offspring is something else entirely."

Valrin noticed that the hallway had several wings that led off to either side. Robed monks stood in the openings, and he had a sudden feeling of slight fear but also awe.

"I sense your wonderings, Stormborn. Those who inhabit this place have only allegiance to the one called Dimn. We see not an elf or dwarf or Rusis, but only the soul, as is intended to have balance in the world."

They reached another door, and Sautoa turned to them.

"You have come at a time of meditation in our grand hall. The one you seek, Evurn, is one of our leaders in such realms, given her powers. Please do not speak until she has finished. I do believe you will be proud of Aeveam, daughter of the Ice Mage, Evurn."

As he pushed open the door, twisting winds glowing a deep pink in the center of a massive chamber met them. There were many others in robes just like Sautoa sitting cross-legged around an elevated platform.

Valrin noticed a single figure sitting atop it. As they approached the assembly, Sautoa motioned for them to sit as he did the same. The figure sitting on the elevated platform had golden yellow hair that curled slightly in the winds. The figure then reached out with their arms and twisted their wrists. From either side of them, windows opened and a rush of spectral blue and red magics swarmed in and twisted into the cyclone at the center.

The assembly began to hum, and the figure slowly rose from the platform. At first, Valrin thought they were standing, but then, as the winds converged around them, he noticed a female now looking out at them. Her eyes glowed white, and her body floated above those who continued their long, bellowing hum. She slowly descended and stood below the platform. The winds began to recede, and she breathed fast. The glow around her faded away revealing her stark blue eyes. Her blonde hair curled around her as the cyclone that before was pink turned to a whitish hue.

She wore white linens curved around metal armor on her shoulders. She pointed toward them and then abruptly began to walk their way.

"My lady," Sautoa said.

But she did not look to him nor Valrin, but to Evurn. "Shadow elf!"

"Yes, Aeveam?"

"Tell me, why do I see you here now when I have not seen any of my father or you for so many years?"

Evurn stood and leaned on his staff. "I had no contact with your father until recently."

"Then you come still and not him. What more must I do to prove my worth to him? I demand him here, now."

"Mind your words, Aeveam," Sautoa said. "The winds bring much news upon your soul."

"Your father has deemed it time. I will reveal more of him to you, but he cannot."

"What trouble have you two gotten into this time? I remember your stories! Your ordeal with the dragon and the crystals! Do adventures keep him away?"

Evurn looked down for a moment. "Aeveam, your father has fallen. Dwarves with poison attacked his island."

"Poison!" She reached out and grasped his head with her hands. Her eyes flashed white for a moment, and he slapped his staff forward with a blast of magic.

"Watch yourself!" he shouted.

"I saw what was needed! Poison like you used for the Barb King, so you are the reason!"

Sautoa stepped forward. "You must find peace and seek wisdom my—"

"Now is not the moment for your teachings, Wind Culler!"

She gripped Evurn by the neck and summoned a ball of sparkling light in her hand.

"Tell me, elf. How much were you paid?"

He gasped, gripping at her hands. Rasi shot out of his robes and wrapped around her neck. She released Evurn and began pulling at the snake. Evurn brought his staff down and bathed her in an orange light. She fell to the ground and struggled but then relaxed.

"You killed her!" Rortho shouted.

"No, dear dwarf. She is asleep." He shot a glare at the Wind Culler. "Sautoa, I am not too impressed that her peace is so violent! This is exactly what Lorlaam feared. This is why her father trusted you and your kind. She is a moment away from being just as her mother!"

Several of the other monks came and picked up Aeveam, carrying her to a resting area where they laid her down and covered her. They then lit incense and began to chant over her.

"Come," Sautoa said. "We will speak further of Aeveam."

He led them down another corridor and to a large circular room. It was a tower with windows on the eastern side that looked out toward the horizon. The monks had designated this area for all of them to lay down. Valrin actually felt very tired, but he, like the others, wondered much of Aeveam. He returned to the lower level where the monks brought a small meal to them.

"Fish," Rortho said, "and berries."

"A good meal for many days out at sea," Fadis said. "Not like our lack of supplies has been a primary concern."

Evurn was the only one not eating. He nibbled a piece of cured meat.

"Salted pork?" Rortho asked.

"Close— dwarf. I keep a bit on my persons for when I'm in a quaint setting."

Rortho's eyes became larger than Valrin had ever seen. "You eat my kin in my presence! Within a place of the holy gods?" He began to stand, and Fadis grabbed him.

Evurn chuckled. "No, not really, dwarf. If I am to eat dwarf, I prefer it fresh. This is a crab-based food, dipped in a weaker poison to up my resistance to certain sea creatures. We all have our dietary needs."

He took another bite of his food, and Rortho sat back down.

Valrin looked over to Edanos, who stared at his empty plate. "Do you want some food?"

Edanos looked up, almost surprised that someone had spoken to him. "Do you not hear it? Do you not hear them?"

"The monks?" Braei asked.

"No, the songs."

Valrin stared at him, noticing a fear in his eyes.

"I have tried to block them out, but I can't. The songs are so loud."

"You must meditate. I will teach you," Evurn said. "It is dangerous to drift to death and return. Very dangerous."

Edanos sat back and nodded to Evurn. Valrin noticed Evurn seemed on edge near Edanos, like he didn't trust the man before him.

About that time, Sautoa came back into the room. "I trust the food was acceptable?"

"It was," Rortho said.

"It is hard to satisfy the dwarven visitors we have, and you are not the only guests we expect. We have visitors from the South coming this way. The winds bring forth many upon the edge of darkness." He looked to Evurn. "If her father has fallen as you said, then it is a dark time, indeed."

"He ascended, as the peoples of old, and combined the magics of his blood to destroy that where he was."

"I know when he brought her here as a young child, he warned against her bloodline. Her mother was an angry woman—an evil resided within her like no other, and she was nearly unstoppable."

"My kin stopped her. You do not openly kill as many as she did within the Shadow Lands and simply continue breathing. She wasn't like that before, but of her demon, I cannot speak of. It is said it was a dark presence that took her. Before that, she was what I would call a friend, at least for a time. I do not know what happened, only that she was stopped. The greatest fear I have is that when a demon of that level of power inhabits you, it leaves a part of itself within you that will haunt your children. I fear that power will return to take Aeveam."

"Well, their daughter has many powers. She learned of her Dwemhar powers first, and though we tried to conceal them, she was able to manipulate the world around her before her first Rusis spell. She has been taught the way of peace but her parents' abandonment has helped create a woman that resents the very world meant to protect her. Had she been a baby and never known them, it might have been different, but you do not take a child from what they know and not expect adverse effects."

"Lorlaam was not the type to raise a child."

Sautoa's demeanor changed, and winds seemed to shift around him. "Then he should have known what he could not take the risk and do. She is powerful, unlike any in these realms. She has been taught that at one time her power would be needed for the gods of the North but her mother's demon would likely return to claim her. Even now she meditates in the upper sanctum to reclaim her peace. It is likely she will struggle with the truth as long as she remains here."

"Well, it is time, Sautoa. With the Stormborn in the world and the events of the Barb King, it is time for her to go into the world. It was her father's last wish—to assure she was well. I hold no allegiance but to those I call friends, and with these new friends"—he motioned to the others—"I have discovered that a poison meant to wipe out all who challenge the Barb

King is upon the Glacial Seas. It is no coincidence this boy has claimed his ship."

Sautoa suddenly glared at Valrin, "Where are you from, Stormborn?"

"I am Valrin of Travaa."

"Valrin? A good name. A strong name. You will need strength to survive these seas."

"Vals," Edanos said.

Valrin was surprised that Edanos remembered. It was a comforting reminder that his friend was still there.

"Vals or Valrin, well, both are good. Evurn and I have much to speak of for the time, but your crew is welcome here. Night is coming, and I do bid you sleep."

The conversation was not a mere coincidence to reach the point where he told them to get sleep. A moment later, Evurn and Sautoa stood and departed. Valrin and the others went to their room in the upper level of the tower. He lay down and felt a ripple of energy from his chest go down his back and then, in the strangest of feelings, move away from him. As he closed his eyes, he saw his ship docked outside. He then, for the first time in many, many days, fell asleep.

A scream pierced his ears. Valrin found himself standing on a beach. Trees burned around him. Elves grabbed at their throats. He saw his ship torn apart beneath a grand tower that reached up into the heavens. A haze, like smoke but with flashes of orange magic, surrounded him. Rortho stood next to Braei, who looked up at him, her skin bubbled from her bones and he saw death overtake her. He tried to walk but found himself struggling to free himself from the dead around him. The water behind him turned to ice. He then saw four elves appear in the distance. Three were boys who appeared not much older than him, and there was a younger girl. He watched as the haze-like magic covered them and they collapsed. Then he began to hear a tune in his mind. A song, like an organ he had heard on a grand ship that had come to Travaa once. Darkness shrouded his sight.

He felt his body shaking and then saw his ship again docked outside the Wind Temple of Swia. In the distance, with the early-morning sun behind him, a ship approached, and he saw dwarves aboard it.

2
SONGS OF HARRODARR

He opened his eyes and realized he had been dreaming. He had been sleeping for a good amount of time, but he felt like it had only been a minute. Everyone slept around him. He sat up, feeling his heart beat in his chest at the thought of the horror he had seen. If this was what sleep would be for him, he didn't want to ever sleep again. He stood up and went to the window, noticing that the morning sky was just beginning to glow from a still-sleeping sun.

He went downstairs and to the room they were in before. He saw Evurn standing with his hands behind his back, staring out to sea.

"Valrin, you stay awake for days upon days and yet still awaken as I'm sure you did before you knew the name Stormborn."

Valrin smiled. "I used to get eels for the fishers in my town."

"Eels? Good for poisons."

"They used them for bait."

Evurn nodded. "A shame to serve such a malign purpose."

"Did you go to Lorlaam's daughter?"

"I did, and she understands much without me speaking. I am amazed of her powers."

"Will she go with us?"

"If you mean will I have to kill her, well, that is still to be decided. But as long as she uses her powers for good, we have nothing to fear. Dwemhar blood is a strange substance. Though they did much good for the world, one who has the taste of darkness can be a force that even the gods can struggle to contend with. You must fear any merging of Dwemhar. Rusis were naturally aggressive, so you can see that the two together, as with her father, is a very careful balance.

"When Lorlaam and I spoke of our foray, it was a fun time and there was much we did afterward. He wanted his staff, and well, quite a few creatures, placed in our path by the trickster god Wura, guarded it. He showed a bit of his shadowy side then, but he could balance out his power, something she must do. If I sense anything but, I will be forced to destroy her."

"Can you do it?"

Evurn looked down at him with a smile but said nothing.

Valrin was not sure if this was overconfidence or sureness. He heard someone approaching and turned to see Aeveam.

At first, he was alarmed, but she was much calmer now and smiled gently at him.

"Valrin," she said.

"Aeveam."

"Please excuse our first meeting and accept this second one." She bowed to him, and he did the same to her. "Evurn tells me you knew my father and that he sacrificed himself for you."

"For all of us, and you. He said so."

She looked down for a moment and then nodded. "You are like me, Valrin—without parents but with a guardian who watched over you for a time. I had Evurn, and you had your aunt, Tua."

Valrin looked to Evurn and then back to Aeveam. "How'd you know that? Who told you?"

Evurn grinned, "None, but vampires have a way of seeking out remedies for their afflictions that do not involve the natural diet they seek. I had heard about you then. I knew the prophecy and of your arrival to Travaa, but I also knew it not my place to say of your true purpose, though I know the elf vampire knew of it. Perhaps this can be one way we can all trust one another."

Aeveam went to the windows and looked out. "I look forward to our journey and wherever we plan to go. I still do not understand my purpose, but I am prepared to try."

"Then we must prepare," a voice said from out of view.

Valrin turned to see Edanos. The once captain of the *Truest Bliss* approached Evurn and offered to shake his hand. Evurn did so with a careful glare.

"You feel more yourself?"

"For now, sleep and silence have helped some. I will still take your offer of mediation, though I've never been a real type for that kind of practice. I know clearly where we must go and how to get there. It is North of here and not too far. A cave of crystals. A place of very old power masked by magic itself."

"Like a ward?" Evurn questioned.

"No, a place of the actual creation of magic, a place where I believe we will find something locked away for the Stormborn. I know I have struggled since my near death, but there are a few things certain. This is the next path of the Stormborn, and I must kill the one called the Barb King."

Valrin and Evurn just stared at him.

"So sure of your path?" Aeveam asked.

"I am. It is what I saw while poisoned and what I must assure is completed."

He looked to Valrin. "Do not fear—I am me. But coming so close to death, I realized my path. I am not to claim a realm ship. That was your fate. But I must go after the one who took my chance. The one who took my version of the necklace you had that your aunt, Tua, held for you."

"Do you know that that king believes himself Stormborn?" Valrin asked.

"I do, and I will not allow any chance of him harming another soul as long as I still breathe."

They were all somewhat surprised by Edanos' sureness.

"I have already woken and told the others. They will join us soon."

Soon was an understatement, as immediately, Rortho, Braei, and Fadis came downstairs.

Fadis approached them with a confused expression and a single eyebrow raised, "So you wake us up to begin this quest before the sun comes up, and we find you just now advising the captain, Evurn, and the one who tried to kill Evurn, of your plan?"

Aeveam bowed to them. "My apologies for our first meeting. I assure you that my emotions are secured away from that of my actions."

Fadis stared at her. "I'm not really sure what that means."

"It is the way she has been taught," Evurn said. "Emotion is a great motivator for many, but to let that control you . . . well . . . can be quite bad for shadow elves or anyone else you might come up against. She is our friend and ally, and we shall see what good Edanos has in store for us to the north."

They began to prepare for their journey. As Evurn, Edanos, Aeveam, and Rortho conversed with Sautoa about supplies, Fadis and Valrin exited the Temple of Swia and went toward the ship. The sun was cresting the horizon, and the ship floated against the dock with fresh snow on its railings.

"How do you like all of this?" Valrin asked Fadis.

"I'm not sure what to say about it, that I can tell you. It is a strange place, these Glacial Seas. All of my years spent here, and there is still something new to learn of it. I do think about going south again. Soon maybe, I will think it's time. I don't know."

The Ranger became quiet, and Valrin jumped

onto the deck of the ship. He pulled open the way to the inner part of the ship and then looked up. Something was approaching. He could hear the break of water getting closer. Fadis, too, heard the sound, but a deep fog rolling over the distant waters obscured their view.

A horn called.

"That is a dwarven horn!"

Fadis reached for his bow but did not have it, and Valrin's sword was back in the room he had slept in.

Valrin exited the ship and went to Fadis, who pulled him back toward the temple.

The large ship emerged from the fogs not too far from the docks and made a hard turn left to avoid striking the dock itself. But this was no dwarven ship. Fadis had his hand on Valrin to push the boy behind him, but now he squinted.

"That vessel was made by men, the people of Srun, the great Island Nation to the south. It is what I guess you might call dwarven in build, but not a ship of Rugag or the Barb King. They had some dealings with those I fought with back in Taria."

The ship, about the same size as Valrin's, moved up to the dock. Sautoa emerged from the temple and looked at them as he moved toward the new vessel.

"Do not fear these; they are not as the ones you call the enemy."

As they slowly followed behind the Wind Culler, Valrin saw that dwarves were indeed on the vessel. They wore heavy black armor, and massive hammers inscribed with runes hung on their backs.

"Hammersongs, I welcome you to the temple of our lord Dimn. I trust your journey was a good one."

The dwarves moved out of the way of another dwarf and a man of about the same build and stature as the staunch dwarves.

"I am a prince of the Island Nation and have now paid my price to the dwarves of Harrodarr. I am a shameful man and attempted to steal from their home city on my visit. I confess my crimes before those who hold me accountable."

"I hear your crimes," Sautoa said, "but I cannot free you of your debt to them, for I do not see it as such."

One of the dwarves stepped forward. "That man is a foul weakling of his kind, and I do thank you for accepting our request to come here."

"Dwarves used to make many pilgrimages here. It is long since we had any come this way. I am happy to have some of your people on this island. Though know we have other guests, some who have dealt with the dwarves you come to speak with."

The dwarf walked toward Valrin, and he couldn't help but be fearful. The man was massive, larger than Rortho, and had notches and scratches in his armor.

"What is your name, boy?"

"I am Valrin."

"Nurocas, Hammersong of Harrodarr. I see fear in your eyes. I am not the first dwarf you have seen. What have those of the Glacial Seas done to you?"

Fadis stepped between them. "Nothing to speak of

as of now, Nurocas. I know of the Hammersongs. Your zeal is unmatched, or so the songs say."

Nurocas nodded. "So it is so, but I have no quarrel with those except my own kind. Is this your boy?"

"No, but crewmen of our ship will want to meet you. Know we are not friends to dwarves in this region."

The dwarf shook his head. "I fear I may not be, either. Those of my order sent to guard the one called the Barb King have failed to send word of their doings. We are here for many reasons, and we will deal with our kind. Do not get in our way."

"Well," Sautoa said, "let us go in and you can pay patronage to Dimn. He has been without the prayers of the dwarves for some time."

They entered the temple, and Valrin watched for the others. It was Braei who noticed them first and quickly approached just as Evurn, Rortho, and Edanos walked out of a storeroom.

Rortho dropped his sacks and brought his ax to hand. In a flash, the Hammersongs brandished their weapons. Valrin stood right next to Nurocas. The runes on his ax glowed, and there seemed to be a hum in the air from their weapons. Braei had summoned spells of ice, and Evurn held out his staff.

Nurocas spoke first. "Dwarf, you serve the Barb King of Gurundothrak?"

"No, I do not. Hammersongs here?" He lowered his weapon, and the others around the room did too. The monks of the temple and Sautoa seemed surprised and partially angry to the shows of the force happening within their holy halls.

"We are Hammersongs directly from Harrodarr. Something is foul within this ocean, and we come to investigate. I am Nurocas, and these Hammersongs are my brothers. If you have no issue with us, we will not resort to violence unless we are threatened."

They lowered their hammers.

Evurn clapped. "Dwarves, so many dwarves, in the icy North. If only I was back home."

"You," Nurocas said. "You are of the East, of the Shadow Lands?"

"I am of the Glacial Seas, and I and this crew you see before you make no question of your deeds as long as you do not question ours. We trade spices; that is all."

Valrin wondered of the lie Evurn had just said. It seemed a good enough excuse.

"No questions, but you are the strangest group of traders."

Sautoa coughed as to gain everyone's attention. "If you will not be killing one another this wonderful morning, can I and the Breaths of Dimn offer a small meal for you all?"

"Offer accepted," one of the Hammersongs said.

"Lorkt, go get our drinks," Nurocas said.

Their human companion immediately went back toward their ships.

"Slavery is not something we in the service of Dimn appreciate."

"Noted as such, Sautoa," Nurocas said. "There is a

place for slavery when debt is owed. But there is also a fine line there. To claim a slave just to do so, or because of their race, is dishonorable to say the least."

Valrin and the others worked to finish stocking their ship with several rations of food and general supplies that they might need, as Sautoa led the dwarves to an actual dining hall. Valrin and the others went to join them before they departed North.

In the hall itself was a large table, and the dwarves sat along one whole side. As Valrin sat down near the end of the table, Nurocas noted and motioned him over. "This way, young one. I wish to speak to you."

Both Edanos and Rortho followed Valrin to sit next to him as the dwarf waved off the tea offered to him and instead sipped a large ale that their human had poured for each of the dwarves from their own personal barrel that no doubt was not the easiest container to get up the long stairwell they took from the lower halls.

Valrin sipped his coffee and noticed that the dwarves really were nothing like the ones he had met before. Their armor, for one, was not well suited for the works of sailing. It was bulky and cumbersome but did not seem to inhibit their movement at all.

"What are you looking at, girl?" one of them asked Braei.

"You armor is a bit cracked. I had always heard dwarves had the absolute best armor."

"We do!" he said back in a harsh tone. "But

dragons have some of the sharpest teeth you might ever be lucky enough to be devoured by." He paused, "Well, if you have to absolutely be devoured by such a beast that is. But that day was not my last, no, and the one that did this now has a permanent place above my family's hall in Harrodarr!"

"Good, good, Rorda. There is no need to scare the Rusis," Nurocas said. "Forgive Rorda. Sometimes I think that dragon came a bit too close to roasting him."

Rorda looked over at Nurocas. "It wasn't like you were much help!"

"There were eight dragons. I took down two, including the one headed toward you. You should show a bit of respect, brother!"

Though it was an obvious tease, Rorda grumbled to himself.

"So you head to the city?" Rortho asked.

"Yes, we need to see what the Barb King is doing. My masters do not trust him. The last time he was heard from, he claimed the sea was his to command. At the time, we thought he was telling a story of old or recounting something in a song. It seemed as such, at least. Now our brothers have ignored our messages. We will figure it out."

"So you go to the actual city?" Edanos asked.

"Yes, in two nights there will be a grand coronation, or so we have discovered, and it is supposed to reveal the greatest discovery in our people's history, or so our spies have told us."

"Would you need another to join you on your journey?"

Edanos' question caused every one of Valrin's crew to stare at him.

"We need none unless you have need to go to the city."

Evurn grabbed Edanos by the arm. "We do not go that way. We told you where we needed to go, and the dwarves are looking for Rortho for stealing that fish. We cannot go there!"

"Yes, I would recommend not returning there for some time until we deal with whatever it is afoot there. If a dwarf is forced to steal a fish, then there is trouble, indeed. We will seek out the truth."

Edanos looked to Evurn and then to Braei as they both rubbed him on his shoulders.

"You spy on them?" Fadis asked to try to get the attention off Edanos.

"In what few ways we can. I do not lie to you here within these holy halls. I fear my brethren have fallen from sanity. There are few of us now, but know that the dwarves of the South will do what is necessary to assure our kin stay within bounds of sanctity. Know these issues are dwarven, and you shouldn't worry of our plight. Us dwarves can handle this issue."

There was a silence at the table, and Valrin stood up. "We should go," he told the others.

"A boy captain?" Nurocas asked.

"No, he is my first mate," Rortho said. "Come on, crew, to the ship!"

The others stood up to keep the deceit legitimate. Valrin knew they could only trust these dwarves so much. Sautoa joined them. They went downstairs and found Aeveam, garbed in a dark cloak, standing before the cyclone. She was wearing leather boots and looked nothing like she did before. She turned to them as they approached her.

"I saw the arrival of the dwarves and the less-than-happy exchange. I saw it better to remain away from the main conversations."

"It is good now," Valrin said. "Are you ready?"

"I have all I need and have done away with the robes of this temple. We do not need that kind of attention."

They exited the temple, and while the others went to the ship, Evurn, Valrin, and Aeveam stood with Sautoa.

"When you were a child, I never thought the day would come when you would leave our home. I had hope for a better departure than this, but the others are assuring the dwarves remain where they are." Sautoa looked to Valrin. "Though I do not condone dishonesty, I am a man of this world who has seen what it is capable of with or without the gods' desires. Your secrets are safe with us. The dwarves will have no view of your departure, and Dimn will watch over your journey."

Sautoa turned back to Aeveam. "Remember what you have learned here. What has brought you pleasure and happiness and what happened when darkness attempted to snare you. The power of your ancestors must not be misused."

She gripped his hands and bowed, kissing them. "I depart as a Saint of Dimn. I will follow what has been laid before me. I will bring honor to the gods of the North, and not terror. I will protect those covered by the winds and, in time, return to my home in the clouds to be with Dimn everlasting."

"Go, my child, onto the ship."

Aeveam turned, and Valrin noticed that Evurn was smiling—something the elf rarely did except when making a joke or a strange comment, as he was known to do.

"I will watch over her," Evurn told Sautoa.

"May the winds of Dimn guide you all."

They bowed and went toward the ship as Sautoa returned into the temple.

"What happened with Edanos back there?" Valrin asked.

"We are fortunate that Fadis came up with something to detract attention from him. That is what happened."

As they boarded the ship, Edanos stood at the helm. The others moved the remaining supplies below deck while Valrin untied the ship and joined Edanos.

As Valrin steered the ship from the docks, he activated the sails and they began north. With a gust of wind to speed them forward, they were on their way.

The Wind Temple of Swia passed to their side, and a quick-forming fog veiled the island. Sautoa was true to his word, but this was more for the dwarves still likely in the dining hall so that they wouldn't catch sight of the ship, than actually hiding the temple.

Edanos looked around nervously and was not at all the confident captain Valrin remembered.

"What is on your mind?" Valrin asked.

"I can't believe I asked to go with the dwarves. I don't understand why I said that."

Valrin gripped the wheel of the ship tighter and tried to figure out the best words to say.

Edanos continued. "I feel so drawn to that place. I see myself killing the Barb King. He has caused and will cause so much suffering. I have seen it and I cannot explain it."

Aeveam came to the helm and smiled at Valrin.

Edanos continued, almost not noticing Aeveam and stuttering. "I ju—just keep seeing him. The vision doesn't leave."

"Edanos," Aeveam said, "I do not know your full story as of right now, but be careful of visions. It is difficult to discern what is a true vision of the future and what is your own imagination."

Edanos nodded as Evurn approached them. "Come, Edanos. I will take you below deck, and we will work on meditation. You must learn to quiet your mind, friend."

As Edanos went with Evurn, Aeveam shook her head. "Evurn said he was cursed with a variation of dwarven poison."

"Yes, it is how we met your father, and I'm sorry for his death."

She looked away and went to the railings of the ship. "I am not. Evurn said he ascended and in his final moments melded his magics together to protect you and this crew, along with destroying the invaders. I take some form of solemn comfort with that. I knew I would leave Swia in time, but I wasn't sure how. Sautoa was good to me my entire life, and so was Evurn, but I always prayed that it would be my father to come for me. I felt like I was trying to be good enough for him. That it was what I was training for. Then I learned of my mother from Evurn, and I wondered if he was scared of me."

"What did she do exactly?"

"Exactly? She slit the throats of a thousand shadow elves' children to prove a point that her race was superior to them and would not fall to their fear. They killed her, paraded her body through their cities in the East, and then desecrated it further by cursing it to walk the realms devoid of life and in constant suffering. That is what Evurn said, at least."

"Evurn has many stories," Valrin said, almost suggesting that what she was told was false.

"Most of them are true. He has been around these lands for a very long time, and when it comes to elves, that means something a bit more profound. He is old by their standard."

Aeveam knelt down and noticed the crystals at the helm.

"This is a Dwemhar vessel, right?"

He wondered of how to answer, but the second he did, she nodded.

"You really do not need to wonder if you can tell me something. The moment it comes to your mind, I can sense it."

"So you are like a fortune teller?"

She laughed. "I have trained to accent my powers

to the point that I am close to the strongest half-blooded Dwemhar in existence. There are no others like me."

Braei, who had been standing off to the side and had not gained Valrin's attention, walked up to them. "Wouldn't you be one-fourth Dwemhar? Your father was half and your mother was of the race of men."

"Fellow Rusis, I guess you would be correct. Of course, I meant more that I'm only half of the race of men, but I guess I should be more specific. I am still learning about my powers," she told both of them. "I work to perfect my elemental magics, but I do believe Braei is ahead of me there. I'm going to do my best to do what is needed. I was always led to this path but never told what it would hold, and not all future can be foretold."

Valrin nodded and moved the switch to activate the map. It came up, and Aeveam pointed to it. "Incredible and a good example of a future that cannot be foretold! I did not know this ship could do that."

"It is a wondrous vessel," Braei said. "I want to tell you that you're new to our crew, but if I can help you with the Rusis side of your magic, let me know. I know a few tricks."

As the two of them walked off, Fadis and Rortho joined him.

"We were waiting our turn," Fadis said.

"Yes, now that we have two of those casters and both of them have tempers like no others," Rortho whispered, "I don't want to put them in a pissed mood!

I did that once to a trio of women back in Taria. Not a good idea."

"I didn't take you for the promiscuous type, dwarf," Fadis teased.

"Not too promiscuous, but I know my way when it comes to delving."

Valrin didn't really get the joke, but he could imagine, based off what he had seen some nights back in Travaa.

Rortho stared at the map. "So we go north but nothing else? No landmark or real clue?"

"Edanos said before that it was an old place of spirits where our fates awaited us."

"Okay, so no," Fadis confirmed. "We will need to wait for him to finish his meditating to have some clue where we're actually going."

"The captain isn't right," Rortho said. "I wonder if it was right, well, helping him to live."

"We can't decide fate," Fadis said.

"But it's what we did. I worry. He isn't the Edanos I knew."

The dwarf's words were less than comforting to hear, but Valrin knew what he said was right. Edanos had not returned to them as his old self. There were glimpses of it from what little interaction they had, but nothing like before, nothing like before the curse.

3
GHOSTS

As was normal in the Glacial Seas, a storm was moving from the west and crossing their path. Though it was not as turbulent as the one a few days ago, there was a good amount of snow and colder winds. The other crewmembers bound themselves and stayed huddled around a torch basin they had obtained back at Shia Temple.

"Damn cold," Rortho said.

"They call it the Glacial Seas for a reason," Fadis said.

"Yes, but holy winds of Dimn, does it have to be this cold?"

"Dimn does not control the temperature," Aeveam corrected. "Just the winds."

"Well, perhaps the good god can change the direction of them, or keep them away from us, for a time."

About that time, Edanos emerged from below deck.

"Complaints about winds on a sailing ship, Rortho?"

"Well, yes, but—are you feeling better, Captain?"

Edanos went to Rortho's side and put his hand on the dwarf's shoulder.

"I told you before that I'm not the captain. Valrin is. He has done a fine job on these waters so far. I'm just a guide now."

"So where exactly are we headed?" Valrin asked.

"A place called Ara-Hik, an ancient mine for Dwemhar crystals and a place I sense will greatly help our cause."

"Now how do you know the name?" Evurn asked.

"In my dreams, I hear the voices of the sea peoples. I receive visions. It is why I know we must go to this place and why I must eventually face the Barb King."

Edanos sat down with the others, and Braei gave him a cup of fresh coffee.

No one said a word, and Valrin watched as it seemed his crew stared at Edanos but avoided eye contact.

"You all fear me," he said.

"No," Braei stated, "we don't, but—"

"You're different," Fadis said.

Rortho looked up, surprised by the bluntness of his words.

Fadis scanned the others and then leaned into Edanos, "I am not afraid to tell you that you are not the man you were before. You no doubt care for your friends, but you are not the captain I met. Everyone else is too kind to flat out say it, but I will. You nearly volunteered yourself to go with the Hammersongs to Gurundothrak."

"I see. But . . . I understand. I am loyal to all of you, but I am drawn to greater deeds."

Aeveam stood up and went to Edanos. "These deeds," she said, putting her hands on his shoulders, "and these visions you have, how do you know their source?"

"I sense them and know it is true. I had a simple dream while I was near death before. I know the path, and I will stay true to it."

Aeveam closed her eyes, and Edanos looked up at her. Valrin watched as she seemed to grimace and her hand on his shoulder began to shake.

"What?" Edanos asked.

Aeveam released her grip on his shoulder. "Your mind is hidden. I cannot reach your thoughts. But you are not the Stormborn—you are not as Valrin. How do you resist?"

Braei cleared her throat. "He was like Valrin, but the Barb King himself stole Edanos' amulet identical to the one Valrin used to obtain this ship. Edanos cannot claim the title without it."

"I do not desire to be Stormborn now. I will help Valrin, yes. But I came back from the beaches and icy plains of Vankou's realm for a purpose. I see my purpose in my mind, and I will complete it. No one else has need to see it."

Fadis stood up and went to the railings. "Your purpose will require this ship getting very close to the dwarven capital. We cannot risk that."

"There will be a way if the gods will it."

Fadis shook his head and leaned back against the railings. Rortho embraced Edanos. "I am happy to have you here and will do what I can to assist you."

"Aye, I'm happy to be here, Rortho. I will work on controlling my abruptness. I—"

"Meditation is the mind's only friend when too many voices cry out," Evurn said. "Remember this and seek peace."

Aeveam chuckled. "Your stories run contrary to that, elf."

Evurn smiled. "It was your father who taught me those words. I have only listened for a small part of my life."

Valrin switched the map crystal and noticed a strange vibration in the image. He looked ahead to see a glow in the darkening sky.

Evurn noticed it, too, and pointed. "We are far north, near the realms of uncharted seas. Few have gone this way."

"Well, we have no dwarven ships chasing us, so that is one advantage compared to the last time we went this far north," Rortho said.

As Valrin guided the ship toward the glowing lights ahead, an outline of a sheer and slightly sheen structure appeared. As night fell, the water beside them began to glow. Valrin looked over the edge and saw sharks of some kind with glowing runes along their bodies.

"Glacial Sharks," Rortho said. "Very rare in the more southern parts of the sea."

"But common here," Fadis pointed out.

Valrin noticed the sharks appeared not to trail the ship for fun or to hunt, but as a guide. Like smaller vessels assisting a larger one into the harbor.

As he turned the ship toward the fast-approaching structure, he jumped as an eruption of sparkling red lights lifted into the skies from the pinnacle of the structure. As they drew closer, Valrin noticed land beyond the structure and monolithic stones that seemed to be sending twirling dust that glowed in the dark environment.

"Magic," said Aeveam. "I can feel its purity in the air."

"I do too," Braei said.

"This is a place of its creation. The moon gives charge to the stones, and they in turn push magic into the world."

Aeveam twisted her hand and created a small glowing orb of white. The spell spun and began to glow brightly.

Braei did the same with her powers, and Valrin witnessed the most massive fireball he had ever seen the Rusis create.

"A powerful place," said Evurn. "Now we must figure out why we are actually here."

Edanos looked around, gazing at the magic that floated freely in the air. A drift of it came his way, and he lifted his hand into it, sending a rippling wave of it out. "There is a cave here. Somewhere nearby."

Valrin steered the ship around the large sheen structure but saw no obvious doorway. "This is nothing but a rock in the sea. There is not a cave nor doorway."

"There is," Edanos said. "It is right here."

Valrin dropped anchor and walked over to where the others were standing as the ship slowed to a stop.

"I saw it in my vision," Edanos said. "There is an opening."

As Valrin walked near the front of the ship, he felt a surge in his chest. From the post where his amulet was absorbed came a radiant light that shot upon the sheen stone.

There was a ripple of blue light, and runes appeared, covering the stones.

Rortho jumped up and went to the edge. "I know these words. I have seen them in the texts.

"To those who come once this place is of ice, know that we remain. We are the last, and we have formed our power to be blessed unto you to use us as needed. We are yours—we embrace the old ways and the Dwemhar way of where we have fallen from. You are the captain, and you shall lead us once again."

It was beginning to snow and the door cracked open as Rortho read the last bit. The entryway was dark, but Valrin had no doubt at all of what he should do. Pulling up anchors, he moved the ship into the open doorway. As they entered the passage, torches began to light along the walls, and they found themselves surrounded by both ice and large crystals jutting out from the ceiling like stalactites in a simple cave.

"This place," said Edanos. "This is the place I saw. I know where we must go. Valrin, move the ship forward and to the right. There will be a circular dock for the ship."

Fadis put an arrow to his bowstring and circled around, looking the way they had come.

Rortho lifted his ax.

"You mustn't fear this place," Edanos said. "I have been here in my mind. We are safe."

Aeveam stood next to Valrin. "There is old magic here, and there are those who are trapped." Valrin jerked to look at her. "It is not those who live but those who have died who await us."

Evurn went to the side of the ship and lifted his staff over the water. An orange glow reflected on the crystalline ceilings and spread across the caves, bathing it in a warm light.

As Valrin moved to the right, following the glowing crystals, he came to a circular stone dock with several torches that burst to life as they approached. Valrin moved the ship toward it, and just like before at Lorlaam's island, the ship was locked into the dock. It was here he noticed that there were other, smaller ships still at the dock. They were not realm ships, and they had not moved from this spot in some time. Each seemed to be sealed in place. Additional stone constructs seemed to come out of the stonework and secured the ships, lifting them out of the water. A type of dry dock.

"This place is of the sea peoples," Braei said.

"Perhaps another one, like the one that was beneath Lorlaam? One of the ones awaiting death?" Rortho suggested.

"I do not know," Valrin said.

Edanos was one of the first off the ship. He moved so quickly that the others struggled to keep up. Braei ran to catch up with him. Valrin and the others disembarked and looked around.

"Keep mindful of your eyes and what your minds conjure," Aeveam said. "A place like this can produce what you see within your mind's eye."

"More religious nonsense," Fadis said.

"No, Dwemhar powers are strong here. I can sense it in the air. This is more than a node for the creation of magic. This place only opened because of the Stormborn. There is something here, but I sense something else beyond that."

They hurried to catch up with the others. They ascended a hill that had a domed tower with a single glowing crystal atop it.

As they reached the ledge it sat on, they looked down to see an expanse of towers and buildings that glowed a distinct bluish color.

"A city," Valrin said.

"A city long sealed," Rortho said, pointing. "There are no crystals above this place. The rock appears fused, as if it was molten at some point."

"A volcano?" Fadis asked.

"Yes."

Edanos and Braei were some distance ahead and were waiting for them as they descended.

"It is here we find what you need, Valrin. It is a parchment of sort. An agreement," Edanos said.

"An agreement?"

"I have only seen flashes, but the key to defeating what we face in these seas is here."

They walked toward what remained of a gateway. The columns of stone that once made an archway had melted into one another. The buildings were shifted to one side and fused in a jumble of rubble. They climbed over the gateway, and Valrin was amazed at the strange twists and turns of the architecture. Brilliantly carved effigies of seated figures with glowing crystals above their heads stared out at them as if they were actually living.

"The images of their gods?" Fadis asked.

"No," Aeveam said, "of them. This was one of the cities of ascension. The last places the Dwemhar were before they left our realm."

Rortho stopped and searched an area of the rubble. He moved a few of the stones and found ominous skeletal remains. "Not all were so lucky."

Edanos stopped as they passed a large area of buildings and simply stared upward. "I have read of the Dwemhar. Their cities could protect them from enemies, but this one could not sense the coming destruction thrown upon it. It must have been sudden and when they least expected it." He looked back to them and then nodded forward. "There is a passage this way. We are close."

They continued walking. Valrin looked around, wondering of that day and the surrounding eternal graves. He questioned if they had any clue of their destruction. When they woke up and went to look out at the sea, did they know they would not see another sunrise?

Aeveam touched him on the shoulder. "I feel what you feel. Release it. They no longer suffer as they did that day. This place is not as quiet to those who are sensitive to it. You must feel what I do."

Valrin became overwhelmed with sadness for a moment, and then it fled him.

Aeveam smiled at him, "Feel what you feel and then release. You should never hold on to sadness such as this. We enter their resting places and they make their presence known to you with the essences of their souls. Honor them with a clear mind as we move forward."

The company moved into the passage ahead and found another cavern. This one was open to the tides. Valrin could see the night sky through the top of the structure, though it seemed like there was a glass window of some kind preventing the torrential snowfall that blew across the ceiling.

Unlike the previous areas, this place was dark. There was a center platform that led up and away from where they stood.

"Stormborn, here," Edanos told him.

Valrin went to where he stood and saw a rolled bit of parchment a few steps up. Markings on the ground surrounded it. There was a large circle with intersecting triangular lines. There were several other markings in some type of runic script, but he didn't recognize it.

"This?" Valrin asked.

"It is what I saw and is the key to something that I know is important . . . Just . . . pick it up."

Valrin gave a nervous look to Braei. Her hands were out, ready to cast her spells at a moment's need. Fadis watched behind them, and Evurn, Rortho, and Aeveam stared at him. Their looks of concern didn't help him feel any more confident. He looked back to Edanos and saw that he was shaking and sweating profusely.

"Go," he told Valrin.

Valrin stepped forward and grasped the parchment. The markings on the floor turned from black to a glowing red, and for a moment, he paused, not moving the parchment. He took a deep breath and pulled it to him. The floor went dark. He exhaled and looked down at the sealed parchment. He broke the seal and rolled it out. It was blank.

"I half expected a bit more," Fadis said. "Edanos, what is this?"

The scroll burst into a blue fire, and Valrin struggled to let go as it lifted him up into the air.

He could hear Braei shouting, and he looked back to see he was being pulled over the expanse of the water. From beneath him, the water churned and bubbled wildly. He was terrified of what had happened, but at the same time, he gripped the scroll in fear of plunging into the water below. A glowing tower appeared from the dark depths, and the sounds of horns echoed around him.

The walls became alive with movement. Spectral entities floated from the ruins and nooks of the caves. A flow of magical energy came from the caves where they had docked the ship, and spun around him as the top of the tower came to just the level of his feet. The scroll released him. He stood looking out over the water now glowing with many spectral figures. The scroll moved up to the top of the cave, and its bluish fire glowed brighter for a moment. A crystal hidden near the glass ceiling turned golden, and a figure appeared where the scroll was. It spoke with a thunderous voice.

"Stormborn of Travaa. You come here on the will of all. This place was one of suffering. You were summoned by those who seek passage to ascension after ages of suffering. They are lost souls, spirits of what they were. This city was a place of knowledge and peace, but it became a place of war."

The spectral figures below turned to that of glowing ships moving in circular patterns across the water.

"The great fleet of Arik was made up of vessels of the clouds. Blessed by Dimn to take flight in the time before the floods. They were as the realm ship you wield but with the power of the wind ships of the South, those that have been long lost to the deserts of time. Though those ships needed an infusion of energy and flew with the sounds of songs, these were crewed by those faithful to Dwemhar desires and floated gently on the winds of Dimn.

"They were lost when the Rusis came upon us. They, the enemy of old, brought fire upon us and turned the city to that of what you see now. Countless souls were forced to the thralls of death in the waters below, but by magic, we have remained. We were cursed to remain by it. . . The Imprisoner. The one who comes."

Valrin looked down to the others. A bridge leading to the platform he stood on had appeared, and the others were hurrying toward him. All but Edanos.

"You are the Stormborn, the one who will protect the ways of redemption. We are not as the cult that was to be destroyed—those the waters whisper are now called sea peoples—but your fate is what we seek to assure is as all Dwemhar would desire. From the realm of death, we called out to those who could hear and found one close to our realm, one like you but who could be used. We wish to serve the Stormborn, but you must defeat it."

Aeveam was the first to him. She moved her hands in circular motions around him, causing small specs of light to form.

Braei was there next with flames in her hands. "Edanos is shaking uncontrollably and we do not know why. Aeveam said that there is a split in the realms here. Something is coming!"

Evurn brought his staff out, casting a wedge of orange magic.

"If something comes from another realm, we must be ready with all the power we can have. If Aeveam is correct in this."

The figure still high above spoke again. It was if the figure was oblivious to Valrin's companions. "Death is a path we must all take, but there are those who love its embrace and are empowered by it. When it came to feast on our exposed souls, our defender attempted to stop it. The defender failed."

Beneath them, the image of a massive metal statue appeared, holding its hands out at its side. From its head came a bright flash and a beam of energy. A moment later, an invisible force threw and smashed it. Valrin was seeing the past, a vision of what the figure spoke of.

"Free us, Stormborn, and forgive us for the betrayal, if you cannot."

The figure vanished. The spectral armada returned to blackness, and the tower of gold fell dark.

"By the gods," Rortho yelled, "Edanos has betrayed us."

"It wasn't him," Valrin said. "They called out to him when he was near death."

"We should have never listened to that bumbling man," Fadis said.

A blast of wind shook the tower, and Evurn turned, expanding his ward out.

Aeveam still created specks of light. She began drawing lines out of the air, connecting the hovering spells.

"I have never seen a ward spell such as that," Braei said.

"It isn't a ward," Evurn shouted. "It is something else, and you must hurry if this realm is split."

"I know, shadow elf!" Aeveam said.

Her eyes flashed white, and she lifted her hands upward. At that exact moment, a bolt of red lightning appeared beneath them. She brought her hands in with a single clap, and the white lights hovering in the air expanded outward with a blast of energy spiraling around them. Valrin and the others were now splashed in a white hue.

The air hummed. Valrin drew his blade as the red lightning increased. It began to dance along the outside of Aeveam's enchantment. Evurn had dropped his ward and instead kept his staff above them.

"Shroud, strike, shriek. Shroud, strike, shriek. Shroud, strike, shriek." He continued repeating the phrase, and around them came another wisp of magic.

"This saved your father and me," he told Aeveam, "long ago, long before any one of you were born."

Evurn's spell circled around them and shot out in several directions, bouncing off the walls of the cavern.

"All of this," said Fadis, "and still we do not know our foe."

Valrin wondered of Edanos and what was happening to him. Even from afar, Valrin could see that he was still shaking.

There was a growl in the air, and the red lightning converged on one spot just beneath them. Their foe emerged as if climbing through a torn parchment. It was a beast of the ocean with a massive head that looked like a man. From his mouth came flying serpents, and its arms were of a green fire.

"I . . . devour . . ." it said.

Evurn brought his staff in a downward motion, and his spell struck the creature. There was a rumbling clamor, the sound of hissing and then the creature was upon them. Its legs were not legs at all but the many tentacles of a squid. It opened its mouth, sending the flying snakes toward them in a battering blast of creatures shredding upon hitting Aeveam's spell.

She brought her hands in and then pushed outward. A shimmering wave of white split across the room, throwing the creature back. In doing so, their protection had failed.

"Off the tower!" Evurn yelled. "This is a titan of the cursed realm!"

Rortho barreled forward, followed by Braei. Evurn remained atop the tower with Aeveam. Valrin ran with the others, with Fadis just behind him. The Ranger put an arrow to cheek and sent a bolt toward the beast. It struck, but the creature just seemed to grin. In a rush, throwing up a wave of water and rubble, it smashed the bridge leading down. Its legs shot up around them, and Valrin swung his sword, slicing at one of the legs.

Fadis drew back two arrows and sent them into the creature's face. They both struck, and it slapped with its hands to remove them. Valrin pulled Fadis back, and they ran back for the tower.

As the creature went to grab them, a blast of flames from the level below struck the titan, sending it into a frenzy. It turned and slapped at the buildings where Braei and Rortho awaited.

The dwarf jumped upon its body and hacked at its form with his ax. The creature stumbled, sliding on the rocks to move back as Braei sent another blast of fire. For a moment, it was aflame. Rortho swung repeatedly, sending chunks of shell and rock shattering off the beast. The creature fell downward toward the water, and Rortho went with it. In an explosive wave of seawater, he was thrown off the beast and found himself slapping at the surface to keep afloat. Braei ran along the far edge of the room, using her magic to create a path of ice to Rortho.

Evurn and Aeveam stood back to back, scanning the water. Fadis pointed to an area of water that seemed to be churning more just as Evurn shouted and shot a blast of magic the opposite way.

Valrin spun and saw the creature's legs surrounding them from all sides and consuming the tower.

Aeveam leaped into the air and lifted her hands up as if she was lifting a heavy weight. Valrin felt himself get heavier, and then a sensation rushed through him, and he and the others were propelled upward. He looked down, struggling to keep a grip on his blade as he flew high enough up that he could nearly touch the glass ceiling above them. Aeveam hovered just below all of them. Her powers centered on keeping them all above the creature. The creature spun around the room, now completely out of the water. Its tentacled form and muscular human-like body lumbered about, pulling apart the foundations of the cave.

"There is no sending this beast to the realm. We must kill it!" Evurn shouted.

"We have not an enchanted weapon to do so," Aeveam shouted. "But I will try!"

Below them, Braei projected a wide ward, shielding her and Rortho from the titan's rampage. Valrin was amazed to be floating as he was, and he wondered how much power Aeveam had to possess to both hold them suspended above the creature and prepare whatever she was.

"By the powers of Arik and in the spirits of my ascendants, I summon what is needed in this hour!"

A shimmering, sparkling bolt of white magic appeared in front of her.

There was a sudden tune in the air, a growing sound that became louder as Aeveam brought the bolt above her head. The titan seemed to sense its close destruction, as it turned just after this. There was a rumbling growl, and the tentacled form propelled itself upward at a shattering speed, overwhelming Aeveam. The spell she had summoned fractured and fell apart, and so did her hold on them. They were falling.

Fadis screamed behind him as Valrin felt a grasp on his chest. He was face to face with Evurn, who held a vial of the poison from before. The same poison used to heal Edanos.

As the titan spun above them, set on crushing them with its weight as they all fell toward the water, the shadow elf shattered the vial off Valrin's sword.

They were still falling. He could see Aeveam attempting to grasp them, as she herself had managed to regain composure. Valrin held his sword out, feeling the colder air of the lower chamber rush over the back of his neck. He closed his eyes as the blackness of the beast was upon him. He thrust his sword up, and a flash of red lightning undulated away from him. He was suddenly jerked to a stop. The creature had expanded its tentacles out and was quivering as an appearance of green spiders burrowed their way into its form, and a nauseating fume erupted from the creature's pores. Valrin held his sword with both hands, still dangling above the water, as in a series of explosive flashes, the creature turned white and disintegrated into tiny shells that sprinkled the water below.

Valrin was falling again, but at the last second, he was caught. Not by the grasp of Evurn somehow or the powers of Aeveam, and there was no splash into the water. He looked to his left and saw the one who had been speaking before. The ghost of the fallen Dwemhar. The one who called this place their grave.

"You have defeated the Devourer of Souls."

The spectral form that caught him had materialized on the deck of a ship. He set Valrin down. Aeveam descended to them with Fadis. Thankfully, Evurn had been caught upon another ship nearby. Valrin nodded and smiled, seeing he was safe. Looking to where he stood, he could see the water beneath him. The ship had the look of fog, but those upon its decks seemed as real as anyone else. The man who before had been the voice of the parchment looked no different from any other living form. The ship went to the edge of the water, and Valrin stepped off.

"Stormborn, you hold a future for all in the worlds. A whisper of a hope to make right what he has doomed to fail. Your ship is one of the last vessels of its kind. Against odds that have grown direr than you yet know, you may have need of those of the loyal fleet of Arik. I promise, as the Speaker of the Arik, that we will be there to serve the realm ship of the Stormborn if ever he desires us. A small token of our eternal gratitude. We are free due to the actions of the few here."

The man handed a small golden sphere to Valrin. "Place this upon your ship, and you need only call out our name and we will serve you in battle no matter the odds. This, deemed by the god Wura, is our last step to true salvation within the ocean."

As Valrin looked down at the sphere, the light of the spectral fleet faded. He looked up to see they had vanished and the cave was again still.

Rortho and Braei made their way to them in a quick jog but with the dwarf limping.

"The bastard is dead," Rortho said.

"A bit of poison worked well," Evurn said. "Our captain did what was necessary."

Valrin smiled, looking to each of them, but then he thought of Edanos. He looked around. "Edanos!"

The others began to search as well, but he was nowhere to be found.

"The creature?" Braei asked. "Did it slap him into the water?"

As the others went to the edge and looked in, Aeveam closed her eyes. It was a mere second before she opened them again. "To the ship, Stormborn! He intends to flee!"

Fadis was the first to turn and run. Valrin was just behind him, but in quick fashion, Evurn, Fadis, Valrin, and Aeveam made their way toward the ship. Rortho shouted from afar, "I'll kill him myself if he tried to take our ship without us!"

Valrin was further confused why his friend would do this. Yes, he had been drawn here by the spirits of the Dwemhar, but that wasn't his fault. Valrin sheathed his sword. He had no plan to hurt Edanos. There was no way he could take the ship, anyway.

As they hurried along the path through the city ruins and began back up the hill leading to the ship, Valrin noticed that since the defeat of the titan and the release of the spirits of the city, there were many more crystals shining around them, as if the city itself, in what little power remained within it, had awakened. As they came to the docks, Fadis drew back on his bow but did not fire. Edanos was nowhere to be seen, and Valrin's ship was untouched.

Aeveam walked onto the ship and glanced around. "I saw him upon the sea."

Valrin walked over to where the smaller ships had been suspended above the water to find that they were not at all as they were before. The ships had been released and one of the ships was gone.

"He took a ship," Fadis said. "He seriously took one of these ships and sailed away?"

Evurn said nothing. As Braei and Rortho made their way to the docks, Valrin walked along the docks and rubbed his finger along a stone platform with many glowing runes.

Aeveam walked over to him and pointed. "These were not like this before. Whatever power left within the city has increased, at least enough to deem it to awaken as if the Dwemhar once again live among it."

"Then we must go!" Valrin said.

"He cannot get far without us."

They moved toward the ship, and in very quick motion, Valrin guided the ship away from the docks and began toward the opening. It was then the current changed and the ship would not move. In the water around them, the Glacial Sharks with their glowing runic bodies began to circle the ship. Something moved in the water beneath them. As the current shifted underneath them, the sharks swam to surround a blackness emerging from the depths.

4
FOR A FRIEND

"Another monster? No more monsters!" Rortho shouted.

The water rolled off a massive form, and to Valrin's surprise, the god of the seas, Meredaas himself, emerged.

"Stormborn," he said.

Valrin and the others took to their knees. Even Fadis followed suit in slight shock of a massive talking fish.

"Stormborn, you have progressed from our last meeting. Stand, all of you."

They did as Meredaas said.

"Darkness gathers upon the vast oceans in a way unexpected by most. The workings of the world have led to these events, and even the flight of the one you all care about is in the order of what is to come."

"Edanos, he fled, great Meredaas. This isn't like him," Valrin told him.

"The one called Edanos drifted too close to the realm of death. The sorcery used to save him has done little to prevent what damage the poison in his blood and the curse upon it have done to his mind. He is but a vessel for action. He will not stop until he completes his goals."

"He is going to Gurundothrak, then?" Valrin asked.

"Yes, his ship moves that way with a speed blessed by the gods. He will do what he feels is right, and the gods will watch over you as these events unfold. Edanos follows his fate, and before any type of peace can be had, the danger of the Barb King and what he plans must be washed away."

"Do it, then, god," Fadis said. "Why must we mortals do what you could do? Destroy the Barb King if he is such a danger!"

Meredaas moved closer to the ship and bumped it.

"Do you mind shutting up?" Braei shouted.

There was a bubbling sound on the side of the ship, and in a splash of ocean spray came a figure in a coat of swimming fish. In its hand was a dagger with a curved blade. A bright blue crystal sent out a radiant light that forced those on the ship to shield their eyes.

"Fadis!" the figure said. "You speak to me as if I am one who has never taken action against this world. In this form, I have fought upon the lands next to men and elves. I have existed long before this place was an ocean, back at the creation, back when the Great Poet sang the songs of creation and spawned me upon the ocean floor. Do not mock what you do not understand."

Meredaas' demeanor softened and he turned to Valrin. "Go and be watchful. Do what you feel is the best choice and embrace your calling as Stormborn. The Barb King is an evil force that will test you in the end. Know that those of the seas are your friends. You have called to us before, and we are with you."

The figure returned to the water, and a flash vibrated beneath the surface. The god of the seas departed, and they were left alone.

Evurn and Aeveam looked to Valrin. He stared at them and then looked to the others. "Edanos will get himself killed if we do not help him. I see no other path but one that leads us to him."

There were no immediate words from anyone in the crew. Valrin took that as no one protested his idea, but as he guided the ship away from the cave and emerged outside under a bright moon, he felt worried. He knew he wanted to save Edanos, again, and while the once captain had led them to the place before and it had worked out, going to the chief city of the dwarves—the dwarves who wanted them all dead—was not perhaps the wisest of decisions, and he knew it. But the threat to those of the Glacial Seas was a very real one. The toxin the dwarves had obtained would destroy too much to be ignored.

He brought the map up and noted his target. As he turned the ship a few degrees for the best path south, Rortho came up to him. "Captain, I do not know what you hope to do by going there. If Edanos goes there, he will have one intent. We are all brave, but I do not believe us strong enough to assail the Barb King."

Valrin said nothing. In truth, he wasn't sure what to say.

"Valrin, I want nothing more but to be able to have our happy crew as it was before, but, and I can't believe I would say this, I do not think Edanos is who he was before."

"I know."

Rortho put his hand on Valrin's shoulder. "I'm with you, lad. I'll do what we need to do."

"The dwarves plan to attack the people of the Glacial Seas, and from what Rugag said back at Lorlaam's Island, it is the elves they target. The dwarven lich said they are the key to some great undoing of what their Barb King seeks. He has been promised armies and claims that he is stronger than the gods of the North."

"His first folly and not his last, I am sure."

Valrin noticed that Braei, Evurn, Aeveam, and Fadis had been talking near the front of the ship. They approached in unison but then simply sat around the helm.

"They told me we go to Gurundothrak," Aeveam said. "I know little of that place but enough to fear it. I have heard stories of the enchantments in those waters—the reason none have assaulted that place."

Fadis exhaled. "I don't know what we can do to help Edanos at this point. Isn't this place a dwarven fortress suspended over the ocean? How can we get in? An underwater tunnel?" He looked at Evurn.

"None exist that I know of," Evurn said, "and if they did, I would not dare jump into those waters so close to the monster that lives in those depths feeding off dwarven magic."

"It is a fortress, but it is also a city," said Rortho. "There will be a way in, but it may not be so obvious. If the Hammersongs from Harrodarr are going there, I suspect the city will hide any otherwise foul practices that might not line up with the beliefs of the other dwarf kingdoms. Our first problem is this ship."

Rortho pulled out a small parchment with runic writing on it. Valrin tried to look over at it as he passed but couldn't tell anything about it.

"I wrote down a few of the crystal alignments that allow for the ship to do different things. I can say for one that I have found a type of veiling spell. Not to necessarily make the ship itself invisible, but more to make it look as every other vessel. Even the sails will change. If I understand the wording correctly," he said, turning two of the larger crystals, "it might even mean we will once again have ropes hanging above our heads as it was with the *Truest Bliss*. Good for us in two ways. One, we will look like other vessels, but two, even with ropes that appear to be needed, the ship will maintain the ability of its advanced construct, although activating any of the weapons will destroy the veil. Once we get closer to the city, I will activate it, but let us try it first."

He twisted one of the rear crystals, and the rails of the ship suddenly turned to a weathered age. Ropes flew down from near where the sails connected to the main masts and slapped down into hooks on the lower levels. From the deck of the ship, pulleys emerged and ropes wrapped around them and shot back up to the top of the ship.

The ship slowed, and the sails draped down before shimmering and turning a dark blue. The ship had transformed and looked like any other ship on the seas.

"A clever disguise," Braei said.

"It is," Fadis agreed.

Rortho switched the crystal again, and the ship immediately became as it was before. The ropes, pulleys, and the colors of the sails blew off the ship as if they were only dust.

The ship increased speed.

"I will keep it disengaged for as long as I can. Our speed does suffer when it is in the other form. It seems that everything about the ship changes to be like others, even its sailing speed."

Valrin took out the orb given to him back at Arik, and set it on the deck where he originally set the golden prisms given to him when he first obtained the ship. The orb began to spin and glow gold before a wooden growth emerged from the deck. It was like a small tree that wrapped its branches around the orb. With the orb now entwined in wood, a stone case moved up and around the orb, producing a small pillar that further secured it.

Rortho snickered, "I hope I never come up to this part of the ship while a bit too sleepy. I just know I will hit my leg on that thing."

"Sleep," Braei said. "Us non-Stormborns should try to get some before we get to Gurundothrak." She winked at Valrin.

"Go on, then," Evurn told them. "Aeveam and I must meditate upon our future works. We shall keep Valrin company."

The crew didn't protest at all. They all knew that the events to come were a bigger unknown than when they had found the ship they were on. As they watched them descend, Evurn and Aeveam stood on either side of Valrin.

"We have both spoken while the others debated this path. We know it to be the right one, but Aeveam has seen more," Evurn told him.

Valrin looked at her, and she closed her eyes. She touched his head, and he didn't expect what happened.

There was a flash, and he was staring at the open ocean before him. The horizon and a setting sun were in the distance. The sky began to turn dark, and then he saw what appeared as an eye sparkling white. Another flash and he saw a shoreline and massive trees. He saw hundreds of elves and a haze over the tree lines. One by one, the elves fell to the ground, gasping. He then saw his ship speeding away, but it was not him and his crew but dwarves. Among them was a larger dwarf, but his face was black. As the ship passed away from the island, he saw blood running from the back of the ship, and the sky darkened before stars began to fall from the sky, streaking above him and smashing all over the seas. He could hear a song on the wind, a tune as if from an organ somewhere far away, and then the elven land before him vanished, leaving only the floating bodies of thousands of elves.

She removed her hand, and his hands were shaking. "Was that the future?"

"It was what may come to pass, but I fear I cannot see a clear path for us to follow to avoid it. He attacked elves, and in some way, this seems to doom the rest of the lands."

Evurn looked around them. "There is a prophecy in the North. It speaks of a half-elf and a great darkness to come. This half-elf will awaken a horrid evil, and death will fall across the lands. In turn, because of these events, a greater darkness will come. Some have wondered what it means. Some spoke of the Stormborn and how it was meant to be the half-elf. That clearly is not true. When they speak of the evil, they talk of the Itsu, but that, too, is something that I do not see a possibility. They are bound from this realm; at least, as I understand it. This dwarf we know as the Barb King uses the title of Stormborn to try to assert power. He asserts himself over other dwarves and claims that some power in the world will increase his own power if he destroys those who might be of the prophecy to prevent the coming darkness. The death that will come is what you, what we, must prevent.

"Valrin, I tell you, I may simply eat any dwarf or elf who may find its way to my island. I may come from the elves known as the most deadly killers in the history of the realms, but seeing the poison of my beloved Vearika used in such a way, to see an entire land destroyed, an entire race, and if possible by the hand of the Barb King." He paused. "To see a race of people destroyed by anyone is not something that this shadow elf will allow."

Valrin gripped the wheel and then looked up at the stars.

"That vision—I can't let that happen."

"We will help," Aeveam said. "My father feared me; he feared my powers."

Evurn glanced at her and then looked down.

"But," she said, "I am not my mother. I do not have a blood lust as she did. I am my father's daughter, strong in my powers and trained to serve the gods of the North, and that I will do. For now, that means serving you."

Valrin smiled. "Then, well, those elves? The ones in the vision—can we help them? Where is that place?"

"My vision is unclear," Aeveam said. "Your ship is the key, I believe, but why are there dwarves on it?"

"We can take no risks as we come near Gurundothrak. There are barrier islands, and we will hide the ship there. From there, we can get in the city," Evurn told them. He then tapped his staff on one of the crystals, and the map appeared on the deck of the ship. "The seas are vast, and elven kingdoms border the waters in many places. I know of no island of elves, but I wonder if the vision was meant to have a vague meaning, to mean, perhaps, that from the sea would come something to destroy elves."

They were all silent.

"I will curve my powers to search out the truth in my vision. I will say that if Edanos is successful, we may have some better luck and the elves will be safe without our intervention."

"He is foolish," Evurn told her. "If Edanos has the sense to not take that ship all the way into the dwarven city, we will be lucky. His newfound encouragement will either propel him to his victory or be his downfall."

That was the last they spoke of it before Evurn went into the ship to sleep. Aeveam sat on the deck, mediating as the stars crossed over the night sky and the winds shifted over Valrin. He closed his own eyes, feeling the ship glide across the water, the break of the sea on the bow, and for a moment, he felt the sails themselves as if like wings as he flew across the ocean. He smiled, feeling at one with the ocean. He opened his eyes to the words of Aeveam.

"Starlight high, the night breeze cold,
Upon the seas above ruins so old.
Ascended masters speak within,
The chosen Stormborn, my captain.

I come from man of Rusis blood,
Of Dwemhar magic
Of once-strong love...
My mind sparks with hellish gleams,
I chant my mantras and slowly sing,

Oh, how bright the wakening light
Above the stars,
Above the night.
The realm so pure that I'll call home,
The one where my ancestors roam."

Aeveam's song continued through the night. Valrin smiled and wondered at the words. He had never heard of something called "mantra" and of light above the "stars and night." The mystery amazed him and took his mind off the tasks ahead. He could see the outline of Gurundothrak with a darkening morning sky glowing above him. As much as he wished to help Edanos, he was fearful of what was to come.

It was a few hours later. Aeveam had gone to sleep, and he had spent the time humming to himself as the ship rolled through the waves. He could see approaching lights in the distance. They were large braziers with trails of smoke rising up and a large lighthouse on the furthest point reaching out to the sea. Valrin moved the crystals to make the ship appear as before. The ropes shot out from the masts, and the ship changed form once again. He hoped the disguise would work.

Further behind the nearest islands, he could see the massive form of Gurundothrak. The dwarven city was wrapped in fog, and as he moved the ship to the right of the lighthouse, he could see that the waters past the islands were much more turbulent.

Fadis and Evurn emerged from below, and sleepy-eyed Fadis leaned over the railing of the ship in an over-zealous stretch. "I slept wrong. My damn back tightened up."

Evurn laughed. "You are much too young to complain about such things. Try having a dragon tooth embedded in your spine."

"I'd rather not, and how would you know how that feels?"

"I wouldn't. But I had an uncle who did. We had to carry him on the back of a unicorn everywhere we went. A most painful situation, I assure you."

Evurn pointed to the west. "The islands to the far edge. Get away from the first one with the lighthouse. There are rocky coves where we can anchor the ship."

The rocky coves were perfect. Though partially covered in fog and not the easiest to traverse, other ships were already docked here, and each arch acted as its own miniature mooring. As the ship passed under the arch, chains lifted out of the water to help secure the ship. Evurn reached up and secured the mooring to the actual deck of the ship. Off one of the rocks was another chain, which Evurn pulled, allowing a pathway to drop that would lead them across the water and to the island.

The others awoke soon afterward.

"How long has it been since you were here?" Valrin asked.

"A while. If you are worried about them knowing

me, do not. They would not expect me dressed as such, and I'm sure they think I'm dead."

"Are you sure? After your duel with the lich before?"

"If I told you how many duels I got in during the old days you would be surprised I am still alive. I even dueled our dearly departed Lorlaam, at one point. It is amazing what some creatures can do to your mind. Thankfully, we didn't kill each other."

"I think he meant they will think you're alive considering you fought the lich," Fadis said.

"I knew what he meant I just chose to answer as I chose."

Valrin shook his head and smiled.

Evurn said nothing else and led them from the ship and across the wooden plank walkway that bridged the water to the island. The village ahead bustled with activity, but strangely, there were no dwarves. As they reached the other side, Rortho walked over toward one of the small rock houses, and two men sitting by a fire jumped to their feet.

"We are sorry, Master Dwarf! We will get to smashing the rocks again."

Their words caught Rortho by surprise. He looked to the others and then to the terrified men.

"Please, Master Dwarf!" the man said with his hands shaking above his head. "Please do not punish us."

The two men both stayed low to the ground and did not dare look up.

Rortho shook his head and stomped toward them.

"I will tell the Barb King of your folly unless you tell me exactly what this island here is."

The men looked up, slightly confused, but then returned to staring at the ground.

"This is where we clean the ships for the slavers. We are the slaves deemed unfit for the city. We find our work honorable and would never complain. Have you come to claim your ship? We know many slavers have brought in extra help for the festivities."

"Festivities?"

"In honor of the Stormborn, the Great King, the ruler of the oceans who will bring glory to all the Glacial Seas."

Rortho looked at them and rolled his eyes. "Get up, you bastards." He pulled them up one at a time, and they both recoiled away from him.

"Get back to work and let no one know you saw anyone else here. I will take my ship to Gurundothrak."

"Yes, Master," they both said.

Rortho motioned for them to follow.

"What is your plan, dwarf?" Fadis asked.

Several ships were moored in docks on the far side of the island. It would be an easy journey to get to the city from here.

"His plan is to make us slaves to cover our entrance into the city," Aeveam said.

Braei shook her head. "That cannot be the best idea we can come up with."

"Would you rather us sail in with fireballs flying from our fingertips? And risk a fate as Edanos? No, we need to get in quietly, and unless someone has a better idea of how to do so, our way in has been revealed."

They walked down the dock and stepped into the low-sitting dwarven ship.

Valrin noticed stockades and icy chains covered the entire deck.

"We'll make the look right," Rortho said. He unhinged several stockades and pointed. "Go there. This will have to look real or it is pointless."

Valrin stared for a moment, and Evurn pushed him. "Come, boy, time to do your part in a stockade."

He laid his neck in the cold wooden plank. His neck was small compared to the size of the opening. He put his hands in the appropriate holes, and Rortho strung a chain through the stockades. The dwarf paused and looked at Valrin's.

"Well, I mean, at least you could escape if you really wanted to."

"Must be nice," Fadis said as he rattled his own stockade.

From where Valrin was, he couldn't see Rortho after he untied the ship from the moorings. The helm was behind them. They were moving to the city now. The waters were rough but not as bad as he had expected. As they drew close to one of the several stone pillars surrounding the city, he spotted a massive chain leading down into the fogs.

"This city is old," Evurn said. "The dwarven magic protecting it is grand in design."

"Edanos said it was like Merea. Crystal magic," Valrin told him.

"Your friend is right, but the construct of a city like this where most of it sits above the actual ocean is a rare and magnificent thing. Too bad the dwarves within are as they are. I say that, but know that the average dwarf here is a common dwarf. They live, work, and have their lives here. It would not stop me from breaking one of those chains and bringing ruin to their happy homes. I would have more dwarves to snack on than I could ever need."

Braei sighed. "You do not really eat dwarves, do you?"

"Of course. I said it before."

"But actually eating elves and dwarves—I have never met anyone like that."

"There need be only one, and just be happy I have no desire to slow roast anyone on this ship here. Well, unless this dwarf taking us in causes us too much discomfort."

"I'll keep the ruse up," Rortho said, "as long as I have to. But is there a spot you know, Evurn, a place not as guarded? I have not been to this place before."

"There is no spot that you seek. This is Gurundothrak, not Corson or some back-island wasteland. The dwarves here are proud. Foolish, but proud."

Valrin noticed the fog was clearing. He could see a red gleam above them. As he continued to stare, he could see the crystals protruding from the bottom of the city structure. It was a massive construct where winds whistling beneath it made a terrifying sound. The ship began to toss in the water just before Rortho made a rough mooring.

"Slaver!" they heard over the winds.

Rortho ran to the edge of the ship and threw the tie lines out.

Another dwarf came to the edge to help him.

"Where is your crew? That was the worst piloting I have ever seen. You missed the main drop-off point by at least one hundred paces. This way is off limits!"

"I am sorry, Harbormaster. My crew was murdered by these fools here. I only sought to bring them in. I normally run spices to the southern lands, so I am not accustomed to your rules here."

The dwarf jumped onto the ship, and Rortho's hand went to his ax.

"This is a disgusting lot. An elf, a man, and two women—well, perhaps not so disgusting. The one in the dark robes and with blonde hair will fetch you enough to afford a new crew, no doubt."

"That sounds enticing. I look forward to taking advantage of that."

Valrin noticed that Braei and Aeveam became restless, moving in their shackles.

"The rest are kind of a waste," the dwarf said.

"Oh?" Rortho asked.

"Yes, our great king has brought in many from the city to prepare for a visit from Hammersongs from the South. Our dwarven brothers do not condone our vast and profitable slave trades, and well, frankly, except for the females, he wants to assure the presence of men, or other less-desirable races, is low. Either way, head up the walkway and take them to The Pits. From there, be sure to head up the city and have a fine drink. Stick around for the festivities! There is a great announcement coming soon. The Barb King has unearthed a rare artifact, and I have reason to believe that our city will soon be the greatest in the world!"

The dwarf laughed and exited the ship.

Rortho, who had not relaxed the entire time, holding his hand on his ax, sighed. He waited a few moments for the dwarf to depart and then released them from the stockade. He bound their hands with cuffs.

"I don't see why we must be bound," Aeveam said.

"We have to keep the ruse up or we risk being seen."

"I can get us into the city with my powers."

"No," Evurn protested. "The city cannot be entered by way of magic, or the guardian stones of the dwarves will burn you as you pass them. The city must be entered through the main gates and without magic."

One by one, Rortho strung them together with a chain and led them off the ship. Evurn tugged the chain as they began up the stone steps.

"Not too rough," Fadis said. "It's not like we're actually your prisoners."

"I fear who watches," he said, without looking back. "The last thing we want is trouble when virtually none of us have weapons."

Valrin struggled to keep pace, feeling a slight pull on his wrists as he began to jog to keep up with Rortho. They came over the top of the steps, and he saw a massive area full of ships. There were fishing vessels, slaver vessels, and elves and men in cages.

Rortho stopped walking as the rest of them filed behind him.

"This many," Evurn said. "I have never seen so many slaves."

They looked to the far left of the rocky port and saw the main gates that led to a bridgeway that went up into the city.

"That is our way in," Evurn said, "but it looks as if they have changed how one may enter."

"They don't want slaves in the city, but they have all of these?" Braei asked.

About that time, several dwarves appeared at their side.

"Halt there! Why do you stand and stare? Why are you not moving?"

Rortho walked toward them. "My first time in the city," he told them. "I was taking in the sights."

"Our lord has stated that those who seem suspicious must be questioned."

One of the dwarves grabbed hold of the chain holding Valrin and the others.

"He has also stated that no one save the Barb Guardians shall make transactions with slaves. You are not one of us, so you will go to the city and speak with our consulate to determine if you can be trusted. Once you have approval, you may leave."

The dwarf holding the chain brandished a whip and slapped it at Valrin and the others. "You five don't even flinch! You will learn your place."

Rortho drew his ax, and the other dwarves did the

same, except the one who spoke to him. This one had a hammer with an orange crystal in its head.

"Dwarf, I am Hammersong. Do not tempt me to smash you into the lava rock of this city."

Valrin and the others were pulled away as this Barb Guardian pushed Rortho in the chest. He worried of his friend, but as they came closer to spiked gates between walls of cages with inebriated slaves all around him, he began to worry about himself a bit more.

5
SLAVERS

The dwarf moved faster than Rortho. They passed through the gate, and Valrin tripped on a stone and began to be dragged.

"Get up!" Evurn shouted.

The ground was slick, and he struggled to stand, sliding and stumbling as he tried to get his feet under him. Before he could actually get up, they were pulled into a holding area with several other slaves who looked much worse than him. Dwarves on elevated platforms looked down into the cell.

"Those two!" one of them shouted. He pointed their way.

Two of the Barb Guardians entered, and one grabbed Braei.

"This one?"

"Yes! Ten thousand gold for the two of them."

The dwarf who had dragged them in immediately nodded his head, and Braei and Aeveam were struck in the back of the head. The chain holding them was loosened, and they dragged Aeveam and Braei out of The Pits.

"Damn fuckers!" Fadis yelled.

He pulled himself forward, lunging forward and pulling Evurn and Valrin. One of the dwarves turned and punched him, dropping the Ranger into the mud.

"No more," said Evurn. "Just wait."

There were several other transactions after that, and not involving them.

What had happened to Braei and Aeveam did not happen to anyone else but then again there were no other females. Valrin figured that must have been a special occurrence at the auction. He was very worried and he had no idea where they were being taken.

"This was a bad idea," Evurn said. "We should have left Edanos."

Fadis was now attempting to stand back up. "We have to get out of here."

Immediately, another shout came their way.

"I want the man and the boy. Leave the elf. He can remain here."

The dwarves came at them and forced them to the ground.

"Do I need to punch you again?" he asked Fadis.

Fadis looked down. "Remain quiet," he said to Valrin under his breath.

They were moved quickly out of The Pits, and Valrin got a last look at Evurn before they were thrown atop a cart with a donkey tied to it. The dwarf who had bought them quickly approached with a paper in hand.

"A happy purchase," he said to the other dwarves.

Valrin's and Fadis' hands were bound tighter.

The dwarf was not dressed as the others. He wore no armor and had a simple garb of a dark tunic. He climbed onto the cart and snapped a whip. They were moving.

"What do we do?" he asked Fadis.

"We stay together and figure a way out."

Braei and Aeveam awoke in a cold and dark room. Braei could hear music but could only see a sliver of light ahead of her.

"Aeveam," she said.

"I am here. I don't know where we are. My senses are still coming back."

"You are trapped," a voice said. "You will be used and then you will die."

Braei noticed her hands were not bound. She created a small ball of flame and revealed the person speaking. It was an elf, but she wasn't alone. There were several others, all females, wearing little clothing, with bruises and blood covering their bodies. Beyond them were others, but they were not alive and in several different stages of decay.

"What is this place?" Aeveam asked.

"We have no place as slaves, but we have value as entertainment," she said.

"What is your name?" Braei asked.

"I have no name," she said plainly. "You will be the same in time."

Braei looked at one of the others. "What is your name?"

But she didn't answer and instead looked down.

"They no longer speak. They will die soon too. They will clear out the pin, and we will be free then."

Braei stood up, as did Aeveam. They both went to the door.

Aeveam pressed her hand against the wood and closed her eyes. "There are two on the other side, and this door is just mere wood. We will get out of here and get to the others."

The no-name elf crawled over to them. "What are you doing?"

"We are leaving. You can come, too. All of you can."

"No! You cannot! Don't attempt to leave! Some did that! It was angered! Don't anger the monster!" The elf recoiled back and moved past the still-living females to the corpses. "Please don't!"

Braei and Aeveam looked at one another, confused.

"Here, I will show you there is no monster here." She made her fireball grow in size, lighting up the cave even brighter.

The prisoners pointed and began to move toward the corpses. Braei and Aeveam looked at where they were pointing and saw a crystalline figure with now glowing red eyes. They both suddenly felt weak and were unable to move. Braei's spell faded, and then the door opened.

"I knew one of them had magic!" a dwarf said. Braei could see them looking her over.

"Which one?"

They rubbed her legs and then grabbed her face. "But she isn't that good. Grab the other one."

Braei looked toward Aeveam. Aeveam appeared as if she had consumed too many ales. Braei tried to lift her hands but could not. They dragged Aeveam from the room, and the door shut.

Valrin and Fadis had determined the best course of action currently was to remain silent. They weren't gagged, but when they had attempted to speak even a whisper, their dwarven master slapped his whip at them.

"You're going to the main kitchen of our king. I need some hands to work in the kitchen, and well, he killed the others I had. We are short on time with a massive feast needing to be prepared. Fish need cleaning and potatoes from the South are needed to thicken up our stews. I do hope you two can handle that."

"Yes," Fadis said.

The whip flung back and struck him across the face, leaving a red mark.

"No talking, not even when spoken to. Your place is to serve your masters. You shall work until your work is done, and do so in silence. Any word of protest or that you're sad or that you feel anything but goodness towards your happy home, especially, and you will be released from your wonderful job with the ease of an ax head."

Fadis grabbed at his face and squinted in pain. Valrin rolled over and watched as they ascended a series of roads going higher and higher into the city. He couldn't see very much, but every few moments, he could see a glimpse of the sea and thought how right now his only desire was to be upon his ship once again.

After some time, they passed through a massive gate and went off to the stone path. He sat up to see they were now away from the main city. A dark and ominous spire to his left reached high into the sky and glowed with red braziers up and down its entire structure. The ground they traveled across was now black sand, and in just a few moments, they stopped and were ordered out of the cart. The dwarf cut their bonds.

"You are servants here. You cannot escape. If you try, you will die. There is no question in this matter. You will be well fed, and in silence, you will revere your god king. He is our lord, our Stormborn king, and master of the seas. In time, you will understand his powers."

Valrin forced himself to remain silent for fear of the whip or worse. Fadis motioned for him to go ahead as the dwarf walked them toward a small wooden door. They entered a room filled with fragrant herbs and the sounds of bubbling broths. There were several other humans in the kitchen, but all kept their heads down. Massive vats of stew were in the center of the room, and even now there were stacks of bowls being prepared.

"The feast is tonight, if I do not have to remind you dogs! This will be the grandest service, and there will be a show of excellence by our grand king. Do not speak or you will be silenced, and I do not want bloodshed on this grand night. You will all soon understand. Be happy you are here and not someplace worse. There are many dark places in Gurundothrak."

Time went by slowly. The entire kitchen communicated with hand signs and rhythmic pounds on the table. If someone pointed and struck the table really fast, it meant the action needed to be completed quickly. There was a lot to learn and it was only made worse by the demanded silence at all times. Valrin didn't understand everything, but when he was pushed to a table of potatoes and handed a dull knife, he understood enough.

The slaves took Fadis to a different part of the room. He had to clean fish and chickens, but it didn't take long before he began working on a plan of escape. Valrin knew little of Rangers, but when he saw Fadis slip the knife into his garments when gathering more fish, he knew something was on his mind.

Valrin worked tirelessly, cursing himself for ever coming here and hating Edanos more every second. He shouldn't have tried this. He feared for the others, but especially for Braei. She had been a slave before, and now she was one again, and it was all his fault.

The time came when the dwarf from before returned. He had several stacks of clothes on a cart. "You will clean yourselves and then dress. You will serve us in the Grand Hall. There, you will standby at all times for the moment you are needed. Do not fail me in tonight's ordeal, and I may allow you time outside tomorrow. There will be few of us dwarves here then. Oh, I know of our king's plan. I have sensed it for some time. You will all see that this is the most wonderful city of the Glacial Seas, and our god king willing, it will be the last."

The dwarf shut the doors, and Fadis stared at him. As the others droned their way to another room, Fadis and he followed.

"We will see this Barb King. If Edanos is here, perhaps we will hear of him. The Barb King sought him out in the past, or so I understand. Surely he will speak of it to show off to his Hammersong guests."

"What if Nurocas recognizes us?"

"Then we must hope he has seen enough to sour his mood toward these dwarves. Somehow I doubt he will do us any favors; we are not dwarven like him. Dwarves and elves care little of others."

―――

A few more moments and Braei could sit up again. The no-name elf stroked her hair.

"You are a young one, but you will not be safe. They will take you, too."

"What are they doing to her?"

"Whatever they wish."

Braei knew what that meant. It had been the fate of many of her kind in other parts of the world.

"That statue," she said.

"It only awakens when one of magic uses power, and then it also will come alive to take those who have rotted too long and created sickness. Be happy in knowing that I have only been here a week and I will soon depart this life. It will be nice."

The elf lay down and did not speak again. Braei began to shake. She had never felt fear like this, and she didn't know what to expect.

Evurn had been taken to a cave far from The Pits. It wasn't a place where others were. It wasn't even worthy of actual guards. They pushed him in, and he found little else other than a muddy mat that was so encrusted, he wondered how long it had actually been there. They slammed the gate and left him. He went to look out and saw that he was high above the slave area they were in before. The sun coming through the clouds was choked by smoke from the city. The sky appeared orange and even the sea in the distance didn't look as it should have.

Rasi slithered down his arm.

"We have to get out of this rancid place," he told the snake.

The snake nodded and slithered up and out of the top.

"This is why I eat these dwarves. I never cared for the elves as much as the dwarves. These fat-blooded little armored lards."

"You eat dwarves?" a voice asked.

"I do," Evurn said, looking around, confused.

"I've done that. Back home."

"Where is home?"

From the top of the cell fell a gem on a gold necklace.

Evurn leaned forward and saw an image of a clawed head.

"From the far east! You are a shadow elf?"

"Surprised?" the voice asked as the gem disappeared.

"Yes, I had thought you all gone from these regions. I have been here for many, many years and never saw another."

"Well, I was sent to finish a contract, and it didn't work so well."

"Did you lose your assurance of never being captured alive?"

"I had not the stomach for death from poison, and I would quite like to avoid it."

Evurn smiled. "A shared sentiment. How did you keep such a gem with you?"

"Trading with the ravens that feed on the corpses of other dead here in the forgotten areas. Even from here I can talk to those I wish. I am stuck in the lost region."

"Lost region?"

"This is where the undesirables go to die."

"Seems a bit much when they could throw us in the maelstrom beneath the city."

There was a laugh from the other elf. "That is a mirage. They keep ships there now. They are building a grand fleet. They obtained something unlike other things."

"You talk in riddles."

"You should know better than anyone that this is the way of our kind. My cellmate did not, and he helped me get this nice gem. The ravens love fresh food. I, too, love foods. This gem is tasty."

Evurn began to hear the elf above chomping down on something, which he presumed was the gem, and wondered if this man was perhaps a bit more eccentric than him.

A few moments later, Rasi returned with a key in its mouth.

"Good," Evurn said, jumping to open the cell door. The key was a perfect fit. He unlocked it and signaled for Rasi to come to him.

"Where did you leave the nasty dwarf?"

The snake seemed to spin in place almost like it was confused and then shot up his leg and into his clothing.

Evurn peered around the rocky edge of his cell to see two dwarves running up the way. "Come now, Rasi, did you forget to bite them?!"

The dwarves pointed. "That damn snake took the keys! I know it went this way."

Evurn looked and noticed it was quite a way down from the level of his cell off the cliff the actual cell sat on. As the dwarves got nearly to the cell, he jumped out, startling one of them, who tripped and rolled off the cliff. The other drew an ax and lunged for him. He jumped up the edge of the cliff and then grabbed hold of the dwarf by his shoulder before drawing his adversary's dagger kept at his back. He made a thrust into the back of his neck, and the dwarf was silent. He threw the dwarf to join the other one off the cliff.

Evurn heard clapping above him.

"Very good, near horrible form. Now be a good elf and toss me the keys so I may eat some delightful gems!"

"You, my friend, have an issue, and I do believe it would be rather unwise for me to release you." Evurn tossed the keys just out of the other elf's reach.

"From one shadow elf to another, enjoy the solitude. Perhaps your raven friends will help you."

He turned away and began down as the man repeatedly cursed him. He would go to the city and find the others. He figured the dwarf would be easiest to find and together they would figure out the next step.

Braei had closed her eyes for some time. She wasn't sure for how long, but she heard footsteps and quickly sat up. Aeveam returned but this time standing. She was forced in, and the door slammed behind her.

"You are alive! What did they do to you? Are you hurt?"

"I have long studied the piggish attributes of the races," she said. "Engorged in wine, a dwarf sought me as a play thing. I played him as he wished."

"That . . . I don't know what to say."

"They will not, either, when they find him. My powers have returned. I have altered their minds' ability to see as things really are. They see as I wish them to see but the spell is temporary. They will learn the truth soon, and when they do we will need to be ready."

Aeveam put her hands together, and a bright light formed in her fingertips. She drew a circle on the ground, reaching from one side of the cave to another, and the entire room filled with a bluish glow.

"The statue, the one in the corner. If it senses your powers, it will attack again."

Aeveam stared up at the corner. "Oh, that trinket."

She pointed and sent a blast of white magic toward it. It glowed and then shattered into several pieces. Looking back at her circle, she began to inscribe runes in a language Braei didn't recognize.

"When we first came to this place, the strike to my head had disrupted my powers. The only potential issue now is the fact that once my spell is fully charged, it will take time to engage. While in that state, it will produce a sound that the others will be able to hear and a light that even through the rocks of this cave, they will see."

"What is this?"

"I will move us from this place back to the ship, the one we were made slaves on. I will need some time to recover, but from there, we can find the others and plan our next moves."

The no-name elf and several others slowly crawled to the glowing circle.

"Stay back for now. We have to wait until the right moment before you enter. Otherwise, it will tear you apart."

No-name had been reaching out to touch it but quickly recoiled when Aeveam said that.

The many faces of the prisoners showed a new light. Their hope, which before had been as dark as the cave they were lying in, now gave them a renewed vigor.

"I can go home?" one of them said.

"Yes, in time," said Braei.

The woman smiled. "I don't remember where my home is."

Braei was smiling, but the deterioration of the others weighed heavily on her.

The door of the cave suddenly swung open, and without looking up, Aeveam motioned with her hand, sending the door and the dwarf opening it flying backward. She then lifted her hands up into the air.

"By the light of time, by a splice of form, open."

She brought her hands down, and a bright white

light covered the entire circle. As she held her arms together, wind circled around her.

"Come now," she said.

The others began to cautiously crawl toward the light. A growling dwarf brandishing a large mace appeared in the void of the doorway. Braei stood up, bringing her hands together and sending a bolt of electricity directly at him. It bounced through and shot down the hall behind him. There was more shouting, and she could hear the clamor of more of them approaching.

"I will need time once they are all within the circle. It will take a few moments. Be ready to jump in!"

"Okay," Braei said.

The dwarves came into her line of sight again, and she sent a line of fire into these. But she didn't stop the flow of flame, and stepped forward, spewing the fiery spell deeper into the doorway. The way was now covered in fire and, at least for the time, impassible.

Several women were still making their way to the circle. Braei ran over to them and began to pull them onto the enchanted ground. There was a last one at the very back of the cave, lying on several corpses. Braei wouldn't have seen her had she not been raising her hand.

Braei crawled over to her and went to pick her up when she noticed that her legs had been taken off and her blood-soaked bandages rotted with infection.

"Me, please—me."

Braei lifted under her arms and began to pull her

back toward Aeveam. Someone shouted, and several throwing axes flew in, striking those within the circle.

They began to scream as blood poured out on the cave floor.

"Do it now," voices shouted from the other side of the flames. "The statue has failed. Switch the manual trigger. Drop them!"

"Braei, the circle, now!" Aeveam shouted.

She was a few feet away. A clank reverberated off the cave walls and it suddenly filled with cold air. A moment later, she looked up to see Aeveam and the ones within her circle floating in mid-air as she began to fall through a trap floor of their cavernous prison. She dropped the crippled woman she was holding.

Braei looked down and cried in anguish. There was a swirling mass of water beneath her. Black, with the jagged teeth of crags piercing up out of the water. As the frigid winds rushed around her, she closed her eyes.

Aeveam only had a few seconds. Standing upon the glowing spell still beneath her and the others, she focused her thoughts. Seeing the form of Braei clearly in her mind, she grasped her with her powers and imagined Braei within the circle. When she opened her eyes, the circle was glowing brightly and Braei was there in shock as she looked at her.

"Bless the powers of the Dwemhar. If only our people would not have been such enemies in the ages before."

Aeveam smiled. "Hold on."

There was a flash, and then Braei opened her eyes to see them on the edge of a rocky hill away from the slavers' area and more to the east.

"This isn't the ship," Braei said.

Aeveam slowly fell to the ground and assumed a meditative position. "I must rest and you must watch for our enemy. I have not the power to go further out at this time, but I feel events are coming full circle and this spot will work for our needs. Be prepared."

It had not taken Evurn very long to figure out that something was afoot in the city. Several dwarves had been running about since he had found a rocky grotto to ponder his best plan forward. He had overheard of an issue at the brothel. He also noticed they were trying to keep the events quiet and covered up to avoid issues with their king. He wondered of the others, and from the franticness of the conversations he heard, there was a chance his friends had escaped. He didn't know for sure, but he prayed Aeveam and Valrin were well. They were his responsibility, or so he felt.

It was now dark, and while he had wondered for a while what would be his best path, a wine carrier walked toward one of the barracks and delivered drinks to several dwarves. He saw his chance.

As the man came back outside and counted his coins, Rasi slithered out and bit the man on his foot. The man kicked Rasi away and stumbled down the path directly toward him. In a quick motion, he emerged from the shadows, grabbed the man, and broke his neck, sending a stream of drool pouring onto his hands. He hated direct-contact killing, but he would be hard-pressed to effectively use a poison without any. He undressed the man and took his garb as his own. Rasi jumped back onto him, and they began toward the city.

It was a perfect plan. The dwarves at the gate stopped him, but only to ask for miniature bottles of spirits. Evurn wondered of such small bottles. He figured if they were going to drink, they should have larger ones, but then he determined that perhaps the guardians of the city shouldn't be drinking and this was a quick way to hide it.

As he slogged his way into the city, the cling of his bottles was rhythmic to him. He smiled and then nodded at the fact he had found his friend Rortho sitting on a bench outside a large stone building with the runic writing of "Consulate" in the dwarven language.

"Will you have a wine with the soon-to-be-dead dwarves? I tell you, I'd rather like to eat them."

"Evurn!" Rortho said. He smiled and then stood up.

"I am free, but I don't know where the others are. There are other ways into the city. A non-slaver way. I am not one for direct attack, but to get our friends—"

"Our friends are at work. The girls are doing their own rescue. I have heard much rumor of it. We must get to the ship, get our weapons, and head to get Valrin."

"They were taken to the Hall of the King. We cannot get there and are you sure of the others? What if they need us?"

"I can sense it," Evurn said closing his eyes for a moment, "Aeveam is well. As for the Hall of the King, there is one way, now that I know that the maelstrom is not what it seems. It is a mirage. A trick of the eye. There is a way there, and we will go that way. First, we go toward our ship, and then we will find our friends."

Rortho and Evurn made their way back out of the city. There were some peculiar looks at them, but nothing else was said. They proceeded past the slaver area and down to the ship. It seemed the tides were calmer now. They boarded the slaver ship and caught wind leading out. The current seemed to be working with them, at least for the moment.

"If there is no maelstrom, then these currents are artificial constructs of a dwarven machinery, at least to the degree of our rough crossing earlier. Maybe that is not true, but my disdain of the dwarves due to their manipulation of the natural world only grows. One should seek oneness with nature, not that which is artificial."

Rortho sighed. "As we go to a ship constructed from that which is artificial using mechanics above our understanding?"

"That is different," he said. "The race that built it

was of the oneness of spirit, which is not entirely the same as manipulating mechanical nature. What wood do you know of that can blast fire as the masts of Valrin's ship? None. The ship is not of this world's understanding."

They made it back to the island to find the ship untouched. After they docked the one they were on, they sprinted to the realm ship and quickly began, not toward the area of the slavers, but around the island, moving to the east side. It was an area of much more steep cliffs and not as many dwarven eyes to spot them. The waves of fog like they had seen before began to pour out from the area beneath the city.

"How do you know this maelstrom is not real?"

"A crazy shadow elf told me." He looked to see the dwarf's reaction, and Rortho's glare of annoyance caused Evurn to laugh. "Trust me, my people may be a bit crazy at times, but we know much, even if we act as fools."

There was a flash above them, and a single flame flew near the ship. Evurn looked up, as did Rortho. Braei was on the cliffs high above.

In a few moments, those who had been rescued by Braei and Aeveam appeared upon the ship in a glimmer of white light and the slight sounds of melody in the air.

Aeveam collapsed as Evurn got to her. "I am . . . weak. I cannot do anything . . . else."

The others around them looked about and were afraid, especially upon seeing Rortho.

"He is our friend," Braei said.

"These were with you two?" Rortho asked.

"Yes, other women used as the bastards wanted and then tossed aside."

Evurn carried Aeveam below deck and then returned with his staff. He moved it over the entire group of once-slaves, and they fell asleep.

"That is what can be done for them for now. I would say it is not a good thing to help so many, but good deeds help balance out the evil thoughts Aeveam can have. We will deal with these when we can, but for now, we must go into the maelstrom. I fear that all of this will soon be revealed to us. Someone led Edanos to make this move here before. It is time we follow this path to its end."

Valrin had never seen such a massive hall. It had taken them quite a while to move all of the cooking vats and dinnerware from the lower kitchen to the large assembly room outside the main hall. They had large mechanical carts that made moving the vats of stew upstairs much easier, and now several of them went back and forth, carrying boxes of herbal garnishes as well as a large cake with many different types of fruit.

The dining hall itself was massive. From the side room, the doors opened up to reveal a long hall with seating that ascended along the walls as if it was a giant amphitheater, like he had read about in a book on singing a traveling man happened to have back in Travaa.

Aside from the actual seating set aside for the guests, there was an elevated platform covered with a large sheet directly in front of the king's table, as a passing dwarf called it. Many guards stood around the strangely covered platform and none were allowed to look under it.

The king's table was a long black stone with jagged edges and sapphires atop it. Some of the best golden dishwares were already set and ready for the Barb King's arrival.

"All servants attend to your attire. Be mindful that the time of service is soon!"

The guests began to arrive, and the dwarf from before corralled them behind closed doors to get dressed for the occasion.

Valrin and Fadis kept their normal clothes on and put the black trousers and shirts over the top of them. It wasn't anything flashy, by any means, but it was clean and proper for their roles. The dwarf over the kitchen returned to them.

"Service will begin! Ale is first, followed by bread and stew!"

He pointed to Valrin. "You, young one, will be the cupbearer for our king. He always prefers the youngest of the kitchen to have this honor. Do not spill his ale. The last person who did so did not fair too well when the king became angry. He gets angry a lot because of his power. The fact he must deal with us mortals angers him when we do not live up to his standards."

The dwarf shoved Valrin into another room with

several large barrels of ale. Fadis looked on from a distance.

"Fill the cup and keep it that way," the dwarf told him. "You will hear drums in the hall when the king arrives. Do not make him wait."

The dwarf stormed off, and the others began to file in with trays full of empty glasses.

They began to fill the glasses with ale, and Fadis quickly pushed himself to the front of the line. "What is our plan? I assume you have one."

Valrin nodded. "Edanos must be near if he is alive. Perhaps he will show up tonight at this banquet."

"That is suicide! There are more dwarves here than in the whole of the Glacial Seas!"

"Then I say our chances are good."

Drums began to roll, and there was audacious cheering in the other room.

Valrin quickly filled a large glass with ale and walked into the hall.

He saw him, the Barb King, lumbering into the room. It was obviously him, considering the man's vast size. He was three times as large as any dwarf Valrin had yet seen. He wore a crown of silver spikes, and even in a relaxed setting such as this, he was garbed in black armor decorated with the skulls of what appeared to be some type of aquatic animal with a long horn, a narwhal, perhaps. There were several of them that stuck off from his shoulders and arms. Valrin understood why he had the name he did.

As the Barb King sat upon his seat at the table, Valrin quickly brought him his ale.

"A new servant for tonight? How wonderful." He poured the ale into his golden chalice, "Keep the ale coming, boy. My guests are thirsty."

Valrin quickly went back to the storeroom and grabbed several more glasses of ale. By the time he returned to the king's table, he actually recognized some of the king's guests. It was the Hammersongs from back at the Wind Temple of Swia. The ones from Harrodarr.

As he served the ale, he kept his head down and moved quickly. The last thing he needed was to be revealed by Nurocas. The dwarf had been friendly to him before, but he had no guarantees of that here.

"Hear ye, hear ye!" an announcer standing near the middle of the seated guests began to shout. "Thank you for joining us in this magnificent event. We have several surprises for you in attendance. Your financial support of our king's adventures has finally paid off! I am happy to announce that in all our searching, we, at last, have found what has been sought! But first, dinner!"

There were exuberant yells as the many slave-servants came from the back room with several bowls of stew in hand. Fadis moved quicker than the rest, making a point to be among the group serving the bread to the king. They then carried a pot of stew to the table itself. Valrin went around to help them with it.

One of the slaves moved a switch, and a large fire appeared beneath the actual table of the king. There was a hook to hang the kettle.

"It must stay warm," the slave whispered to Valrin.

"You! Drink, boy!" the Barb King shouted. "You are new, so I will give you a pass, but take it as your only one. I need more ale!"

There were many shouts of agreeance from the table, but those on the king's left, the Hammersongs of Harrodarr, did not share the same sentiment as the others. They actually appeared disgruntled, but Nurocas at least continued to talk with the king.

As Valrin brought more ale just in time for the main course, Nurocas was pointing across the king and to the Barb Guardian, the Hammersong who had originally captured Valrin and the others.

"You are not in line with our order!" Nurocas said. "These slaves have no place in a dwarven hall, nor do you have a place as any type of slave master, Nirot!"

The one Valrin now knew as Nirot looked at the king. The king smiled and nodded. "Nurocas, Nirot keeps to his charge as my protector, but in the Glacial Seas, there is much that the lessers of the world do not know. I will show you what I mean, Hammersong."

The king stood, and the slight roar of the dinner guests quieted almost immediately. He made a motion with his hand, and the dwarves standing near the covered platform turned and grasped the cloth.

"Many of you know the power I have, channeled from the gods themselves to ascend into the powers of the ancient race of the Dwemhar, but there are powers in the world within our reach that are unlike anything I have seen. I am Stormborn, destined to protect the

Glacial Seas, but I cannot do this alone, and I have lost many friends in these attempts."

The king waved his hand, and the platform was unveiled.

There were gasps, shouts of horror, and a pungent smell unlike anything Valrin had smelled. On the platform were charred bodies nearly indistinguishable from one another. Blackened and crusty, the only way Valrin could tell what they were was by the bends of the arms and legs frozen in place.

Nurocas stood up. "King, this is an outrage! You bring the dead into this hall! Where are their burial sashes, their rights as dwarves!"

Valrin couldn't tell they were dwarves, but perhaps Nurocas could.

The king made another motion toward the far door, and the guards nearest to it opened it.

Something approached. It was dark with trails of purple rolling off of it. As it entered the room, there were more gasps and Valrin knew who it was.

"I would like to welcome Irikow, my master of magic and necromantic powers, to each of you this evening."

It was the lich from before, the one Evurn and Braei had dueled, the one injured by Fadis' arrow. Valrin could see no evidence that the creature was harmed in any way.

Irikow went before the king and bowed. "I am prepared."

"Then proceed."

Irikow brought forth his staff, as well as a bag of

some kind. His staff began to glow a deep purple color as he sprinkled a pink glowing dust onto all the charred bodies.

"Crushed fairies," the Barb King told Nurocas.

Irikow made several circles around the platform until all the bodies teamed with the glow of the fairy dust. He then lifted his hands with his staff still glowing.

"I chase the coldness of Vankou from these bodies, restore them with the power of fae, and bring life through the gods of the South, forgotten in time but embraced by us of the Glacial Seas. In the power of the Barb King, I trust that he will bring honor to my work."

At the exact time Irikow brought his staff down, the Barb King stood with his arms opened wide above him. "I hear my servant's prayers, and I bestow my power upon this place!"

The entire platform burst forth in a brilliant light. Valrin shielded his eyes and then tried to focus again as the light died down.

There was instant chattering among the guests. Several dwarves ran with blankets to the actual platform.

Valrin gasped. Those who were dead before now stood, nude, before the Barb King.

Nurocas stood, as did his companions.

"You return life to the dead?"

"I did. Had the lich used his own powers, they would have been resurrected as killing machines but brainless. By the power I hold now, dear Hammersong,

I can assure that none will threaten our kingdoms ever again, and I intend to use it to that end."

One of the quivering forms now garbed pointed to the king. "My king, you returned me from the plains of icy death. I had been left on the edge of screaming terror with an organ playing from the one of death's tower."

It was Rugag. Valrin glanced over to Fadis, who was actually not paying attention. He was staring up into the upper levels as if watching something.

"Rugag, you are one of my proudest captains! The evil done to you was unjust, and you deserve a long life and a death when you are old in years and warm by a fire. You will not die upon these cold seas! There is a darkness, my brothers and sisters!" He was now shouting. "A darkness approaches our seas that will be brought forth by the elves of a realm that is so protected from us that no mere man can reach it! But I have found something that I will reveal now!"

There were cranking sounds, and the floor began to vibrate. Valrin noticed the king was low in ale and quickly went to the ale storage to grab more. As he went to go back out, Fadis grabbed him.

"There is someone else here. They move in the shadows."

"What? Edanos, perhaps?"

"No, something else. Stay here with me. The king cares more of his show than his drink at the moment."

Valrin stood with Fadis as the king continued.

"From the depths of the great seas, locked in silt and rock, we dwarves worked to free this from the grips of time." A rush of salty air flew in from the opening area of the floor. At first, all Valrin could see was a single mast. It was a ship.

"Years have I searched for this. I have had the key for so long, I had thought it impossible, but now I give you a device of old, a relic of our past, and my own ordained vessel."

Valrin could not believe what he saw. It was a realm ship, much like his but with obvious changes of dwarven design.

"What in the the cursed gods?" Fadis said angrily.

"With this ship and a new weapon of magic and poison, I will lead a crusade to decimate all who have stood against us, starting with the elves of the West. A place called Urlas! A land not on any map where, without knowing it, you will just find the sea. I have this ship, and I have this!"

The king lifted an amulet up into the air. It glowed with a brilliant blue light.

"That is Edanos' amulet! The one he had been searching for. He said it was taken from him!" Valrin said. "But how does it glow unless he truly is Stormborn, as well? But he has not been in the presence of Meredaas. This is all wrong."

"Are you sure?" asked Fadis. "We know little of the gods. How can we be sure?"

The dwarves of the hall were shouting and cheering now.

"We have built our fleet up to be the grandest in a thousand years! Rugag, my captain, you shall lead the fleet, and I will board my ship. But there is but one other thing that must be done!"

In an abrupt move, the Barb King reached under the table and dragged out a cowering figure bound in chains and bloody. He grabbed the figure by the neck and then stood up on the table, lifting the figure up like some prized game.

"The sacrifice for my ship!"

"That is Edanos!" Fadis said.

Valrin went to run forward, but Fadis grabbed him. "No! You'll be struck down before you can get to him."

The Barb King jumped aboard the vessel, and several other dwarves joined him. Valrin now understood why the amulet was glowing. Edanos was near his amulet and an unclaimed realm ship. They chained Edanos to the center masts, and then Nirot lifted a hammer into the air. They forced Edanos' hand against the wood behind him and held the amulet in place.

"My powers beckoned you here and in your weakness, you are now mine. It is time to merge you with my ship," the Barb King said. Nirot swung his hammer, crushing Edanos' hand into the wood with the amulet. The ship began to glow, and more cheering erupted.

"It is done, and we will embark immediately for our glory! Hammersongs of Harrodarr, join us!"

Nurocas and the others didn't move.

Valrin still fought to get away from Fadis. "We have to help him!"

At this moment, figures dropped from the ceilings,

trailed in red flames. There were shouts and then a cackling laugh.

"Assassins!" a dwarf yelled. Valrin stared in confusion as four figures ran along the floor, all moving for the Barb King. His guardians were upon him in a flash, and in quick work, two of the assassins were struck down.

"Shadow elves in my holy hall? Kill them all!"

Fadis pulled Edanos into the ale room.

"We have to get out, now. This is our only chance."

Valrin shook his head as a figure rushed into the room behind Fadis.

He was tall and wore a suit of dark brown and red leather. He held a jagged blade that was glowing green.

"I was told to give you word," the assassin said with a muffled voice, "You know of another shadow elf. He was given wisdom of the maelstrom by our captured master. You should make your way to the lower levels and escape. I will attempt to slay this beast. Stormborn, seek out the shadow elves known as the Verit Gamblers of Aieclo in your travels. Know we have been watching. As the gods would wish us to say, you are not alone."

In a flash of flame and magic, the shadow elf rushed back into the room and jumped upon the Barb King's guards. Valrin and Fadis carefully made their way out of the room and began to run along the far wall. There was a door ahead.

"We go for that!" Fadis shouted.

Valrin ran just behind the Ranger, trying to keep up as he sprinted to the door.

"Slave!" a voice shouted.

It was the kitchen slave master, the one who had taken them before. Fadis pushed open the door, and they entered into the hallway. They looked left and then right. There seemed to be a stairwell leading down.

"This way!" Fadis said.

As they began to run, they heard the slave master again.

"Come here, now!" he shouted. They turned to see the dwarf approaching with his whip. Fadis pushed Valrin away and ran forward. The man slapped his whip along Fadis' arm, pulling him down to the ground.

"I will stomp the escape right out of you! Our king is in danger and you flee? You move against us and you will be taken down. I have been more than clear in our rules."

Fadis pushed himself up. He gripped the whip on his arm and pulled forward, throwing the dwarf off balance. A moment later, Fadis drove his small filet knife into the dwarf's neck. The dwarf gargled on a stream of blood and then collapsed.

"My work is done," he spat on the dwarf and grabbed Valrin, "Let's go!"

They were running again. The stairwell took them down and to another hallway. As they reached the corridor, another door opened and several armored dwarves stared at them, particularly Fadis, who was covered in blood.

"Murdering slaves! Get them!"

They were running again, but the next passage down had more dwarves ascending. Bells rang in the distance, and their escape was not getting any easier. They sprinted, moving quicker than their pursuers and reaching another door. They pushed it open and found an exposed balcony. Fadis ran to it and looked over.

"There is a way further down."

Valrin looked over the edge as the dwarves closed in. They had no time to think. They went over the side, and Fadis landed first with a roll. Valrin was not so graceful and stumbled his landing, collapsing.

Fadis pulled him up.

They could see the water below them, but they would need to keep moving down. It appeared there was a stairwell not too far away that, while open to the shifting winds of the maelstrom beneath, would work for them to keep moving down.

"Are you sure we can trust that shadow elf?" Valrin asked.

"No, but we have little choice at this point. I just hope that maelstrom is not just another trap." They ran into the corridor attached to the hallway and began to run when the doors on either side of the hall opened, revealing two large groups of at least twenty Barb Guardians in full armor.

"Caught the murderous ones at last. You two are not normal. You two are not as depressed as the others. Perhaps you were of the one's Rugag told us of. The boy captain and his ship?" Fadis put Valrin behind him, but it was no good. The door to the stairwell they needed was beyond them and behind one of the groups of dwarves. On either side, a slow-approaching capture was inevitable.

The one speaking removed his helmet. It was the one from before, Nirot.

"Know that the attackers are dead. Your assassins failed. We captured the first one, that Edanos, without so much as a struggle. Know our poison worked just as needed. He was unable to resist the powers of our god. He was drawn, pulled by what he didn't understand, leading him eventually back here. Whatever gods you think are helping you are false beliefs. Edanos was going to be drawn here the entire time, and now he will serve our king and our king's ship. But do not worry; you will not live to see those times."

They were closing in, walking slower than they were before, hoping to turn Fadis and Valrin into squeamish rabbits attempting to escape a trap.

There was an end table nearby. Fadis lifted it and threw it at the dwarves. They stumbled over it and laughed.

"You afraid of a fair fight, dwarves?" Fadis asked.

"It is never fair when a dwarf fights a mere human."

About that time, the door beyond the dwarves blocking their way opened. More dwarves approached. There were around ten of them, and they, too, were armored, except they were not dwarves of Gurundothrak.

"What goes on here?" a familiar voice asked.

"Hammersong. Go back to the hall and await our announcement that the intruders are dealt with. These two worked with the assassins. These two slaves threatened your king."

The Hammersong removed his helmet. It was Nurocas.

"That bastard is not my king, nor are any of the poor miscreant excuses of dwarven folly my brother Hammersongs."

The Hammersongs brandished their hammers. The runes upon the hammers' heads brimmed to life with a slight hum. The dwarves nearest to them fled around Fadis and Valrin, joining Nirot and the others.

"This is not fair. For you dwarves to die with such terrible odds as this is." Nirot said. "I have nearly fifty of my Hammersongs. You have only ten of your Harrodarr rabble."

Nurocas laughed and replaced his helmet. "You make sense for once, Nirot! Rorda," he said with a summoning voice.

"Yes, Master?" Rorda said.

"Stay back. We want a fair fight with these bastards. I don't want anyone claiming that we used too many of our brothers against these fools of the sea."

"Right away, Master."

Rorda motioned for Fadis and Valrin. They ran past Nurocas and the others.

Nurocas grabbed Valrin. "Stormborn, I came to determine what my fellow dwarves were doing. Know I am ashamed. I will deal with this rabble, and if I can, I will attempt to help you with the Barb King. He has escaped and with him went a large fleet of ships. Head below and find a way to get to your ship."

Valrin nodded, and Rorda opened the door for them to descend down. Rorda handed them both small axes. "Just in case you need them. Now hurry!"

They began down the stairwell and ran with the sounds of thunderous clamor behind them. The rocks around them shook with the pounding of the Hammersongs' weapons.

They continued down and around until they were beneath the city itself and entered into a layer of fog.

"Keep your hand on the wall so you do not fall!" Fadis said.

Valrin struggled to keep up and not trip as they journeyed down. Eventually, they were well below the fog and could view the sea beneath them. The maelstrom was no mere maelstrom but a toothed beast with its mouth ajar and seemingly sleeping beneath them. A path led to the water's edge. They made their way as quickly as they could and noticed that a massive fleet was pulling out of the far side of the harbor. There were hundreds of vessels and, to Valrin's terror, one realm ship.

"What do we do?" Valrin asked.

Fadis looked around and scanned the ocean around them. Valrin walked to the opposite edge and then looked back up the way they had come. The fight still continued. Not that he could actually hear it, but the rocks of the corridor were beginning to crack from the battle itself.

"The Hammersongs," he said to Fadis.

Fadis smiled. "I would hate to piss them off."

As the last of the ships departed the harbor, Valrin suddenly spotted glowing Glacial Sharks at the edge of the platform. Then, his realm ship, with all of the crew he had come with.

"Come! Now!" Evurn shouted.

As the ship slowed, Fadis and Valrin jumped on.

"Follow them!" Valrin said.

Rortho turned the wheel, and the ship lurched forward. As they passed around the edge of the sleeping beast, Valrin looked into its gaping maw just above the surface of the water.

"Be happy we did not have to deal with it," Braei said.

He embraced her. "I can't believe we escaped that."

She smiled. "I'm happy we did, all of us."

Valrin noticed the many sickly looking elves and females of his own race.

"Slaves?"

"Worse, I think."

Aeveam bowed to him. "Stormborn, our path will take us west, I have seen."

"We must go to a hidden place. Another realm, a place called Urlas."

"That is why he needed this ship," Evurn said. "He sought passage into a protected realm."

"So Edanos, is he dead?" Rortho asked.

"He is captured. His hand and his amulet were smashed into the ship. The lich and Rugag are with the Barb King."

"Rugag was dead," Rortho said. "No one could have survived that explosion!"

"He was resurrected," Fadis confirmed. "I would not believe it had I not seen it."

They moved away from beneath the city and came to a series of barrier islands on the west side.

"We cannot take these ill women into battle," Evurn said.

As they came along the shores, Evurn went to the railings as several men and women looked on from the shore.

"Your slavers have departed, we recommend you all to do the same. Come, take these we have aboard this ship, and take whatever vessels you can and head south. This may be your only time to escape this place."

The slaves seemed reluctant at first but one by one they came aboard the ship and the sleeping slaves were removed. As the last of them were taken off the ship, they began away from the shore with haste.

Braei was staring at the island as they pulled away.

"A better fate than going with us," Evurn told her.

The ship pulled away from horror that was Gurundothrak for good and they soon gained on the fleet itself.

"How did you escape, Valrin?" Evurn asked.

"Shadow elves attacked the king, giving us enough distraction."

"Who contacted them? I had thought the one I had met was a rogue like myself."

"I don't know," Valrin said, shaking his head, "but they said to seek out the Verit Gamblers of Aieclo at some point."

"Those bastards? Well, that is an adventure for another day, Captain." Evurn smiled. "If this Barb King goes to Urlas, I daresay he goes with good will."

There was a sudden gust of the wind in their sails. The ship lurched forward as a rolling fog overtook the dwarven fleet.

"Dimn sends his blessings," Aeveam said now standing next to them. "He veils our path and speeds our ship along."

"It is what we will do when we meet the other ship that worries me," said Rortho. "We are but one ship."

"Not exactly," Valrin said. He went to the standing orb on the ship.

"The ancestors, they can help us. They must help us."

6

REALMS

It had been a few hours. Valrin had taken the helm for the past hour, and as they moved ahead of the dwarven fleet, safe from their view with the veil of fog around them, Rortho studied the writings of the shipwrights to determine the way for the ship to do as its name indicated, to breach the actual realms and go unto another.

"This place we go to," Fadis said, "this realm of Urlas, what is it?"

"A protected realm," Aevcam said. "In this case, by the texts back at the temple of Swia, Urlas was a realm of elves who fought in the wars long ago. Some of them were known as Blades, the most deadliest swordsmen of all the elves of old. They, in legend, were awarded a realm safe from the rest of the world. It is said the Dwemhar destroyed their homeland long ago, back before the Glacial Seas. Their land is a hint of the world before, and though they can leave their land, it is safe, ordained protected by the ascended Dwemhar."

"Except when they created ships that could pierce such a realm," Evurn said. "Why create such a device?"

"When they could not master the science to ascend to the realms of the gods, they tried to force their way. Many attempted, but eventually, it was abandoned. Rather than scrap their technology, they repurposed the ships to guard their holy places. In time, all of that was for naught, but now there is a reason."

"All of this prophecy of the North and darkness. It is bleak," Valrin said. "I just hope I can do something."

"Stormborn, you can and you will," Aeveam said. "I will help you."

Valrin flipped the crystal to bring up the map. They were south of Corson.

The fogs were between them and the city, and the winds shifted in the sails. He turned north, allowing the wind to once again fill the sails. The fogs were vanishing, and the might of the dwarven battle fleet was laid bare to them. The massive armada was anchored, and the realm ship of the Barb King was moving further west.

"Valrin, I think I know the positioning for the crystals to enter the realm, but I don't know where it is, and I'm not sure if I did, I could actually get the ship to do it."

"If this ship has any more speed, give it," Fadis suggested. He strung his bow and went to the deck of the ship. He set an arrow to the string and released it. The arrow flew forward, propelled further by the favorable winds, but they were still out of range of the other realm ship.

Rortho stood near Valrin and closed the book. "This is it," he said. "If we can stop them now, we will have no need for moving into the realms."

"Wards! Get wards up, now!" shouted Evurn. Valrin jerked his glance right as several arching bolts fired from the dwarven fleet sped toward them. Evurn, Braei, and Aeveam were on the side of the ship, casting layers of protective magic just in time to deflect several off of them.

"Damn, they're firing again," Fadis said.

Another volley struck, but most fell short.

"They did not expect the need to follow their master. They pull anchor and attempt to close the distance. The same wind favoring us will favor them," Rortho said.

They were gaining on the other vessel as the dwarven fleet pursued them.

Fadis squinted and pointed. "They have massive barrels on that ship!"

"Barrels?" Rortho asked.

"It is the poison," Evurn said. "They do not need this armada to destroy the elves. They just need the poison."

"Well, the armada is closing in on us," Braei shouted.

Another volley of bolts struck their wards, and one broke through, smashing into the side of the ship.

"We're taking on water!" Rortho shouted.

Valrin looked for the shipwright's assistants, the

turtles that had repaired the ship before. Immediately they appeared, rolling into position near the breach. They went to work with their crystals, spinning, fusing the woods, and patching the ship.

"When did we get those?" Rortho asked. "They are amazing!"

"Back when I went adventuring alone, but they worked well to patch the ship before anyone noticed back at Evurn's island!"

"I knew the ship had to have been damaged!" Rortho said.

The assistants rolled back into balls and went back to the rear of the ship. Evurn now stood on the far back of the vessel. His ward was large, but it seemed unstable compared to Aeveam's. The night was falling quickly, and it seemed that the Barb King's vessel was beginning to circle.

"What are they doing?" Fadis asked.

"Maybe they cannot open the way. Perhaps they do not know how?" Braei asked.

"That is likely considering we barely know how," Rortho said.

The ship seemed to slow and then stop. Valrin was gaining on them rapidly now. It was then the sails of the ship he was pursuing began to glow.

"Incoming fire!" Valrin shouted.

A blast of red flames shot toward them into a spinning wall of fire, striking the ship. Braei, Aeveam, and Evurn returned fire with their own spells, and a series of purple orbs screamed over them.

"Bane shots," Evurn said. "If it strikes you, it saps your magic!"

Valrin turned the ship a hard left, angling for his own attack. He twisted the crystals and released a series of white blasts that screamed across the water, covering over the opposing ship. He could see some of the many dwarves on the ship were now convulsing. Aeveam jumped toward the left side of the ship and cast another ward up as several flaming bolts flew toward them.

"They are cornering us, Valrin!" Rortho shouted. "Now, summon the ancestors!"

Valrin gave the wheel over to Rortho and went to the orb on the deck. He placed his hands on it. "Speaker of Arik, hear my call. Come to my aid this dark night upon the Glacial Seas. Come with the fury of the fleet to support the realm ship of the sea peoples and the Dwemhar!"

A blue bolt of lightning shot out in all directions, and the winds died completely. A storm rolled in out of a clear night sky from all directions. The sea began to toss and churn wildly. A horn called out unlike any aboard the ship had ever heard. From the orb itself came several sparks that shot up like a wall over the deck of the ship in a line going north and south. There was another horn sound, this one like it was on top of them. From the wall of sparks came the ships of Arik, and the dwarven fleet fired their fiery bolts in the largest volley yet. A blast of white energy shot from the massive fleet of Arik, and while multiple ships of their own burst into flames from the dwarven attack, the dwarves suffered as well.

Rortho turned them back toward the Barb King's vessel. "He tries to flee!"

The ship was heading back west, and there was a sudden bright flash in front of the ship. A spinning vortex of white and black appeared, and the ship entered it and vanished.

"They have pierced the realms!" Evurn yelled. "Valrin, now! We must follow them immediately!"

Rortho bent down to the crystals and glanced back at his book. "Okay, it is done. Now just . . . do it."

"Do what?" Valrin said.

"Grab the wheel," Braei suggested.

Valrin did so, but nothing happened. He gripped one of the crystals and twisted it slightly. Nothing. He could feel the power growing in the ship. His heart began to pound, and he felt like he couldn't catch his breath. Suddenly, his eye caught sight of the center masts where his amulet was placed. He could see it shining a golden hue. He ran to the mast and placed his hand on it, closing his eyes. There was a flash, and he opened his eyes as the portal just as before he had seen the other ship pass into swallowed the ship.

There was a moment of breathlessness, of absolute stillness. Valrin glanced around at blackness and starlight surrounding them. A second later, bright sunlight and the sudden splash of the ship striking the water blinded his eyes. He shook his head to clear his vision, and he saw a massive forest and a green hue in the air.

They were in a bay of some kind with a large river ahead of them. There was a massive tree in the distance, and several structures crumbled around them. The dead were everywhere. Elves crawled over each other along the shoreline, coughing and gasping as they began to seize and fall to the ground.

There was something else. A dwarf with a staff pulled the dead back to life.

"Irikow!" Evurn shouted.

They entered the river passage, and Evurn jumped from the ship and on to the shoreline. He sprinted toward the lich, who sent a blast of necromantic magic his way. Braei disembarked to follow, seeing a large contingent of dwarves swarming the woods and coming behind Evurn. They disappeared from immediate view but Valrin spotted several blasts of magic and explosions of wood and rock.

It was then several massive trees fell, blocking the river path. Fadis looked up, his bowstring at cheek as he fired an arrow and then drew his sword. Elves boarded the ship. They were faster than any Valrin had ever seen. Three of them were upon Fadis and quickly knocked him from the ship. Rortho moved forward and engaged one of them, as Aeveam sent a blast of magic at another, sending them flying off the ship. A moment later, a blast of magic flew her way from a figure on the coast. It was a female and she was headed towards them with a glowing staff.

Fadis was now on the ground with two elves chasing him. He parried and ducked behind trees, but the two attacking him were relentless.

Valrin knew the ship was of no use, and Rortho still engaged the elf on the ship. Valrin drew his blade and jumped onto the shore to help Fadis. One of the elves had its back turned. He spun his blade in a taunting fashion, and Valrin ran for him lifting his sword to strike.

No more than the snap of a twig caused the elf to catch wind of him, but that was all that was needed for Valrin to be knocked off his feet and flying backward. Valrin looked up to see Rortho was forced down on the ship. Fadis ran to strike the elf now coming after Valrin.

The elf turned, parrying the ranger's sword and drawing a second blade in an arching slash, forcing Fadis back. It seemed the elf who had faced Rortho was not finishing him off but instead stood on the railings of the ship, his blade held behind him as he stared toward Valrin.

The dual-blade-wielding elf came at him again. Valrin tried to parry, but the quick slashes of his opponent knocked his sword from his hand. He fell back again and saw the elf midair above him. The blades were like the fangs of a spider coming at his head for the final strike when a staunch voice shouted out.

"NO! Stop!"

The elf drove its blades into the ground at either side of Valrin's head. Valrin stared up at what would have been his killer. The curved ears and slightly long hair. The face veiled behind a cloth meant to block out the poison. He then looked at the two swords and the slight red glow to the blades. The elf stood up, ripping his swords from the ground and sheathing them.

Fadis, too, had been spared at that moment. But he kept his sword up. That other elf they were fighting now sheathed its blade and walked over to Valrin.

The voice that had called them to stop was the elf who had faced Rortho. He jumped down to the shore and behind him came a female garbed from head to toe, but holding a staff aflame with magic. Aeveam walked with her.

"You," the obviously older elf said, pointing at him.

Valrin tried to catch his breath but could not. The poison from the area had dissipated, and the approaching elf removed his own face covering.

"I know you!" Valrin said.

"You are the boy of eels, from Travaa?" the elf said.

"Yes, yes, I am! You were the swordsman! The one with the boys my age, or so you said."

"I am. Tell me quickly, why do you attack us here? How have you come to this realm?"

"We do not attack you," Valrin said. "I follow the Barb King, a dwarf. He intends to destroy this realm with poison. He travels up the river, but to where I do not know."

"The capital city is there, and from what I've seen of the poison already, its results are absolute. I am Jalin, and this is my wife, archon of Urlas, Iluri." He helped Valrin to his feet.

About that time, Evurn and Braei returned. Aeveam approached from the ship.

"Irikow has escaped," Braei said. "They go toward a massive tree in the center of the lake. There are elven vessels slowing its approach, but they are burning as quickly as they come. We must get to that ship with our own and stop them."

"I agree," Jalin said. "My wife and I can assist you."

As they walked back toward the realm ship, Jalin stopped and embraced the other two elves.

"Go back to our home. Protect them. If we fail, you know how to get out," he said to the one.

The other elf drew his blade. "Father, we cannot just wait while you and Mother go to fight. Let us help you. We bested these people easily enough. Let us help you!"

"Master Rukes and the other Blades will help us. You protect your brother and sister! They are too young to be left alone if the dwarves come back."

"Father, they hate us. We will show the purebloods that we—"

"Kealin! You do not need to show anyone anything. Remember, if times become dark, your most important allies are those you love and your blades. Go, both you and Taslun. Watch over Calak and Alri. Your mother and I can handle this."

The elf known as Kealin did not seem too happy by his father's words, but he and the other one made the quick journey back across the river and disappeared into the forest.

As Jalin and Iluri boarded the ship with the others, Valrin went to the helm and used the ship's power to burn away the trees blocking their path. The elves were surprised by the power of the ship.

"Amazing," Jalin said.

"This is the last bit of our toils," Rortho said. "We must pray the gods are with us. I do fear we are far from their grace here."

The ship lurched forward. Valrin guided it up the river where more elves lay dead along the shore. As they broke into open water upon the lake, they followed the trail of broken and burning vessels. The Barb King was ahead and had reached an inlet of sorts. Even from afar, they could see the flashes of elven swords as the Blades of Urlas, the swordsmen of the elves, fought the dwarves for control of the shore. It seemed Irikow floated above the water a good distance away. He held his staff below him, and as he neared the edge of the shoreline, he brought an army of undead elves to battle, striking the flank of the larger elven forces.

Valrin could see that there were few dwarves on the actual realm ship, but that most of the poison had been rolled onto the shore. The Barb Warriors had formed a shield wall to protect the poison being left on the shore, and the undead army was meant to cover their retreat from the realm. Aeveam closed her eyes and touched Valrin.

Destroy the Barb King and do not wait for me.

There was a flash of light and then an explosion of dust amongst the undead army.

"Where did she go?" shouted Braei.

Flashes of white and undead flew in all directions

as the daughter of Lorlaam drew all those attacking the elves on herself. She was in the middle of the undead. Blasts of fire, ice, and bolts of raw energy decimated the lines of Irikow's summonings, but there were still hundreds swarming around her.

Valrin could see Edanos on the Barb King's ship, his hand still smashed into the center mast and with no signs of life. Valrin brought his ship alongside the other realm ship as the Barb King returned to his vessel.

"Foolish boy, I am Stormborn! You will not live another day! You will all die!"

The massive dwarf ran forward, jumping onto Valrin's ship. Jalin and Iluri engaged him, and Braei let out a burst of icy magic, attempting to slow him.

The dwarf barreled through the spell and knocked the elven Blade Jalin away. Rortho rushed forward and locked his ax into the Barb King's ax.

"You fight on the wrong side, dwarf!"

The Barb King laughed, "I am the god of all. I am Stormborn!"

Fadis pulled back an arrow sending it into the Barb King's back. "Fuck you."

The enraged dwarf swung his ax around, striking the railings and shattering the wood. The arrow distracted him for a moment as he grabbed at it and broke off the bloody shaft. Fadis rolled backward and drew his blade. In a sprint forward, he joined the others in a combined assault, striking the dwarf.

"Irikow!" he shouted out.

The lich had been attempting to attack Aeveam to no avail. He returned to the entwined ships, but Evurn was on him. The shadow elf jumped at his foe, swinging his staff with a blast of green that entwined the lich.

"Go, Rasi!"

The snake shot out from his robes and bit the dwarf over and over. Irikow fell and convulsed as his skin—at least, what remained in his almost already dead form—bubbled with poison. Evurn shoved his staff into the lich's mouth and, with a twist, blasted the head off Irikow, finishing the lich completely.

"You will not ever touch the holy sanctum of Vearika again, you beast!"

The Barb King let out a shrill yell and jumped to his ship. The others followed just for him to make a swiping swing, sending all of them flying backward. Evurn jumped at him and landed a smite of his staff on the dwarf's back just to be grabbed and thrown across the ships.

"The undead will continue to feed on the poison. Any still within these woods will be devoured in time. I must only finish this now!"

Valrin knew when the dwarf turned to run toward the helm what he was going to do. The controls to blast the poison were there. He was going to use the ship. Valrin drew his blade.

"Barb King," he shouted, standing on the railing. "I am the Stormborn, protector of the oceans and realm of Meredaas. I will destroy you!"

Valrin jumped to the other ship, slashing his blade at his opponent, who did not expect the sudden attack, taking the entire edge of Valrin's sword across his face. Blood poured from the slash, and he grabbed his mouth as he fumbled with the crystals, still trying to ignite the poison. Rortho jumped aboard the ship, and then the Barb King managed to pull one of the crystals, but not the correct one. A golden orb of light surrounded the ship. Those aboard Valrin's ship attempted to enter it, but they could not get into the protective shield. Rortho gripped his ax and moved along the middle deck. Valrin held out his blade as the Barb King walked down toward Rortho.

"No more games and no more help from your friends."

Valrin jumped from the helm down to the lower deck and slashed again, but this time the dwarf parried and punched him in the face, throwing him across the deck. He looked up to see the form of the dwarf nearly upon him when Rortho swung, just missing Valrin and striking the Barb King center chest.

Blood and tissue sprayed onto Valrin's face, and the Barb King yelled and gripped the wound, falling to his knees.

"For the Hammersongs and all dwarves of honor," Rortho shouted.

But as Rortho went for the finishing blow on the Barb King, Valrin noticed a slight smile on the old dwarf's face. The many Barbs that lined his armor suddenly grew in length, piercing Rortho in his chest and neck. Bright red blood began to seep from the wounds, and Rortho fell backward and collapsed.

Valrin pushed himself up and reached for the

nearest weapon he could find—Rortho's ax. It was heavy, but he tried to lift it up.

On the outside of the ship's shield, Braei, Evurn, and Iluri attempted to blast their way into the shield, but Valrin didn't expect them to be able to reach him. He thought of running back, dropping the ax, and making his way to the crystal to disable it. Perhaps he could do it and get their assistance.

"Come now, Stormborn. If you are truly that, you can defeat the god-king of the Glacial Seas!"

Valrin lifted the ax up. It was getting heavier at each passing moment, but he had to strike. He ran forward, lifting the ax above his head and swinging for the Barb King only to have the ax caught by his opponent midair. He let go and grabbed for his sword, rolling back against where Edanos was. He looked at Edanos, the one who had found him on the island of Travaa, the one who had taught him about sailing and the stars. Edanos was still alive, but he looked closer to death than ever before.

The Barb King laughed and grabbed hold of Valrin's head, ignoring Valrin's attempt to cut into his hands. Valrin dropped his sword and began to scream as he was lifted higher into the sky.

"Stormborn, you have failed!"

Valrin gripped the dwarf's hands, trying to pry them off when suddenly there was a splash of blood that shot up into his view. Valrin was falling and rolled to the ground. He looked up to see Edanos had brandished his sword and thrust it into the neck of the Barb King.

The proud dwarf collapsed as blood bubbled out of the wound. With a few last convulsions, the Barb King was dead.

Valrin coughed, still trying to breathe, and crawled to Edanos.

"Vals, you did it. You stopped him," Edanos whispered.

"No, you did. You killed the Barb King!"

Edanos smiled. "I did. I also got my ship and experienced the feeling of being Stormborn, I guess, as much as it was ever meant for me to feel. Rortho would say my ship needs a name. *Aela*, for an elf I saw once. She was beautiful." He smiled. "But it is too late for that now." He gripped Valrin with his one arm. "It is time for me to die as I should have before. Goodbye, my friend."

Edanos' head fell to the side, and the golden shield protecting the ship dissipated.

"Edanos!" Valrin shouted.

Braei was the first to reach Valrin, gripping him from behind. "We have to go, now!" She paused for a moment, staring at Edanos. She realized he had died. Tears welled in her own eyes and she struggled to breathe.

"Quickly, to the vessel," Evurn said. "Now!"

Fadis was at Rortho's side. "He's still alive. We need to get him off this ship."

Valrin looked up. The undead were swarming the shoreline, and the poison was now a massive green cloud surrounded by a shimmer of white. Aeveam was high in the sky and glowing like the sun above her.

"What is going on?" Valrin asked.

"When you were trapped on the ship, one of the dwarves managed to release the poison. Aeveam has shielded it, but we must open the path to our realm and remove it from this one. We can release it in our realm to drift off within the seas, but if it remains here, we have failed, for it will simply spread through the trees and destroy all life."

Valrin grabbed his sword and touched Edanos' head one last time. "Be at peace," he said.

Jumping back to his ship, he looked to the two elves who had come with them.

"Thank you, Valrin!" Jalin said to him. "Surely, the gods are with you and with all of us this day."

The two of them then jumped to the other realm ship and joined the other elves as they killed the remaining undead. Evurn held Irikow's staff with his own and smiled at Valrin.

"A souvenir and something to remember that fool by."

Valrin turned the ship and then did his best to remember the exact positioning Rortho had used before. He closed his eyes, feeling the positioning until he could feel the ship itself around him, his heart thudding at an even pace. He opened his eyes and ran to the center mast. It was then Aeveam floated down and grasped the mast of the ship, still holding the horrid poisons of the dwarves within her protective spell.

In a flash, the portal opened and they were in the darkness.

But it was different this time. Those around Valrin

had stopped moving. They were no longer flowing through the void between the realms, but instead, the others on the ship faded away.

A figure appeared in a hazy vision before him. "Dis is my lands," the figure said.

"What?"

"Dis . . . dis . . . dis are my lands. These are my lands, the Urlas woodlands."

"Your speech," said Valrin, "it is strange."

"When I am attempting to talk without a clear focus of my powers, that can happen. I feel I am okay now. It is easier between realms than it is within my own."

"Who are you?"

The figure smiled. "I am whatever is believed by those of Urlas to be true, many know me as a shaman but I am much more powerful than that. My name is Iouir. I guard the future as you defended it here today. The dark happenings will not be known by those who witnessed them within the realm. Those who have died cannot be brought back, for I do not have the power to defeat death. The one who does has spurred these events. The one of death, the one called Vankou, the bringer of future darkness. He wished to use this Barb King in another way, but his methods of manipulation are poor. The prophecy of the Glacial Seas and the ones who will release the darkness will come to pass in time. But of how this will come about is still unclear.

"I will heal the trees, restore the rivers, and return the broken ruins and ships to their original elements. The river will hide the bodies of the dead, and it will be believed by those who remain in Urlas that a sudden sickness came upon them. None shall know of you and none must ever know that you were here. Know that I take great risk in doing this, but such it must be for future events to come to pass."

"I do not understand," Valrin said as he walked toward the figure.

"You will await the arrival of those of Urlas. It is not yet time. The will of the Great Poet has not come to pass, but soon, very soon in their lives, they will be sent upon the oceans to Corson. You have many years before this, but once your amulet shines brightly and falls from the wood it's in at this moment, you will know it is time.

"Your crew will know of these terms, for I speak to them as I speak to you, save one who is aboard the ship, for he is too far away from the living realm. Go now, Stormborn."

There was a flash of light, and Valrin looked up to see a starry sky with the polar lights shining in a ribbon of red above them. Aeveam shouted out, and as the poison was pulled fully into the realm of the living, she released it upward. A sharp wind blew upon them, and the poison was blown away, having never killed the thousands it was meant to kill.

Aeveam fell to the deck, completely weak. Evurn went to her as Fadis stroked Rortho's chest.

"He isn't breathing," Fadis told them.

Valrin went back to the helm and fought back tears

as he turned the ship back east. There were no signs of the dwarven fleet, and the fleet of Arik had vanished. Valrin wasn't sure if they could be summoned again, but for the moment, he didn't care. He would sail to Corson. Rortho's cousin should know of his death, and Valrin sought to be free of the ocean for a while.

It felt like a few moments, but they sailed into the port of Corson with a dwarven vessel just behind them.

Fadis was alarmed at first, but then he lowered his bow.

"That is the same ship the Hammersongs at Swia had," he told them.

They pulled into the port of Corson and docked with the Hammersong vessel. Nurocas and the others with him knelt as Fadis and Evurn carried Rortho from the ship to the dock. In a procession, they went toward the *Spitting Crab Fish*, and an emotional Uris rushed everyone out of the inn.

There was silence as they simply stared at the body of Rortho they had laid on the actual bar of the inn.

"It is the closest to Harrodarr and our homelands that he can get," Uris said. "He died defeating the Barb King in combat?"

"He landed one of the last strikes," Valrin said. "And he saved my life."

Uris choked back tears and laughed. "Good. He would have wanted to die like that."

He began to cry, and Nurocas knelt before him. "Your cousin has served us all with a great sacrifice, and I would like to return him to Harrodarr to receive a proper dwarven memorial in his honor. I came to these seas to seek out the truth, and of the many dwarves I met, this was but one of the last who I could feel the vigor of our dwarf god Throka within."

Uris nodded quickly. "Yes, I am honored by this, and he would have loved to be thought of as such."

"Then we will make preparations for the journey and leave immediately."

In the coming night, Valrin lay down and went to sleep. When he awoke from his slumber, he ran downstairs to the inn to find only his crew awaiting him.

"Four days, Captain!" Braei said.

"What?"

"You slept for a long time," Evurn said. "I guess it is well deserved."

"Where are the others?"

"The dwarves departed. They take Rortho for his last rites in the lands to the south."

Valrin walked up to the table the others were seated around and grabbed a piece of bread from the center.

"He told us to lock the inn when we leave," Braei said. "I figured you might want to stay a bit longer after so much time on the sea."

Valrin ate the bread and then sighed. He went to the door and opened it. The others followed him. Standing on the shoreline, looking past his ship at dock and to a rising sun, he took a deep breath.

"I think it has been far enough time we've been on this rock. Let us get back to the sea."

"We're ready, Captain," Braei said, embracing him. Fadis walked past him to follow Braei, and Aeveam went, as well. Evurn was the last to walk past him.

He turned and looked at the inn and remembered the soothsayer's words. In his heart, he felt it would be many years before he was needed again here, but there were still many upon the sea who could need him. He smiled and went to the ship.

As they began away from the city, the winds pushed them south, and as the sun rose a bit higher, he thought of Edanos.

"I think I figured out a name for the ship."

They turned to look at him.

He smiled, "the *Aela Sunrise*."

"*Aela Sunrise*? That's a strange name," Braei said.

"Named for an elf Edanos once saw and said was beautiful. One of the last words he spoke to me was that he wished he could have named his ship after her. I'll do it for him. If it wasn't for him, I would not be standing here with each of you. It is the least I can do in his honor."

"The *Aela Sunrise*?" Evurn said. "It could be worse."

As Valrin smiled again, thinking of the name of his ship, Fadis joined him at the helm. "I think it is time we go south."

"South?"

"Yes, I have a son who needs his father. I think I have long paid for my folly. If we can, I would like to try to find him."

Valrin nodded and brought up the map. The ship of the Glacial Seas was headed south. At least, for now. The Stormborn would be called upon again, and in that time, Valrin would surely answer.

I hope you loved this story! Please review this title here: My Book

Mailing list: http://www.subscribepage.com/Stormbornsaga

So, what about Fadis? The story continues with Ranger's Fury, the next addition to the Stormborn Saga!

Looking for an omnibus edition and want to save some money? Get the Ranger of Taria boxset which contains books four, five, and six!

Printed in Great Britain
by Amazon

16866b2d-3844-4b00-b62e-4086dbab7ddcR01